"Y..."  ...out."

"..." ...s utterly
blan...

"..." ...id. "I'm
not asking you. I'm telling you."

"Do you still have that crick in your neck from the flight?" he asked. "Turn around." As she complied, he smoothed his hands along her skin and across the shoulders of her blouse. Then his lips were at her ear. "My God, why are you so tense?"

She gave the smallest shrug. She'd nearly been fired today, she had an impossible job to do or else she would be fired tomorrow, and the hottest guy on earth was touching her. No stress there.

"Relax, Wendy," he whispered. "It won't look like we're lovers if you don't let go."

With a shiver of pleasure at his voice, she took a deep breath, exhaled slowly, and softened under his hands, as instructed.

"Better?" he growled as he took his hands away.

She nodded a little, so sorry the session was over. A kiss would have been better . . .

She was just telling herself not to go there, because she was going to be disappointed. But as she faced Daniel, he was looking at her mouth.

The beat of the music, the volume, the frenzy of it seemed to escalate with her heartbeat as he bent toward her. But he advanced lazily like a hot southern afternoon. They were a special effect in a film, moving in slow motion, just the two of them, while their surroundings whirled. His lips touched hers.

JENNIFER ECHOLS
Star Crossed

POCKET BOOKS
New York   London   Toronto   Sydney   New Delhi

Pocket Books
A Division of Simon & Schuster, Inc.
1230 Avenue of the Americas
New York, NY 10020

This book is a work of fiction. Any references to historical events, real people, or real places are used fictitiously. Other names, characters, places, and events are products of the author's imagination, and any resemblance to actual events or places or persons, living or dead, is entirely coincidental.

First Pocket Books paperback edition March 2013

POCKET and colophon are registered trademarks of Simon & Schuster, Inc.

For information about special discounts for bulk purchases, please contact Simon & Schuster Special Sales at 1-866-506-1949 or business@simonandschuster.com.

The Simon & Schuster Speakers Bureau can bring authors to your live event. For more information or to book an event, contact the Simon & Schuster Speakers Bureau at 1-866-248-3049 or visit our website at www.simonspeakers.com.

Designed by Meghan Day Healey

Manufactured in the United States of America

10   9   8   7   6   5   4   3   2   1

ISBN 978-1-4516-7775-1
ISBN 978-1-4516-7777-5 (ebook)

Acknowledgments

Heartfelt thanks to my brilliant editors, Lauren McKenna and Emilia Pisani; my wise literary agent, Laura Bradford; my high school BFF and constant inspiration, Catherine Burns; and as always, my critique partners, Victoria Dahl and Catherine Chant.

1

Wendy Mann cleared her throat to get the attention of the mega movie star strolling in from the theater's back entrance. "You're good," she said, "but you're not that good." Then she relaxed against the wall of the musty stairwell, scrolled through her phone messages, and waited for the door onto the street to slam shut behind Zane Taylor.

BANG. Now Wendy looked up. Zane was gaping at her, a combination of outrage and disbelief showing on his chiseled face.

Just as she'd suspected when she'd first met with him and the producer of this Broadway play two weeks ago. Nobody had ever told Zane no: not his handlers, not his bodyguards, not his former public relations people. He'd paid them to say yes.

But he didn't pay Wendy. The producer did. So she was going to tell Zane the truth.

That was her job.

"You're fired," he sneered, mounting the stairs.

"You can't fire me as your PR specialist," Wendy countered. "You didn't hire me. And the play will fire *you* before they fire me."

"They won't *fire me*." Reaching the top of the stairs, he looked down on her with his legendary green eyes. Wendy bet women wouldn't have gone so wild over his movies in the past decade if he'd glared at them like this, as if they weren't fit to polish his Golden Globes. "I'm *Zane Taylor*."

"You *were*," Wendy acknowledged. "You were a brand name that sold out movie theaters. You ruined all that with your divorce. Now you need to stop acting like a diva and get yourself to rehearsal on time every day, or your boss will find a replacement who will."

"A diva!" Zane exclaimed, looming closer over her, murder in his eyes.

Right. He was an old-school ass for whom the supreme insult was calling him a name usually reserved for a woman. Her ex from West Virginia, Rick, had the same attitude. The closer Zane came to her, the more her body tensed with the memory of Rick's hands on her, even as her brain registered that Zane was not Rick.

But she wouldn't back down. She couldn't show weakness by panicking and taking back her words. If Zane felt more offended than she'd expected, so be it.

She met his gaze. "Your agent went to a lot of trouble to arrange this gig for you. Now that the movie roles have dried up, you wanted to retool your career by going after the serious acting cred that's eluded you. This play was your first role in high school, the one that got you hooked on acting. You have the chance to do a play you love on Broadway and prove your critics wrong. And you're going to throw all that away for a few weeks of partying hard and forgetting to set your alarm?"

He took a deep breath, let his shoulders sag as he exhaled, and tilted his head to one side. "Look, I may not be your boss, but you're not mine, either. You're PR. You're not supposed to change what I'm doing. You just make me look good doing it."

Wendy still held his gaze, but she could feel his fingers stroking her hand.

He said silkily, with only a hint of menace underneath, "Maybe we could compromise."

"Do *not* proposition me," she said.

His fingers stopped moving on her hand.

She wasn't going to jerk away from him. She would let *him* jerk away from *her* after what she said next. "If you want a relationship, ask women out on dates. Don't come on to the women you work with just to manipulate them. That's how you ended up with a lawsuit from your hairdresser, a divorce from your wife, and your current downward spiral."

His hands were off her now. If he'd had any history of violence, though, she would have suspected he was about to throw her down the stairs. Her heart raced again as he pointed his finger in her face and started, "You—"

She interrupted him before he could say *bitch*. "Remember Brad McCain?"

"Yeah." Zane put his hand down and stood up straighter with the shock of that unexpected memory.

"You started in the movie business at the same time, right?" she prompted him. "You were in that teen blockbuster together, surviving the apocalypse."

Zane nodded, his handsome face twisted in pain. "I wanted to go to his funeral last month, but I was stuck here in court."

"I was Brad's PR consultant. And he called me too late. Part of my job *is* to change what you're doing. I can't dress up a pig and make it look like Marilyn Monroe. If you're headed for a fall, sending you in a different direction is better PR than covering your tracks leading off the cliff. The producer of your play called me in time. Here's what I can do to help you change your life."

Wendy handed him the business card for one of her assistants. She explained that Stargazer Public Relations could get him whatever help he needed—post-divorce therapy, legal counsel to fight for increased visitation with his children, intervention if his substance abuse had escalated to that point—all without detection, so he could rest assured he wouldn't read a sensationalized version of his private life in the tabloids the next day.

As she spoke, the worry lines in his forehead smoothed. He wouldn't need to drown his troubles in a drink if he had assistance solving his problems discreetly. By the time she finished her lecture, he watched her with something like respect. "Thank you," he whispered, squeezing her card between his fingers until it bowed.

"That's what I'm here for," she said. "But Zane, getting your life back in order will take time. Your number one priority right now is to make sure you come to rehearsal every day on time, sober, with a positive attitude."

"I promise," he said.

After a supportive hug good-bye and an attaboy pat on the back, she jogged down the stairs in her high heels and pushed open the door onto the street. She hopped into her waiting taxi and immediately texted the producer of the play. Zane had been late again today, but he wouldn't be late tomorrow.

That was the plan, anyway. Wendy wasn't convinced of Zane's sincerity. She would be here at the same time tomorrow to make sure. If he still refused to cooperate, she had other ways of exerting pressure. She might pop in on one of the nightly after-hours parties that were making it so difficult for him to show up to work at one in the afternoon.

She looked up at the skyscrapers and bus-sized advertisements in Times Square spinning by outside the cab—the first time all day she'd had a chance to realize how much she'd missed New York, her adopted home. After a month in Seattle repairing PR for metal super-group Darkness Fallz, which had been like herding cats, she'd arrived back in the city on the red-eye that morning, only to be thrust into meeting after meeting on a breakneck schedule. Usually her bosses didn't meddle in her day-to-day business. They only wanted results. For some reason, today they'd required her to touch base with many of her important clients in the city. Zane hadn't been on the list. She'd scheduled that ambush herself.

And she would pay for it now, because she was going to be late for her one thirty meeting with her bosses. She texted Sarah, her colleague and best friend since college.

R u in office? Could you tell bosses I'm in taxi & will be there in 10? They won't mind too much if they have called meeting to promote me ha ha

Wendy tried to relax against the seat, scrolling through the thirty e-mail messages that had appeared on her phone in the ten minutes she'd spent on Zane's dressing-down. But she willed the taxi to sprout wings and fly above the traffic to the Stargazer offices in Midtown. She would even pay extra. She hated being late. It was unprofessional, even though the time she'd stolen might have saved

Zane's career. And then she received an answering text from Sarah:

Done. Warning: bosses don't seem happy.

As Wendy stared at the screen, her mind whirled with the possibilities. She'd been joking when she told Sarah she might get promoted, but she hadn't thought it was out of the question. Could she be in *trouble* instead? Her methods might be unconventional sometimes, but she had a high success rate—despite Brad's demise. In college she'd been second in her class among public relations majors, and the runner-up for the prestigious Clarkson Prize, awarded to the program's most promising student. She did not get in *trouble*.

And she sounded just like Zane Taylor.

No, that was the jet lag talking. She desperately needed a fifth cup of coffee. Shaking her head to clear it, then pushing her hair behind her shoulders, she settled into her e-mail again, confident she could knock out half these messages before the taxi deposited her at Stargazer's door. That would help free up her afternoon so she could deal with her other clients. They were counting on her to solve their problems, so she certainly didn't have time to dwell on her own. Especially when they weren't even real.

* * *

"I am *very* freaking likable!"

Wendy knew instantly she shouldn't have said this to her three bosses across the conference room table. And she shouldn't have said it so loudly.

Her direct supervisor, Katelyn, sat back in her leather chair and touched two manicured fingers to her perfect red lipstick, which had not smeared while she took dainty sips of coffee. *Her* supervisor, Jonathan, ducked his head and looked furtively over his shoulder at the Flatiron Building out the long bank of windows. But Archie, the head honcho of Stargazer PR, just put his chin in his big, hairy hand and scowled at Wendy, unflappable as ever.

She pretended she hadn't noticed their reactions. She sipped her own coffee, trying her best to remain calm, though her blood pounded in her ears with over-caffeinated dread. She understood now that her bosses hadn't called this meeting to talk strategy for Stargazer. They hadn't brought her here to promote her, as she'd hoped, or even to talk her into representing Lorelei Vogel, the latest self-destructive client on the roster, as she'd feared. They'd ganged up on her so she wouldn't pitch a fit—at least, not as much of one—when they fired her.

It had been ten years since Wendy had moved from West Virginia to Manhattan, coming for college and staying for her job with Stargazer. Now that she was losing her job, she didn't have to move back to Morgantown. There was nothing left for her there. She wasn't eighteen anymore, and she wasn't vulnerable to Rick. But the way her panicked heart was racing, she might as well have been boarding the next bus back home.

"I mean," she said, and her backtracking petered out. She'd already said what she'd meant. She did too much of that, which was her whole problem.

"Wendy," Katelyn said, "you know we love you like a daughter."

Wendy squinted at her. "A daughter you're firing?"

"Yes!" Katelyn exclaimed. "If Arabella wasn't up to snuff, I swear I'd hand her ass to her on a platter." Her eyes shot sideways to Jonathan, who shook his head, warning of another outburst from Wendy. Taking the hint, Katelyn leaned forward across the table and patted Wendy's hand soothingly. "Not that I'm trying to hand *you* your ass."

Archie slouched diagonally in his chair with one ankle propped casually on the opposite knee. He punctuated each syllable with a plastic coffee spoon as he told Wendy, "You're not *really* ~~silly~~, but we did want to make this as pain~~less~~ ~~as~~ possible for you, and this is the thanks ~~us~~ of her chair, Wendy took a deep

Grin~~g~~ ~~s~~aid, "My job is to salvage the public im-
~~d~~ stars who are about to go off the deep end. I'm dragging them back from the brink of drug addiction, alcoholism, whoring, or just plain stupidity before they fall into the abyss. Sometimes I go into the abyss

after them and drag them out. They emerge kicking and screaming. You can't expect them to *like* me."

"That may be true," Katelyn acknowledged. "By nature, your relationship with them is adversarial. However, if they hate you so much that they don't want to work with you at all, we can't send you anymore. You're no good to us."

"Who doesn't want to work with me at all?" Wendy protested. Unfortunately, lots of possible answers rushed to mind. Zane topped the list.

"Brad McCain," Jonathan piped up.

"That guy is dead," Wendy told Jonathan. She was losing interest in being especially polite. Brad McCain was a sore point with her, and she wanted to set the record straight. She said quietly but firmly, "He was hell-bent on being dead, too. He was halfway there when you sent me to him."

In fact, that was *why* they had sent Wendy. If anyone could have prevented Brad from getting plastered in a West Hollywood club and driving his Porsche off a mountain, over a privacy fence, and into the swimming pool of an up[...] coming handbag designer, it was Wendy. As it turned [out...] she *had* done, after his death [no]body could. But what set up his mom in a florist business [...] licize that he'd beautiful oceanside home in Florida. Beca[...] her a lic saw him in a more positive light, a movie [...] rushed to release special editions of his older gross-ou[t] comedies, sending even more money to his deserving family.

Wendy had counted the case a partial success. Being accused of failure made her feel like crying in frustration. She couldn't allow herself to tear up with her bosses watching her, so she did what she always did when she felt like crying. She lashed out. "If you want to present this argument to me, fine, but you can't use the opinion of a dead guy as evidence." She sounded bitter and defensive, and she knew it. She wasn't just on shaky ground now. The ground crumbled under her feet. As she flailed, she couldn't find a handhold.

"We've got a long list," Archie said. "Not all of the complainants are dead. But the reason we've decided to terminate you today, Wendy, is that Darkness Fallz doesn't want to work with you anymore. They never want to see you again. They've gone to the length of writing that into their new contract with their record company."

Now Wendy felt like she'd been slapped. Darkness Fallz had sunk so low getting fired from pub ———— ——— ——————— *Wendy was* sent to than't drag his ass to work at nine o'clock at night. The rest of the group had been grateful to Wendy when the funny, self-deprecating video she arranged to be shot for them went viral. They were invited to tour the talk shows, then to sign a new recording contract. She'd thought the lead singer might have been grateful to her, too, in the end, despite some of the things she'd said to him about acting like an overgrown Halloween trick-or-treater.

As the sting of the slap faded into a deep ache, again she felt like crying at the betrayal. Instead, she laughed shortly. "Their contract actually *says* they don't want to work with me again?"

"Show her the contract, Katie," Archie said.

Katelyn peered into her designer tote, thumbed through a stapled sheaf of papers to a particular page, and handed the contract across the table. Wendy took it as if Katelyn were dressed in a red rubber Satan costume like the lead singer of Darkness Fallz himself. She peered at the underlined sentence: *Manhattan Music agrees that it will not employ Stargazer Public Relations to work with Darkness Fallz for the period of this contract.*

To be on her bosses' desks this morning, the contract must have been on its way while Wendy was still in Seattle, helping Darkness Fallz through their issues. Which i̶̶̶̶̶̶̶̶̶ more.

"The contract more.

"They meant you," Jon̶̶̶̶̶ me," she grumbled.

Katelyn told Wendy, "You've lo̶̶̶ everybody at Stargazer. We hear Manhattan̶ already retained another firm for them. Can you gu̶ what firm that might be?"

Wendy knew. Katelyn wouldn't have posed the question otherwise. Manhattan Music must have hired Stargazer's biggest enemy, whose heir apparent was Wendy's own arch-rival from college. Daniel

Blackstone was the undisputed expert among PR experts at getting stars out of trouble. He was also one of Wendy's least favorite people, along with her ex, Rick. But she was trying to save her job, so she swallowed her medicine. She attempted to look contrite rather than ill as she ventured, "The Blackstone Firm?"

"The Blackstone Firm," Jonathan repeated in a whisper, as if he dared not say the name of the dragon too loudly for fear of calling it down from the icy mountain to slay them all.

"We can't keep you on staff if you're losing us business," Katelyn explained.

"What about my current business?" Wendy asked, realizing as she did so that her bosses had already finished up her current business. That's why they'd sent her all over town this morning, touching base with her clients. Her stars would feel taken care of for a few days, until Stargazer was able to send in someone else. But there was one client she'd met with on her own. "What about Zane Taylor?"

"We're giving him to Tom," Jonathan said.

Which was why her bosses hadn't put Zane on her visitation list. She wanted to say something cutting about Tom Ruffner's chances of whipping Zane into shape, but she couldn't. She was Tom's mentor and friend. And despite his youth and inexperience, Tom was good at this.

Wendy was beginning to feel expendable.

"But I *get* you business," she said weakly. "Maybe my sunshiny personality doesn't, but my results do.

I'm the best you have at pulling stars out of scrapes. Am I right?"

"You're right," Archie said, "but you're not doing us a lot of good if the stars employ us for a month, you pull them out of their scrape, and then they fire us. We need long-term relationships."

"One more chance," Wendy insisted. She realized her voice had risen again when a flock of pigeons burst from the window ledge behind her bosses in a flurry of wings.

Startled, Katelyn and Jonathan turned toward the window. As they faced the table again, they looked at each other and, barely perceptibly, shook their heads no. Archie told Wendy, "It's so much easier to fire you."

Lowering her voice, Wendy said, "Most workplaces would counsel an employee and allow her the chance to improve before giving her the ax." Wendy understood that most employees didn't cost their workplaces hundreds of thousands of dollars overnight, but she left that part out. "I'll prove to you that I can help some guy out of the gutter and make him love me, too."

Katelyn and Jonathan shook their heads more vigorously. Archie said, "The only star we'd even *think* about letting you near—" Now Jonathan was wagging his head no in an exaggerated fashion so Archie could see him out of the corner of his eye. Archie put his meaty hand on Jonathan's shoulder to stay him, then continued, "—is the star who asked for you specifically, Wendy."

"Lorelei Vogel?" Wendy guessed. It was that kind of day.

Archie watched her grimly, which meant yes.

Often when a huge star like Lorelei approached the agency, Wendy, Tom, and six other operatives fought over the account like lions over a piece of meat while a laid-back and calculating Sarah watched them as if she weren't even hungry—which often resulted in the bosses handing the job to her. But nobody was touching Lorelei. Stargazer never turned down a difficult case, and the tacit message to employees was *Deliver or die.* Wendy knew if she saved her job today, Lorelei would likely be the death of her career anyway.

And she had another, much more personal reason to stay as far away from that chick as possible.

But Wendy's future lay on the metal table in front of her, with Jonathan pulling the IV out of its arm, Katelyn holding her finger on the button to turn off life support, and Archie waiting with the body bag open and ready. Lorelei Vogel was Wendy's only sad, unlikely chance at resuscitating her job.

"I'll take it!" She slapped her hand on the table. The wood reverberated, the coffee sloshed, and all three bosses jumped. "You said Lorelei asked for me specifically. What do you have to lose?"

"A lot, honey," Katelyn said. "This girl is the headlining act for the Hot Choice Awards on Friday. If she melts down, she's doing it on national television and taking our good name with her."

"Maybe that won't happen," Wendy said. "Send me. I'll meet this pretty delinquent with a smile on my face and a song in my heart. Maybe I'll even straighten her out, and in that case, I want a raise and a promotion."

Katelyn glanced at Jonathan, who watched Wendy as if a lunatic stranger had sat down to this conference with him. Wendy got this look from him a lot.

"Come on, you guys!" she pleaded. "You're concentrating on failure. What if I turned this girl around and made her a showbiz darling? Think of all the recs Stargazer would get from that! And aren't the Hot Choice Awards in Vegas? That's perfect. You can't win big if you don't take a gamble."

Archie raised his eyebrows at Katelyn. Satisfied with what he saw in her face, he told Wendy, "Sure. You're hired. But on a trial basis only, sweetheart. We've made clear how we feel about you."

"Thanks! You won't regret it." Wendy jumped up and crossed the conference room before her bosses could change their minds. She took slow, deep breaths and tried to rid herself of the feeling that the dark mountains of West Virginia crouched over her. Then closed her into a narrower and narrower valley until she slipped into the only escape available, a mine shaft, and fell forever.

* * *

Daniel Blackstone was rolling his suitcase into his Las Vegas hotel room when he remembered he was supposed to call his father in New York first thing on arrival. Daniel rarely forgot to touch base with his father. He knew he wasn't as good a PR rep as his brother would have been. He wouldn't be as good a president of the company when he took over next month, either, which was why his father deemed it necessary to monitor him. Normally this thought made him feel sorry for his father and sad for his lost brother. But today he was jet-lagged and exhausted, and all he felt was angry.

He would not be calling his father until he was good and ready.

He surveyed the room. In a corner, the hotel staff had set up a bar for him with bottles of expensive liquor and a fresh bucket of ice, as he'd requested. He wasn't much of a drinker, but the job required it. When he was forced to play host, the setup looked cool. He hoped he wouldn't need it at eleven in the morning Vegas time. If he did, he was in trouble already.

Satisfied with this arrangement, he surveyed the rest of the place. It was smallish for a luxury suite, smaller than one in L.A. but a damn sight bigger than one in Tokyo. There was a sitting area, a desk where he would spend most of the next week or however long he was stuck here, and a king-size bed. Windows extended the length of the room, with a killer view of the Strip.

At midmorning, the casinos across the street didn't seem like the wonderlands they were advertised to be. They only looked vast, mostly blocking the dun-colored mountains in the distance. But he knew from experience that in the older, mellow part of the night, after however many drinks his job had demanded of him, he could lie on this bed, look out at the lights glowing in the signs and reflecting against the glass faces of the buildings, and dream that he was on his last trip to London with his brother.

It had been the best week of his life. He'd visited his grandparents every year of his childhood, but this time he and his brother had gone alone to England, in advance of their parents and their little sister. They'd explored the countryside, nearly wrecked their rental car driving on the wrong side of the road, gotten drunk in countless pubs, and marveled at the punk girls in this strange part of the world. That shining vacation, all color, was the last time he'd seen his brother alive.

Since then, all his trips had been filled with black-and-white business for his father. Looming overhead was the inevitability of not doing everything as per-fectly as his brother would have, and letting his father down. The women Daniel had dated had told him how jealous they were of him, flying to the world's priciest and toniest resort destinations, hanging out with the stars, and enjoying fine dining and the best entertainment the world had to offer. He would have preferred some actual downtime and the chance to wander off the beaten path. He did love to travel, but not like this.

What he wouldn't give to explore Vegas with his brother.

He wanted to ride the roller coaster around the faux skyline at the New York casino. He wanted to see every cheesy washed-up pop star in concert, and maybe a few magicians. He wanted to visit Hoover Dam, even fly over it in a helicopter like a tourist. He wanted to hike Red Rock Canyon. He wanted to win a thousand dollars at craps and feel the high, then lose two thousand and actually miss the money. He wanted to pawn something for cash to win his money back. He wanted a massage in a serene spa. He didn't deal with call girls, but it would have been nice to share his nights with a beautiful, loose woman, lost like him and lonely.

The thick window was the only barrier between his business trip and the tourists far below who were just waking up and heading onto the Strip for lunch and more gambling.

The hotel room might not be spacious, but he would take it.

He placed his bag on the suitcase rack and zipped it open. He lined up his shoes in the bottom of the closet, then hung his shirts neatly on hangers with ties around the hooks and suit coats draped over the shoulders. He tried to make his job easier by dressing well and giving the most professional, least approachable impression possible. This helped immensely when lecturing stars on why they needed to stop fathering illegitimate children. Leaving his things crammed in his suitcase bothered him and would mean more ironing later. He didn't have time to send things out for pressing. He was in crisis mode.

The drama with Colton Farr was still unfolding downstairs. Colton's bodyguard had texted to say that Colton was in the casino, down almost a hundred thousand dollars at blackjack. *Not* something that would help with Colton's image problem—as if urinating in the fountain at the Bellagio last night and getting evicted from the hotel hadn't been bad enough. When witnesses had called police, Colton's bodyguard had called Colton's agent, who'd contacted the Blackstone Firm for crisis management.

This case was so high profile that Daniel's father himself might have taken it last year. But he was retiring in a month. He was backing away from company duties he didn't want. It had been Daniel who'd taken the 4 a.m. call and talked the Bellagio manager down from pressing charges—even though Daniel had just finished a monthlong stint in Hollywood, threatening four different people into working together or else. He'd gotten back to Manhattan two nights ago, exhausted and happy to see his cat. Now this.

Personally, he didn't care whether Colton Farr crashed and burned. He had a handful of clients whose work he respected, like Victor Moore, who'd made some very good action movies. In contrast, Colton Farr went around insulting women and pissing in public places, and Daniel did not do either, so he really didn't understand why this guy deserved saving, except that it would pay for Daniel's father's new Maserati.

Daniel ducked into the bathroom to glance at his hair, which he'd kept short and neat since he'd grown out of his teenage punk phase. Satisfied with his reflection, he turned for the door.

An afterthought stopped him, an image he'd glimpsed in the mirror but had been slower to process. He leaned back into the bathroom and took another look at himself.

That's what he'd half noticed: the dark shadows under his eyes. He'd always loathed his own harsh face, all angles and planes that looked whiter against his black hair. By the same token, looking naturally mean gave him an edge when he needed to twist a star's arm. But the shadows under his eyes were new as of a few weeks ago and had gotten progressively worse. There was looking harsh, and then there was looking haggard. Not good for business. He needed to appear as if he was about to run the company, not like it was running him.

He touched the dark skin under one eye, then released it and watched the color flow back into his white fingerprint. *GQ* was always recommending products for issues like this, products that would inevitably be declared useless by *Consumer Reports*. He wished for a miracle cream—tubs of it if the stress continued at this level when he took over the Blackstone Firm. Enough for all the years he stayed in charge.

Which would be until his father either died or didn't know the difference anymore when his beloved business closed for good.

Thirty years from now, possibly.

When Daniel himself would be nearing retirement age.

He straightened and shot himself a disdainful look for being so vain. He had no time to worry about it, anyway. He had a spoiled actor to corral.

Shrugging on his suit coat, he walked to the elevator—a short walk rather than the mile-long trek some vacationers endured in these massive hotels, because he'd made friends with the staff many trips ago—pressed the button for the casino, rode down dozens of floors, and stepped into the cacophony. Slot machines beeped and sang cheerfully. Gamblers laughed and clapped each other on the back. Skirting them all, he headed for the high-roller gaming tables, where the employees still smiled but the clientele grew serious.

He spotted Colton right away, despite the disguise. Colton was average height but broad from working with a personal trainer for the past seven years, ever since he first became the fourteen-year-old heartthrob of a teen sitcom. His UCLA sweatshirt didn't hide his shoulders any more than his trucker hat hid his high-lighted blond hair. He wore designer shades in the dim and flickering light of the slot machines, which could only mean he was a professional gambler, a star, or a wannabe.

But even if he hadn't looked the part, his entourage at the blackjack table would have given him away: his bodyguard standing behind him, arms crossed, with a conspicuous earpiece that probably wasn't even turned on; his driver, who'd transported everyone from L.A. and deposited them safely in Vegas, and wouldn't serve a purpose again, except as a drinking buddy, until the Hot Choice Awards were over five days from now, when he would drive them back home; and a call girl. The woman sat next to Colton at the table, placing her cleavage in his line of sight as he looked to the dealer and signaled for another card.

Daniel paused beside a sparkling bank of slot machines and surveyed the rest of the casino floor. He counted three security guards posted around the vast room, back near the walls, making themselves known in their cheap suits and speaking occasionally into real microphones attached to real earpieces. Two different groups of tourists seemed to have recognized Colton and discussed approaching him, which was why the security guards were there, and why, if Daniel had been consulted, he never would have let Colton out in public in Vegas. Not when the whole country knew he was here for the Hot Choice Awards. And not when he was insulting his ex-girlfriend on the Internet and pissing in fountains.

A couple of other men sat at the table with Colton, both tourists. One was dressed almost exactly like Colton in a sports cap and a sports T-shirt. He even looked a bit like an older Colton, all blond muscle, but without Colton's soft and pampered features. This guy looked like he opened beer bottles with his teeth. The other man, skinnier and balding, wore a loud Hawaiian shirt.

There was nothing inherently suspicious about tourists sitting at a Vegas table with a celebrity. Stars liked to mix with real humans once in a while.

But as Daniel watched, Hawaiian shirt man, who was sitting on the other side of the call girl from Colton, touched her shoulder. This surprised Daniel. They definitely hadn't seemed to be together. Daniel had a lot of experience browbeating pimps away from his clients. This guy didn't give off a pimp vibe.

Sure enough, the touch that passed between Hawaiian shirt guy and the woman had been a signal. Without taking her eyes off Colton, the woman leaned back in her chair until her breasts were no longer blocking him. Hawaiian shirt man pulled something out of his back pocket.

Before Daniel realized what he was doing, he was moving across the floor toward the table. He didn't shout because that would draw attention to himself rather than the paparazzo pulling out the camera and the woman backing away to give him a clear shot.

Daniel hoped Colton's bodyguard would see the man before he got his photograph and escaped through the casino. The guy might not make it outside, but all he needed to earn his pay from the tabloids was to upload his photo. The casino would ban him and perhaps have him arrested for taking a photo on their property. Too little, too late, if the photo was already out in the world by then.

A photo of Colton losing a hundred thousand dollars, with a prostitute.

Daniel rounded the table. The bodyguard would see the photographer any moment. The security guards would come to assist. Daniel only had to get a hand between the camera lens and Colton. He reached out.

Colton perceived Daniel's reaching arm and the camera. He half stood and awkwardly swung up his fist from behind him. The photographer leaped sideways off his stool.

Daniel had enough time to cringe at what was coming but not enough time to duck out of the way as Colton's meaty fist connected with his eye. The impact launched him backward. His body met something solid that grabbed his arms—probably the bodyguard, finally doing his job.

Daniel pressed down the almost overwhelming urge to fight, to jerk out of the bodyguard's grasp and slug him, then go after Colton. Long years of practice hadn't rid him of that instinct but had given him superhuman strength to suppress it. Before he could see or clear his head of the throbbing, he said in as commanding a voice as he could muster, "I'm Daniel Blackstone. I just arrived from New York to handle PR. Get this guy's camera before he can upload."

Released from the bodyguard's grip, he stood blinking, half wishing the bodyguard still propped him up. He struggled to stay upright while bringing the suddenly too-bright casino lights back into focus. The security guards had come forward to help the bodyguard manhandle the photographer and the call girl. The gawkers stared from behind an imaginary velvet rope, unwilling to join the fray but eager to find out what trouble Colton Farr had gotten himself into now.

Daniel had to hustle Colton out of there before more cameras were produced. He stepped around the table to where Colton, fists on his hips, scowled over his driver's shoulder at the photographer. Daniel said softly, "I'm your new PR specialist. Come with me."

Colton looked Daniel up and down, assessing. His gaze lingered on Daniel's eye, which was probably bruising by now. Colton's lip curled. "I'm down a hundred thou. I was just getting my mojo back. I'm not going anywhere."

Daniel felt his own fists clenching down by his sides. He'd thought his impulsiveness had been shamed out of him by his father many years before. But at the moment, it was all he could do to keep from slamming this smug asshole square on his nose job. He quashed the startling thought that he wasn't going to leave Vegas without doing just that.

But not now. Now he had a public relations disaster to avert, whether or not Colton wanted to cooperate. He gave Colton his coldest stare as he said, "*You* called *me*, Farr. I have plenty of other business. Come with me, *immediately*, or I will take the next flight back to New York and bill you for my wasted time."

Colton stared back at Daniel for several seconds while Daniel calculated what his own next move would be. He didn't have a friend in the place, and his dizziness was progressing into vertigo. The only tool he had, really, was the illusion of control, which was somewhat difficult to sustain with a black eye developing.

Colton turned to his bodyguard, whose foot was resting on the photographer's head. "We've got to talk shop. Can you take care of this?"

"Sure thing," the bodyguard grunted.

Daniel spoke to security. "Even if you don't see the picture, get the camera. And tell the casino to ban the photographer and the prostitute, or Mr. Farr is checking out." The Bellagio had asked Colton to vacate after the fountain-pissing incident last night. But some casinos were pickier than others. This one was happy to be associated with any star, even a tasteless and mentally unstable one.

Impressed with Daniel's confidence, but not sure whether they were supposed to be taking orders from him, the bodyguard and security guards nodded at him.

Daniel wasn't satisfied. He would have preferred a "yes, sir." He wasn't satisfied with his own handling of the situation, either. The other tourist, the one who resembled a battle-hardened Colton, might have been involved in the conspiracy to snap Colton's photo, too. But he'd disappeared. Daniel had lost track of him. And there was only so much Daniel could ask of himself under the circumstances, with his eye throbbing and threatening to fall out of his face. He turned to usher Colton toward the elevator.

Colton stayed planted to the spot. Daniel thought he knew why. Colton's ex-girlfriend, Lorelei Vogel, was also a guest at this hotel. Colton had been furiously feuding with her online since their all-too-public breakup a few weeks ago, but that only gave away how invested he was in the failed relationship. As long as she was staying here, he wouldn't want to leave.

Daniel put his hand on Colton's shoulder—trying not to flare his nostrils in distaste as he did so—and assured him quietly, "The casino will take care of this, and you'll still be here tomorrow."

As if in answer, from behind them came the sounds of a scuffle, several chairs turning over, and a shrieking call girl.

"Don't look," Daniel advised Colton, afraid that his client's image could still get snapped by a curious passerby, and the headline on the cover of the tabloid would be COLTON FARR INVOLVED IN CASINO BRAWL WITH PROSTITUTE. The article inside would explain that Colton was involved only tangentially, but nobody would read the article. They would only glance at the headline and photo in the grocery store check-out line and reach a verdict about Colton.

And turn the channel when the Hot Choice Awards aired Friday night.

Daniel managed to prevent that catastrophe, at least. He steered Colton all the way into the elevator, growling, "Don't turn around," as the doors slid shut behind them.

2

Feigning her usual confidence, Wendy strode out of the conference room and stopped to talk with one of her assistants. "I'm on the Lorelei Vogel case, so I need access to all those files on the server, please. And tell the travel office I'm flying to Vegas this afternoon. Have them text me the deets."

"Vegas!" the young woman exclaimed. "You are so lucky!"

"I feel lucky." Wendy walked through the wide room of cubicles, toward her own office. She consciously quieted her high-heeled footsteps as she approached the open door of Tom's office. She loved Tom like a younger brother, but if he wrapped his arms around her and hugged her close in the hallway to comfort her, she would lose what little composure she had left. She hoped he wouldn't call out to her as she sneaked past.

"Hey, Wendy." He had senses like a Navy SEAL.

Reluctantly she peeked into his office. He sat with his elbows on his desk and his chin in his hands. As she appeared, he turned his head slightly to shift his mischievous blue eyes from his computer screen to her. Tom had been hired a couple of summers before, fresh out of college and four years younger than Wendy and Sarah. At the time, her overall opinion of him had been twofold: that his still-in-college girlfriend was very, very fortunate, and that he was a complete mess.

Fearing for his job safety, Wendy had tried to impress on him the importance of looking professional at work. He'd responded to her suggestion with as much alacrity as Sarah had, which was none. Today he wore a wrinkled blazer over a rock band T-shirt, and he hadn't shaved. In fact, he never seemed to shave, which was impossible. He must have shaved *sometime* or he would have looked like a member of ZZ Top. Wendy called him Scruffy. Sarah argued that *Scruffy* sounded like a border collie, but Tom was more of a German shepherd. He looked friendly, he acted playful, but he had a dangerous air about him. When Wendy talked about him like he was a little brother, Sarah pointed out that he was like a little brother who had been to prison.

"What happened at your meeting with the bosses?" he asked Wendy. His eyes widened as he saw her expression. "Wendy, I—"

She shook her head. She shouldn't need to be comforted by him, when *she* was supposed to be *his* mentor. She just needed to get to Vegas and perform a miracle. She fled past Sarah's office to her own and quietly closed her door.

She stood in the small space beside her desk with her hands pressed to her eyes, trying to remember whether there was anything hidden in her office that would incriminate her or any of her clients if the bosses fired her while she was in Vegas. Looking around the office would do no good because on the surface it was clean and pristine, with her huge bulletin board sectioned into the clients she was responsible for and their current whereabouts—though she hadn't yet updated Brad's column to read *six feet under*. Disentangling the nightmarishly junky drawers of her desk and filing cabinet would take years. Even *she* didn't know what was in there. But she didn't *think* she was in possession of anything that would get anyone in trouble, now that Brad McCain was dead.

A knock sounded in the hall—on Sarah's door, not Wendy's. "Come in," Sarah called. Then, through the thin wall, Wendy could make out only the murmur of Sarah's and Tom's hushed voices. But she knew Tom was telling Sarah that Wendy had had a bad meeting. Sarah would knock on Wendy's door any second.

Wendy didn't want to recount the meeting to Sarah. Then she really *would* cry. She sat down at her desk, hoping she could give Sarah the impression that sh was busy with work. She opened the top drawer and quickly closed it again. The mess was depressing. She truly was a neat person, but the appearance of neatness was more important than neatness itself. And maintaining that appearance sometimes meant she raked everything on the desk into the drawer. Repeatedly. And then she got sent to Nashville or Paris and never got a day for spring cleaning. Usually the disorder didn't bother her, but at the moment it seemed overwhelming.

The inevitable knock sounded at her door.

She covered her face with both hands, willing that despair away, that feeling of being forever lost down a mine shaft. "I didn't cry until now," she called softly.

"Of course you didn't cry," Sarah whispered, closing the door behind her. Wendy heard the swish of Sarah's too-casual-for-work, thinly disguised gym pants against the guest chair as she sat down.

Wendy suppressed a sob. "Don't hug me or I'll lose it. I have to get out of here and go home and pack and catch a flight."

"I won't hug you," Sarah said in the soothing Alabama drawl she hadn't quite shaken after ten years in New York. "So you're not fired? Tom thought you got fired."

Wendy explained the clause in the Darkness Fallz contract. Then she burst out, "You and I should break off and form our own PR firm. Take Tom with us." Even as she said this, her stomach knotted in dread.

Going out on her own might mean failure, and she couldn't fail. If she failed, she would lose her savings, her apartment . . . that was all she had.

"I'm not cut out for it," Sarah said, waving the idea away with one hand. "I love my job, but I want to do it only so many hours a week, you know? I want to be off when I'm off. I want to train for marathons. I want to hang out with Harold on the weekends."

Wendy tried not to grimace at the mention of Sarah's husband, Harold. Wendy hated that guy. Sarah was beautiful—or she *could* be, with a little makeup and any hair care at all and a proper brassiere to replace her sports bra—but Harold treated her like he was in college and she was the high school girl back home that he'd grown tired of but didn't have the guts to break up with.

"You still have a job, though?" Sarah asked. "How'd you pull that off?"

"Lorelei Vogel asked for me," Wendy grumbled.

"But that's great!" Sarah said. "I mean, that's a deep hole to dig out of, but if you were going to have to represent Lorelei anyway, you're not significantly worse off than you were earlier this morning. Yet."

"If I hadn't been fired," Wendy said, "I would have done anything to avoid this case. Lorelei's ex, Colton Farr, reminds me of Rick." Wendy had thought she would feel better getting this off her chest. Instead the memories of Rick threatening her loomed over her.

No wonder she'd had a visceral reaction to Zane standing so close to her an hour ago. She'd heard around the office that Lorelei wanted representation. Wendy had subconsciously made the connection to Colton, then to Rick, and then she'd started seeing Rick in everybody. The way her day was going, it had been inevitable that she would land in the one assignment that would scare the hell out of her.

"Rick?" Sarah exclaimed. "No. I see the physical resemblance to Colton, but no. You can't let yourself go there."

Sarah had met Rick only once, when he'd appeared in their dorm before classes started freshman year and demanded that Wendy come with him to talk alone. Sarah had rushed to call campus security, but not before Rick had backed Wendy against the wall with his thick arm across her throat.

"They both say their girlfriends are beautiful angels until they misbehave," Wendy grumbled, "at which point their girlfriends become stupid bitches."

"Hey!" Sarah exclaimed. "Snap out of it."

That's when Wendy realized she'd huddled into a ball in her desk chair, hugging herself, just as she had whenever Rick called her names.

"Colton isn't Rick," Sarah pointed out.

"Right." Wendy straightened in her chair and lifted her chin.

"And if they do have anything in common," Sarah said, "you'll be doing Lorelei a service by helping her distance herself from Colton."

"I would have preferred running away."

"Yeah," Sarah agreed. "Do you want the rundown of what Lorelei and Colton have been up to?"

"I need to get home and pack. I don't have time for the rundown. But . . ." Wendy cringed. "I can tell from your face it's bad."

Sarah nodded. "And as of today, Colton is repped by—"

"The Blackstone Firm?" Wendy exclaimed. "I have to rep Lorelei Vogel, I have to make her like me while I do it, *and* I have to extricate her from an Internet brouhaha with my ex-boyfriend's doppelganger, who's now a Blackstone Firm client? The only way that could get any worse is if Daniel Blackstone is the rep."

Sarah opened her hands. "I heard his dad is retiring and Daniel is taking over the firm soon. I doubt that's happened yet or we would have heard. It's feasible that Daniel is in Vegas right now, notching his belt with one last triumph."

"Notching his belt," Wendy muttered. "Better than his bedpost, I guess." She dabbed her fingertips under her eyes, checking for smeared mascara, feeling completely dead.

"I know this sounds unlikely," Sarah said, scooting to the edge of her chair, "but I actually came in here to make you feel better."

"It's okay," Wendy croaked. "I'm glad you warned me."

"Don't sit here thinking about it," Sarah said. "Thinking helps most people, but you tend to do better with no thought whatsoever."

"Thanks."

Sarah rose. Wendy did too, and they embraced after all, just as they had when Sarah got married, and when Wendy got Sarah the job at Stargazer, and when all Wendy's college boyfriends broke up with her with final salvos of *bitch!*—every single one of them—and when Daniel Blackstone beat out Wendy for the Clarkson Prize.

Rubbing Wendy's back, Sarah pulled away and looked her in the eye. "If you get in trouble, Tom and I will come help you on Stargazer's tab. Now go. You can do it." She turned and disappeared into the hallway.

Wendy went after her. "Sarah," she called.

Sarah paused at her own door.

"If I do get fired while I'm gone," Wendy said, "and you're sent to clean out my office and you happen to come across some crack, just flush it down the toilet."

Sarah arched one eyebrow. Tom must have been standing near the door of his office, listening, because he slowly leaned into the hall to peek at Wendy, and slowly disappeared again.

Half an hour later, as the doors of the elevator in Wendy's apartment building slid shut in front of her, she grinned at her reflection in the polished brass. She couldn't afford to dwell on the very real possibility that she was about to lose her job. She had to capitalize on her small chance to *save* the job she'd worked her ass off to snag in the first place. A positive attitude could do just that if she managed to couple it with whipping Lorelei Vogel into shape.

When she smiled like this, with her long blond hair cascading around her shoulders, a stranger might mistake her for a model, or even a starlet like the ones she shoveled out of trouble. She'd been told her features came from the mother she'd hardly known—though Wendy gave those natural looks a generous helping of maintenance and grooming and product. She took very good care of herself. She'd overheard boys in high school saying she was the most beautiful girl at the party until she opened her mouth. Ever since, she'd worked hard at staying the most beautiful girl, because her mouth was going to open sooner or later, and she couldn't seem to control what came out of it. Facials were so much easier than staying silent.

That had to change. For the entirety of this trip to Vegas, she would need to pretend she was a benevolent, motherly person. As the second floor, the third floor, the fourth floor slid past, signaled by dark spaces through the crack between the doors, she winked at her reflection good-naturedly. Now she looked like a stranger. Which might be a good thing at this point.

At her own floor, she opened her apartment door carefully in case her turtle was behind it. He wasn't there, but an unopened package was, piled with scarf and a coat she hadn't worn since March. W' she wasn't on a difficult case, she was very neat. '

she *was* on a difficult case, which was most of the time, she lived at the office or on location with her client and used her apartment as a dump. Sarah said Wendy's apartment looked like the inside of Wendy's mind, which was probably true. She tried to straighten up between jobs, but this time she'd missed her chance. She had a plane to catch.

She could clean for the turtle, though. She scrubbed his terrarium and filled his reservoir with fresh water. Then she scanned her apartment for him. He wasn't in the potted tree by the window, where he usually hung out. She looked around the ramp she'd propped there so he could get out of the pot if he wanted. After a cursory search of her living room, she realized she was going to need to conduct more than a cursory search, because there were too many sweaters, sheaves of paper, files, and packages of books on the floor. He could be behind or inside any of them.

Oh God, she was going to miss her flight because her turtle was lost. She'd nearly been fired today, and now her turtle was going to starve to death in her absence. She resisted the urge to call to him. She didn't know whether he would come or not. She'd never had the patience to test this. Even if he did come when called, it would take him five years.

On a hunch, she opened the closet door wider and peered into the dark corner behind mounds of her shoes. There he was, exactly where she'd found him years before when she moved in—the last owner's cast-off pet and a kindred spirit for Wendy, who'd felt like her father's afterthought.

She inhaled deeply and exhaled slowly, relieved her turtle was safe.

She picked him up, a small but solid mass, and gave him her usual stern warning: "Don't pee on me." She carefully placed him in the terrarium, secured the jar of turtle food under her arm, and picked up the tank with both hands. She negotiated the door of her apartment with some difficulty and gently kicked the next door, hoping she wasn't waking Bob.

She heard him move toward her from across his apartment. The footsteps paused as he looked through the peephole at her. Opening the door, he was already holding out his arms for the tank. She tried not to stare, but it was always shocking to see him without his wig and makeup and corset.

"Thanks a million," she said. "Sorry to do this to you again so soon. It's almost like he's your turtle instead of mine."

"Hi, Wendy," a voice called from the depths of the apartment.

She leaned around the doorframe and called back, "Hi, Marvin." Bob's boyfriend probably didn't want to greet her in person because of what he was wearing. Or not.

"It's no problem," Bob told her. "Turtles don't bark." He slid the terrarium onto a table near the door and took the jar of food from her. "Plus banana?"

"Just a tiny bit of whatever fruit you're eating, yeah

"How long this time?"

"Maybe a week. I'll be in Vegas." Wendy gave him her optimistic grin. The effort in front of a friend made her so tired that she sagged against his door-jamb. "Longer, I hope, because I'm probably going to get fired at the end of it."

"Oh, honey!" He stuck out his bottom lip sympathetically. "I can get you a job if you need one."

"Thanks." Wendy kept grinning. The threat of working at a strip club was one of the many reasons she'd been so eager to escape Morgantown.

"Kidding!" Bob exclaimed. "You would never pass for a man dressed up as a woman, unless we strategically placed your hair, Lady Godiva." The turtle food rattled as he switched the jar to his other hand so he could tug her blond locks. "Vegas, huh? Who are you bailing out of trouble? Colton Farr?"

"No, the Blackstone Firm handles him." She thought again of her nemesis from college, Daniel Blackstone. He was gorgeous in an ultraconservative way, his dark hair cropped close and perfectly styled, his dark eyes haughty, a hint of his father's British accent breaking through when he gave a formal presentation in class. She felt a wash of pleasure at the thought that if he was indeed the rep whom the Blackstone Firm had sent, he had worse problems than she did today.

"What's the latest you've heard on Colton?" she asked Bob.

"He got arrested last night for pissing in the fountain at the Bellagio," Bob said.

"You're kidding!" Wendy squealed in delight. "There's a wall around the fountain. How did he balance up there long enough to whip it out?"

"In addition to his storied acting career, he has his own line of exercise equipment, remember?" Bob wagged his eyebrows. "He's in good shape."

"That is revolting and fantastic. Maybe I can engineer other inappropriate places for him to pee, and that will draw people's attention away from my client. I feel so much better." Wendy leaned in and kissed Bob on one baby-smooth cheek.

"Who's *your* client?" Bob asked.

"Lorelei Vogel."

Bob's eyes widened. "Girl, she's *much* worse than Colton Farr. Best of luck straightening out *that* little hellcat. You're as good as fired."

Wendy stuck her fingers in her ears. "La la la, I am not listening to you." She backed through the door into her own apartment.

Glancing at the texts from the travel office on her phone, she saw her plane was leaving in two hours. She would have barely enough time to negotiate a taxi to the airport and the line through security, and she could not screw this up. She sprinted for her bedroom, snagged the suitcase she hadn't yet unpacked from her trip to Seattle, slung it onto her bed, and dumped it out to start over for a new city. She'd spent enough time with debauched stars in Vegas that she had a good idea what she needed to pack.

Bathing suit.

No, bikini.

No, string bikini.

Cocktail dress.

Three-inch heels.

Cocktail dress.

Four-inch heels.

Cocktail dress.

Five-inch heels.

Rhinestone tiara.

Body glitter.

Teddy with matching thong.

Headband with bunny ears and cottontail to clip onto the back of her thong. Some celebrity parties got a little weird.

She didn't really want to take the ears and tail. She lifted them from her suitcase and put them back into her dresser drawer. But if she didn't take them, she would certainly need them. She would waste money and, more importantly when she was working, waste an hour buying another set. Shaking her head, she set them in her suitcase again.

Latex gloves.

Rubbing alcohol.

Scissors. Wendy's hair was long, and Vegas was sticky.

As she packed, butterflies fluttered in her stomach. In the past, she'd loved going on salvage missions. She'd thought she was helping people. And she felt high whenever she grabbed the point of someone else's rising star and held on for the ride. People all over America bought the tabloids and followed actresses' every move online, fascinated with the lifestyle and the glamour. Wendy had grown up one of those starstruck girls. She still was one, even now that she'd seen divas at their worst.

But as she folded the complicated bra she wore with her lowest-cut shirt and tucked both garments into her suitcase, she realized this time would be different. She was desperate to save her job. And Daniel Blackstone might be there, stepping on her toes, getting in her way, looking down on her for making a ninety-seven on Dr. Abbott's speech-writing midterm when he'd gotten a ninety-eight. If he actively tried to screw her up—which wasn't out of the question, considering how strongly his father and her bosses hated each other—she would prove no match for him. Though she was in a terrible hurry now, the recurring thought of him drove her to her bathroom to touch up her makeup and brush her hair.

No, not just because of him, she assured herself. She never knew whom she'd run into on the flight from New York to Vegas. It was a common route for people in PR. Many of the biggest stars lived in New York and chose Vegas as the location for their nervous breakdowns.

As she wheeled her suitcase through her apartment, she slowed at the bulletin board beside the door. It was always the last thing she saw when she left her apartment, and she'd tacked things there that made her happy: A few photos of herself with Sarah. A few shots of herself with stars she'd saved and who hadn't thrown her to the wolves afterward. Printouts of e-mail messages from those stars and from Katelyn, Jonathan, and Archie, praising her for jobs well done.

Squeezing her eyes shut against the tears, she kept rolling right out of the apartment. Her meeting with the bosses today was just a blip on the map of her career that nobody would remember this time next year, when she was enjoying her promotion and her raise. She would save Lorelei Vogel from herself. Lorelei would *enjoy* it and beg to retain Wendy's services forever. Vegas would be welcoming. Wendy would not have occasion to use the rubbing alcohol after all. And maybe Daniel Blackstone wouldn't even be there.

Daniel wanted to sag against the elevator wall and gingerly touch his mauled eye to assess the damage. But he wasn't alone—Colton was with him—so he was still on display. He stood up straight in the elevator with his hands down by his sides. Breathing evenly through his nose, he tried not to think about thirty more years of keeping his cool in this job.

"I'm sorry I hit you, man," Colton said quietly.

Bullshit. Daniel glared at Colton. But searching Colton's face, he saw no malice. On a pained sigh he said, "It's okay. All in a day's work."

Colton's bleached blond brows shot up. "Really?"

"No," Daniel said, losing his battle with showing his annoyance.

The doors parted. He stepped through them and led the way down the hall. As he slid his key card through the door lock and pushed open the door for Colton, he was glad he'd taken a few extra minutes to make sure he left the room neat. Shoulders sagging, Colton looked like a kid in the principal's office in these professional quarters. Colton had been in his own suite only a few hours, but Daniel suspected it was already littered with beer cans.

Gesturing to the sofas overlooking the blinding day-lit Strip, Daniel muttered, "Have a seat. Excuse me just a moment." He took a deep breath, then peeked through the bathroom door at the mirror.

His eye looked exactly as bad as it felt. At least his whole socket wasn't bruised, but the knuckle mark underneath was turning from red to purple. For the life of him he couldn't remember a single piece of advice that *GQ* had ever dispensed about this.

Classy.

He hated this job.

He drew his phone from his pocket and checked his messages. He'd silenced it because it had been chiming all morning with new negative publicity for Colton.

Now, among the many e-mail updates of how strongly the public hated Colton, Daniel's office had flagged the message containing the worst news of all. Colton's unhinged ex-girlfriend had hired Stargazer, a public relations firm second only to the Blackstone Firm for averting Hollywood career disasters. They were scrappy, resourceful, irreverent—the opposite of the Blackstone Firm in every way. And Wendy Mann was one of their top agents. She was a likely candidate to take on Lorelei, since some of her time would be freed up now that she'd lost representation of Darkness Fallz to the Blackstone Firm.

Daniel had thought of her only occasionally in the six years since graduation, whenever she came up in work-related conversation. But he'd thought about her a lot in college. Battled with her over an academic prize that he had to win or risk embarrassing his father. Wished that they weren't enemies, because the very sight of her turned him on, not to mention the knowing tone in her husky laugh. She'd been the star of all his hormone-fueled college fantasies. He was sure if he saw her in person now, he would turn beet-red with embarrassment at what was going on in his head, as if she could see it herself.

He crossed the hotel room to the bar and dropped a few ice cubes into two glasses. Then he sloshed in a generous helping of Kentucky bourbon, in honor of Wendy, who was originally from down south some-where. As he poured the amber liquid, he wasn't sure whether he meant the drink as a bane to keep her away or a charm to bring her closer. One thing was certain: if she really was representing Lorelei, Wendy was about to make his job a whole lot harder.

He sipped his drink. The bourbon had a sharper kick than he'd expected from its refined look—like Wendy, he thought briefly, before snapping back to reality. He rounded the sofa to hand the other drink to Colton.

"Thanks." Colton took a big gulp. "You might want to put yours on that eye." He held his own cold glass near his eye to show Daniel what he meant.

Daniel sank onto the opposite sofa, careful to give the impression he was sitting rather than collapsing. He gave Colton a tight smile, though smiling was the last thing he felt like doing. "Tell me why your agent brought me out here."

Colton let his head loll back against the sofa, suddenly weary, though he'd seemed chipper enough when blackjack and a call girl were available. "I'm supposed to emcee this stupid televised awards show Friday night, but they have a stupid morality clause. They're threatening to replace me. They say nobody's going to tune in because of what I'm saying *online*?"

Daniel cleared his throat. "It may have more to do with your peculiar choice of where to relieve yourself. What was that about last night?"

"I was *so wasted*, and my driver dared me. I never back out of a dare. Usually my bodyguard stops me from doing stupid shit. My driver and I snuck out. I'm ashamed." Colton gave Daniel a lopsided grin that might have been charming if they hadn't been talking about a grown man pissing in a fountain, and if Daniel hadn't wanted to kill him.

"I don't care about the awards show so much," Colton admitted, "but my agent's got me on the short list for some big flicks, okay? Action movies that would make my career. My agent thinks if the awards show replaces me, the movies won't want me, either, because I'll look like a liability."

"Your agent is a smart man," Daniel said.

Colton grimaced and gulped his bourbon. "I'm working with you to make my agent happy, but he's overreacting. No way is the awards show going to replace me this late in the game."

"Really?" Daniel asked. "How much rehearsal have you done so far?"

"None. Rehearsal starts tomorrow, but—"

"So," Daniel broke in, "if you're pissing in a fountain that's somehow become one of America's most beloved landmarks in the past decade and a half, and you're posting tasteless insults online about your beautiful ex-girlfriend, why *would* anybody tune in to watch this unpleasant guy? Why *can't* the show replace you at the last minute with another actor, one who's on TV *now*, one who's not struggling to make the transition from teen shows to the adult market and failing miserably?"

Colton swallowed. "I guess it could happen."

"Which is why you promptly went down to an open

section of the casino and nearly got photographed losing a hundred thousand dollars while sitting next to a prostitute."

Colton frowned. "I didn't know she was a prostitute."

Daniel watched Colton levelly over the rim of his glass while taking a sip. "I might believe you if I were my father, or if I were twelve. What's with the girl, Colton?"

Colton shrank several more inches. "Okay. I let her pull up a chair. I also noticed the photographer pretty quickly. I was hoping a picture of me with the prostitute might get picked up by the tabloids and make Lorelei go nuts. I wasn't trying to lose the hundred grand, though."

At that admission, Daniel took another, bigger sip of bourbon. He might not be much of a drinker, but for once he wanted to chug the contents of the glass and pour himself another. He couldn't, though. He had too much work to do today. He asked Colton, "What's the deal with Lorelei?"

Colton's jaw tightened. "We were great for the past three years. Then, as soon as we left the TV show and she started her own band, the whore cheated on me with her drummer."

Daniel winced internally at Colton's brutal language for his ex-lover. "Maybe we're having trouble with definitions here," he said. "A whore is what was sitting next to you downstairs at the blackjack table, where everybody in America could take pictures of you together. Lorelei is your costar from a children's TV show—"

"It wasn't a children's show," Colton said testily. "It was for teenagers, and a lot of adults watched it, too."

Daniel waited for Colton to hear how immature that statement sounded. After a few seconds of silence, he realized that was not going to happen. He cleared his throat and went on, "—and Lorelei is also your ex-girlfriend. You shared your life with her for three years. The public expects you to have sore feelings about your breakup. Anybody would. But they don't expect you to call her names on the web. You can't say things like that about a young lady. She's twenty-one years old, Colton."

"She's plenty old enough to know exactly what she's doing."

"She's not much older than my sister." Daniel said this with more vehemence than he'd intended. He could tell, because Colton raised his eyebrows in surprise.

Daniel was surprised, too. He wasn't sure where that outburst had come from. Since when was he human? He cleared his throat. "When you insult a young lady, you're trying to make her look bad, but *you're* the one who ends up looking bad. And things are about to get worse for you. I heard that Lorelei has hired Stargazer, which is one of the best PR firms she could have brought on board, besides my own."

Colton frowned. "What does that mean?"

"Stargazer's very good. If they send certain people, I won't know quite what to expect. But if they send Sarah Seville, I'll know we're in trouble. Sarah is a smooth talker, very friendly, and she'll become Lorelei's new best friend and persuade her to use a soft touch with the press. If they send Wendy Mann, we're in *more* trouble. Wendy is a drill sergeant. She has a reputation for whipping people into shape and getting them to do things they never dreamed they could do themselves. Before you know it, she'll have Lorelei dressing in lace and pearls and hosting tea parties for charity."

"If she's so good, why don't I fire you and hire her?" Colton asked in the tone of a petulant child. "Maybe *she* wouldn't have dragged me away from the tables when my luck was turning."

"Your luck wasn't turning," Daniel said. "There's no such thing as luck. The probability that you'll get a good hand is exactly the same every time you play." He could tell by Colton's wandering gaze that Colton was losing interest, so Daniel stepped back from the lecture on applied math and returned to the subject that Colton seemed most interested in: Wendy Mann. "And if you hired Wendy, you wouldn't like her. I guarantee you wouldn't lay eyes on a blackjack table the rest of the time you spent in Vegas."

"But with you, I can? I don't think it would be good for publicity if I stayed in my room until Friday. That would make it look like my handlers had shut me down because there was something seriously wrong with me. It would be an admission of guilt."

"That's very insightful, Colton. If you'd been that smart for the past month, you wouldn't need me."

"It's Lorelei. I wouldn't have gotten so plastered last night if my driver hadn't gotten me talking about her. She makes me crazy, man." Colton took off his trucker hat, rubbed his hair, and put his hat back on, a gesture Daniel had seen many times before. Other actors got this agitated about women. So did rock stars, celebrity chefs, and professional football players. Daniel himself did not, so he couldn't empathize.

"You've got to help me get her back," Colton pleaded.

"After she cheated on you and you called her names all over the Internet?"

"Yes!"

People in love were foreign and strange. "I'm not a high-priced relationship counselor," Daniel pointed out. "I can't help you get her back. I'm a public relations specialist. The best I could do is make it *look* like you've gotten her back."

"Then do that," Colton said, "and maybe the rest will follow."

He had a point, actually. Daniel didn't care whether Colton fixed his relationship with Lorelei, or whether that was even a good idea. But the two of them getting back together right before the awards ceremony that they both were starring in would be terrific PR. He surveyed Colton coldly, like he was a penguin behind the glass in the Central Park Zoo, and began to plot how he could use the star's heartbreak to repair his reputation.

"Let me think about it," Daniel said vaguely, as if dismissing the idea. "In the meantime, we need a short-term game plan. I don't want to institute martial law"—actually, he did, but instituting martial law only made stars more likely to go on a bender and land in jail—"but I do want to be notified of where you're going and why."

"Giuliana Jacobsen reserved the back room of the Big O club here in the hotel for tonight. I was planning to go to her party."

Daniel kept himself from wincing or laughing out loud at the name of the club, so provocative it was ridiculous. He said only, "Giuliana Jacobsen, the reality star?"

"Yeah, I know. That's kind of slumming. But it's Monday night, so there aren't a lot of parties to choose from."

"You mean, Lorelei will be there."

Colton grinned sheepishly. "I don't know that for sure, but Lorelei's staying here in the hotel. It would be easy for her to go. Lorelei likes stuff to be easy. And she doesn't miss a party." He gazed out on the Strip. His voice turned dreamy as he said, "I love that about her."

The trucker hat cast a shadow across Colton's eyes. Daniel studied him. He knew Colton was twenty-one, but in his hat and sweatshirt and mauled jeans, sitting on the tailored sofa, he looked like a fourteen-year-old after a growth spurt. "What are you planning to wear?" Daniel asked.

Colton looked at him in confusion and gestured to the attire he had on.

Daniel frowned at him.

"What?" Colton demanded. "I'm Colton Farr. I wear what I want."

"You're a young actor with public relations problems," Daniel corrected him, "and you look it. If you want to keep your emcee job for the Hot Choice Awards and land an A-list movie role, you need to look like *that*. Never dress for the job you already have. Dress for the job you're trying to get. At this point, it wouldn't hurt for you to act like you're trying."

Colton nodded shortly. "I get it."

Daniel picked up his glass, drained it, and set it back down with a *bang* carefully calculated to startle Colton while not quite denting the table or shattering the heavy tumbler. "If you're going to this party, we need to agree on three things." He counted them on his fingers. "You will not get too drunk."

"Agreed."

"You will not piss anywhere except a urinal."

Colton laughed until he saw the serious expression on Daniel's face. Colton's smile fell away as he repeated, "Agreed."

"You will not call Lorelei names."

"Of course not," Colton said. "I told you I wanted her back, didn't I?"

Daniel almost felt relieved at Colton's genuine reaction, and sorry he'd brought it up again or ever mistrusted the actor. But that was just it—Colton was an actor.

Daniel stopped himself just before he reached for his empty glass on the table. The bar was here in the room with him. It was tempting to drown this job in alcohol. But he'd always been able to resist. He wouldn't make an exception for Colton, Lorelei, and Stargazer PR.

Unless they truly sent Wendy Mann. That woman might drive him to drink after all.

3

Wendy sat up—she'd given herself one hell of a crick in her neck from bending over her computer so long, poring over the files on *Lorelei*—and pressed her forehead to the cool window as the plane circled Vegas. The Strip was gorgeous at night with every casino outlined in glowing color. The hotels looked so tiny from this altitude that she could hardly imagine how vast they really were, even though she'd lived in some of them for weeks at a time. Her heart beat faster in anticipation. After many missions to pull celebrity addicts out of poker rooms and bordellos, she should have been jaded. She *was* a little jaded, actually. But Vegas still held much of the charm for her that she'd felt on her first business trip here years ago, as excited at the idea as her assistant had been earlier that day.

She loved the luxury the casinos offered to everyone, not just the high-born. She loved that the seedy part of town was around the corner from the luxe side, so she could lean over and peek into the sort of life she'd left in Morgantown without actually taking a step in that direction. She looked forward to the excitement and noise and music and fashion and lights, blinking like a beacon below her. New York got on her nerves sometimes, Chicago was cold, Los Angeles smelled, but Vegas was still magic.

She grinned again, no longer faking her positive attitude but really feeling optimistic that she would figure out Lorelei soon enough. Lorelei might not need money, but surely she cared enough about *something* to rein in her bad behavior. Her silver-screen heartthrob dad might have pressured her to hire the agent who had placed her on a teen TV show, which was where she'd met Colton. But six years of experience in this business told Wendy that Lorelei herself had formed her new band, secured a recording contract, and arranged for a tour. And she'd asked for Wendy's help when ticket sales were so disappointing that the tour was threatened.

So Lorelei cared about her music, or her father's approval, or living up to the legacy of her dead rock icon mom, or what Colton thought of her after all. Or possibly about the drummer from her band, with whom she was alleged to have had an affair. Everybody cared about something. All Wendy had to do was tease out what that thing was, and then yell at Lorelei until the sinking starlet realized she was throwing that thing away. Except this time Wendy was banned from yelling, damn it.

The plane touched down smoothly in the black night and taxied toward the terminal. It was midnight in New York—Wendy could vouch for this by the itching of her contacts—but only nine in Vegas, and Lorelei's night of partying would just be getting started. Before the flight attendant had finished announcing that passengers were allowed to use their electronics, Wendy clicked her phone on and checked Lorelei's various social media accounts. Most of the star's messages that day had been innocent enough, complimenting the other artists scheduled to perform at the Hot Choice Awards, expressing her excitement. Wendy wasn't ready to sigh with relief, but at least she knew Lorelei could act like a normal person when pressed.

However, Lorelei's most recent message gave Wendy pause.

Heard Colton Farr punched out his new PR guy. Sounds about right.

"Ha!" Wendy shouted, drawing the attention of the other businesspeople pulling their bags down from the overhead bins. She'd wanted to punch Daniel Blackstone herself many times in college. She was only sorry that Colton had beaten her to it.

That was her knee-jerk reaction. Then she realized the news wasn't what she'd initially thought. The Blackstone Firm hadn't sent Daniel after all. Daniel would never allow anyone to punch him. He would keep much tighter control of the situation than that.

She hurried down the aisle to exit the plane, mentally skipping through other men the Blackstone Firm might have sent. Her disappointment disgusted her. Surely she hadn't been looking *forward* to seeing Daniel Blackstone. Did she *want* to get fired? The fact that he wasn't on the case was *good* news. The fact that Colton was going around punching people was good news, too, because it made him look negative and Lorelei look better in comparison.

It could also be bad news. Lorelei and Colton obviously weren't done with each other, and the last thing Lorelei needed was a volatile—even abusive—boyfriend. Wendy had had one of those herself, and she wouldn't wish it on anyone. The sick feeling that she had another Rick on her hands crept into her stomach.

As she pondered the possibilities, watching the screen on her phone, a new post from Lorelei popped up with a link to a photo. Wendy followed the link and came face-to-face with a full-screen image of Lorelei's cleavage, if one could call it that. The breasts were so diminutive that *cleavage* was an optimistic term, implying that there were two separate objects and a clear division between them.

On second thought, Wendy puzzled over the picture, not absolutely sure anymore what part of the body it showed. She turned the phone this way and that, frustrated when the photo turned along with the device. Finally she read the caption. Yep, it was Lorelei's cleavage all right.

Poor ex is here at Giuliana Jacobsen's bash wishing he had some of this.

Marching up the jet bridge, Wendy called the number she'd been given for Lorelei's cell phone, though that was an exercise in futility. If Lorelei was at this reality star's party, she wouldn't hear her phone ring. Even if she did see the call coming through, she wouldn't call back an unfamiliar number. Wendy texted Sarah.

Lorelei is tweeting pics of her v v small boobies. Girlfriend is off the rails. WHY DIDN'T U WARN ME

She had to wait only thirty seconds for Sarah's answer.

LOL! You said: "I need to get home and pack. I don't have time for the rundown." :P

Wendy hated it when Sarah mocked her with emoticons. But she needed Sarah, so her texts were only mildly sarcastic as she asked Sarah to figure out the location of Giuliana Jacobsen's party. Luckily it was in a club at the same hotel where Lorelei and therefore Wendy were staying. She slid out of her taxi and wheeled her suitcase through the grand entrance to the casino and across the wildly patterned carpet, toward the Big O. The club's ridiculous name was spelled out in huge letters and outlined in lights over the doorway.

She slowed as she drew closer. She thought she saw a familiar figure seated at a table next to the glass wall. No, it couldn't be. She'd imagined in her darkest hour that Daniel Blackstone might be here to represent Colton, but that had been her panic talking. Tall, dark, handsome men in impeccably tailored suits were a dime a dozen in Vegas.

Then he turned his head, eyes following the ass of a passing bar waitress. Wendy caught a glimpse of his profile and those high cheekbones. Damn, it *was* him.

The table where he now sat was a booth way too big for one person, but nobody was going to tell Daniel Blackstone to move. The booth was elevated several feet above the main floor so he could see over the pulsing crowd and watch everybody who came in the door. He would look things over from the outside first, observing, getting the lay of the land, figuring out who surrounded his client, who had jealousies, who was a potential leak. Only then would he move to the inner room, sticking close to the client, persuading him or pressuring him or, in select cases, blackmailing him into changing his ways.

In short, Daniel sat exactly where Wendy would have sat, doing exactly what Wendy would have been doing, if he hadn't beaten her to it.

And one of the people he was looking for was *her*.

Her first instinct was to slip past him into the club room. Just then, his eyes passed over her. She could still duck into the club without speaking to him, but the two of them likely would circle each other slowly over the next few days, running into each other at the same elite parties, as she pulled Lorelei out of her mess and he tended to Colton. Might as well get the formalities over with.

She wasn't going to drag her suitcase awkwardly up the stairs to his booth, though. First she gave the bartender a sizable tip to lock down her suitcase, computer, and suit jacket, which was too hot for the crowded bar. Then she turned for Daniel—grumbling to herself that he'd put her in a position where she had to look up at him—and noticed his black eye.

This time she didn't laugh that Daniel had finally gotten smacked. She felt his pain. In college she'd heard his older brother had died in the Blackstone Firm office at the World Trade Center when Daniel was a teenager. Her own father had died when she was a college junior. She understood how a death that close could affect a person. His black eye reminded her of his unexpected vulnerability, and her heart softened.

He must know Wendy saw his eye. He probably knew about Lorelei's post blaming Colton for the injury, too. Any other PR operative would cringe in embarrassment, afraid to be seen in public. Yet Daniel still watched Wendy coming, confident as ever.

She climbed a short set of stairs to his table, feeling as if she were ascending a dais for an audience with royalty. *It's for your job, to keep your job*, she kept telling herself as she willed her body forward.

At the last second, she remembered how she and Sarah had jealously made fun of Daniel in college. In the privacy of their dorm room, they would throw up their hands, shriek "Daniel Blackstone!" and pretend to faint like teens in the fifties swooning over Elvis.

That's why Wendy was laughing as she put out her hand to touch the king.

If Daniel had meant the morning's Kentucky bourbon to call Wendy Mann to Vegas—and he still wasn't sure about that—it had worked. His mind spun with the implications. Now that Wendy was directing Lorelei, the plan he'd been cooking up to get Colton out of trouble would be harder to implement.

But the fact that he and Wendy were enemies didn't mean he couldn't enjoy the sight of her. Her long blond locks blew back over her shoulders with her own speed as she climbed the stairs to his table, and her slim hips swayed in a tight black skirt.

He stood and put his hand out to meet hers, keeping his face a blank.

"Daniel!" she called over the throbbing music in that throaty voice he remembered. "Wendy Mann." Her hand slipped farther into his.

He squeezed her hand and hesitated. Not long enough to be rude. Just long enough to make her doubt whether he remembered her.

"We were in Dr. Abbott's speech-writing class together? And Dr. Benson's image management class. Several others." Her blond brow furrowed in annoyance that he couldn't quite place her.

Good. Now that he'd knocked her off balance, he turned on the charm, as if he were doing a favor for someone underneath him in the business. "Of course. Wendy. Please." He gestured to the velvet bench beside him.

As they both sat, he signaled the waitress—who was wearing a teddy—and ordered the silliest thing he could think of. "Two glasses of champagne." He named a good label but didn't go the last step of ordering the bottle. He needed his head clear, for one thing. And though it would probably help him in his job if Wendy's head *weren't* clear, he didn't want to attract the attention of having a bottle popped open for them. They weren't getting married, after all. Ordering ridiculous drinks was enough.

After the waitress had left so it was too late to say no, he turned back to Wendy and asked, "Is champagne okay?" He expected her to have settled far away from him on the long bench, embarrassed and browbeaten by his superior air.

Instead he found her as close as she could sit without touching him. Her elbow was on the table, her arm bare below a white puff of sleeve. Her chin was propped on her fist. She looked utterly comfortable, which made him very uncomfortable—the same way she'd always made him feel. The way *he'd* been trying to make *her* feel, damn it! They'd exchanged only a few words in college, but he'd always known she was poking a little fun at him. He wished she would stop. He'd lost his sense of humor years ago. He would sound like a robot if she made him laugh.

She brought her other hand up from her lap. He watched it coming, feeling slightly dazed. He caught a whiff of her expensive perfume as she placed her hand over his on the table.

"Champagne is perfect," she said. "In celebration of seeing an old friend. Thank you."

He *knew* she was making fun of him then, because they'd never been friends. She'd intrigued him in college. But he was competing with her for top honors in their major. His father wouldn't have thought much of her as competition—a little girl from Appalachia— but Daniel had read her papers and seen her projects, and he'd witnessed her funny and fearless delivery. He couldn't let her beat him, because he couldn't explain that defeat to his father. So he'd done everything he could to win. He'd studied harder and worked longer. And he'd stayed away from her.

Now he almost would have thought she was coming on to him, but she was way too good at her job for that. Her hand disappeared into her lap again. She wasn't scooting any closer.

He leaned toward her so she could hear him over the music. "Or in celebration of the end of your six-hour flight."

She grinned. "You're not kidding! I have a crick in my neck that would kill a horse."

"You should get a massage while you're here." His eyes flitted to the creamy skin of her neck before he forced them back to her face. "You're in town just for pleasure, right?" he deadpanned.

"Right!" she said enthusiastically. "And I see you're in town for the recreational opportunities."

He raised his brows, waiting for her to explain so he wouldn't look stupid by telling her he had no idea what she was talking about.

She took her hand away from her chin and gestured to his eye. "I've heard it's the latest craze in high-end fitness. Boxing!"

He bristled at that comment before giving it right back to her. "Yes, I'm here for pleasure, too. I'm taking a short break because I just got assigned to a difficult case. Have you heard of Darkness Fallz?" He inclined his head toward the enormous speakers in the corner, which were blasting the latest Darkness Fallz abomination.

She was good. She hardly even winced when he mentioned the supergroup that had just ditched her. And then she said in a reasonable facsimile of an innocent tone, "No, I haven't heard of them. Are they contemporary Christian?"

He nearly laughed and ended up only choking on the word *no*. Luckily his voice was drowned out by the Darkness Fallz chorus: "You're moving on and it's like a knife in my eye/I hope you get sick and DIEEEEEEEE."

Blinking lights made him turn away from Wendy momentarily, toward the window onto the casino. A slot machine was going crazy, flashing as it spit out a river of tokens. The elderly couple in front of the machine embraced. The man picked up the woman, spun her around, and kissed her.

"How sweet!" Wendy exclaimed, beaming. "I hope they enjoy their loot. What a good omen, that this is the first thing I see after I step off the plane into Vegas."

Besides me, Daniel wanted to point out. He rather liked being her bad omen. But they were pretending to have friendly small talk, so he kept the conversation light. "Are you a gambler?"

She looked him straight in the eye. "I like people to *think* I'm a successful gambler," she said. "Actually I'm stacking the deck. How about you?"

"I'm with you. I gamble only if I can figure out a way to cheat."

"You're my kind of man."

He wanted to stick to that line of questioning. They might only be toying with each other, assessing the enemy's weapons before they struck, but he was enjoying it.

The waitress picked that moment to interrupt them. She placed one glass of champagne in front of Wendy and one in front of him. After she left, Daniel lifted his flute. "To pleasure," he said.

"To pleasure." Wendy tapped the rim of her glass against his. The bell-like sound rang through a rare quiet moment in the Darkness Fallz track.

Sipping his champagne, he watched her over the top of his flute as she drank a few long gulps with her eyes closed, then turned her head to one side and stretched her neck. She really did have a crick. Sitting with Daniel and having a drink was her only break—if one could call it that—before she searched out Lorelei. He knew how she felt.

The next second, she set the drink down, her eyes opened, and she was grinning again. "So who of note is here at the bar? Not that you've been paying attention. I know you're on vacation."

"You're right," he said drily. "I've just been sitting here relaxing and getting plastered."

"You do seem three sheets over there. Totally out of control. You might want to cut yourself off."

"Thanks for your concern. But I did happen to notice Lorelei Vogel pass by."

"Really!" Wendy blinked her long eyelashes, feigning shock. "What a big star! Did you get her autograph?"

"No. And Colton Farr is here. Giuliana Jacobsen."

"You don't say!" Wendy gasped. "Did they go into the back room?"

"Yes." He leaned closer again, catching another whiff of her perfume, and said conspiratorially, "I heard Giuliana is throwing a party."

Wendy gaped at him. "Wow! A reality star of her stature is liable to bring all the A-listers over from the Bellagio!"

"I've seen them." He gave her a litany of the D-list celebrities who had filed through. "But like I say, I haven't been keeping track."

She slapped her hand on the table as if coming to a spontaneous decision. "This may sound crazy to you, but I think I'll slip back there to the private room and see if I can get in." She laughed uproariously at her own joke, it seemed, without letting Daniel in on what was so funny. Then she eyed him knowingly and clarified, "They don't let just any girl into the private room of the Big O club, you know."

Daniel laughed. Then corralled his laughter into a polite, halfhearted chuckle. He didn't want her to know how funny he thought she was. And he hoped she couldn't see him blushing in the dim and shifting light of the bar.

He watched her very carefully, and he could have sworn she didn't blush at all as she said, "I wonder if the interior of the club is red velvet. Or pink. Pink velvet."

He bit his lip. He refused to let her make him laugh again.

"And they have fountains running over the velvet, to lubricate it, for effect."

He cleared his throat.

"Like a *vagina*," she said with gusto.

That was it. He burst into laughter. Several men passing turned to stare because his outburst was so loud, or because he looked so strange wearing a genuine smile. He reached for his champagne and polished it off.

"You okay there?" She pursed her lips, suppressing her own smile as he nodded. She didn't press him further, though. She let him off the hook. Sighing, she said, "I probably won't get in, but it's fun to try. Maybe I'll see you there later?"

He considered making a joke about her inviting him into a vagina. But that was a joke *she* would make, or some guy with a sense of humor. The kind of guy she was probably married to or—dating, he decided, glancing at her ringless hand supporting her chin.

He managed, "It does sound like fun, but I'm sure I won't get in, either." Of course he was on the list to be admitted. She was, too, or she would argue with the bouncers and make phone calls until they let her behind the velvet rope.

"Thank you for the champagne." She stood—first bending so that he got a glimpse down her white shirt at her cleavage and the lacy edge of her pale bra, then straightening.

He stood with her. Maybe it was his imagination, but he thought there was a moment when she looked up at him in the near darkness, her blue eyes big with something other than teasing. A spark passed between them.

And then she was sliding out of the booth and rounding it to make her way through the crowd to the back room where the action and the catastrophes were.

Sitting again, he watched her go. Then blinked. Slapped one hand to his jaw to make sure it hadn't dropped. Her tight skirt had seemed like normal business attire from the front. Now he saw that an exaggerated zipper ran all the way down the back. It was a detail some crazy designer had added to make the standard offering a little different. It was also way too risqué for conservative New York offices, including his own. She was wearing it anyway.

And wearing it well.

He longed to watch that zipper sway all the way into the back room, but he couldn't afford for her to catch him staring at her like she was a scantily clad celebrity and he was her starstruck fan. With supreme effort, he tore his eyes away and looked through the glass wall at the casino floor again, wondering what minor luminaries he'd missed while Wendy had his full attention. He put his elbow on the table and his chin in his hand and was just realizing he'd unconsciously imitated the position she'd taken sitting there when he heard a voice close by.

"Hey."

Wendy was standing beside him. As he looked up at her, he couldn't help wondering whether she'd engineered their positions on purpose, so that he would be gazing up at her instead of the other way around.

But she'd lost the mocking tone in her voice. "I just wanted to say . . ." She frowned down at him. "Take care, Daniel. You don't seem like yourself." Her gaze focused on his battered eye.

And then the teasing came back. Before he could stop her—and how would he have stopped her?—she reached out and ruffled his hair.

She walked quickly through the writhing crowd, toward the Big O. The long golden zipper on the back of her black skirt wagged violently as her hips shifted.

He felt his cheeks burn with anger that someone in the bar might have witnessed her overly familiar gesture. Yet he still felt the soft touch of her fingertips brushing along his scalp. And he couldn't tear his eyes away from her ass.

She was so tiny that she disappeared behind the dancers. He glimpsed her white blouse again, glowing among all the black. She vanished again. And then he saw her talking to the bouncer at the entrance to the inner room. He hoped against hope that the bouncer would refuse her entry, and Daniel could save face after that hair ruffling by interceding for her, coming to her rescue.

The bouncer held the door open for her, and she slipped inside.

Daniel pushed away his champagne flute and stood, eyes never leaving the door of the inner room. He'd heard stories about Wendy's exploits his whole professional life. Now that he thought about it, he was amazed their paths hadn't crossed before. But he was finally feeling something he hadn't felt since he'd gone head-to-head with her for the Clarkson Prize.

Challenged.

4

As Wendy walked away from Daniel's table, she started to get that sinking feeling, with mountains looming over her. She knew she had no filter. She had very good instincts about what made other people tick, and very bad ones about what made herself tick, or how far she could take her natural inclination to tease, like stopping on her walk to elementary school and poking an ant bed with a stick. It was only afterward, as she was retreating from an encounter, that she realized she'd made a mistake.

She looked back toward Daniel. She couldn't see him past the wall of bodies dancing around her. It didn't matter anyway. She didn't *really* want to know whether he was still glaring at her, did she?

Flushed with embarrassment and adrenaline and the certainty that she'd ruined everything in her first hour in Vegas, Wendy stammered through her introduction to the burly bouncer at the door to the inner room. Luckily, her name had made it onto his list. At least someone in Lorelei's camp wasn't too coked up to sweat the details. But Wendy felt coked up herself at the moment and was in no shape to introduce herself to Lorelei as her savior.

Stepping through the doorway into the second party, she noticed with disappointment that the club was decorated in blue rather than pink velvet and did not glisten or otherwise look like anything remotely resembling a vagina. Clearly the designers were not as creative as she was. She fought her way through the even tighter crowd and retreated to an empty bench in a corner. She couldn't make a call because being overheard would be disastrous, and the music was too loud anyway. But she could take deep breaths and text Sarah.

Daniel "Cheekbones" Blackstone is here. Was trying to draw him out and when I left I patted him on the head. Probably should not have done that.

In less than a minute she had Sarah's response.

YOU WHAT? He will be MORE likely to one-up u now. Why couldn't u just have too many friendly drinks w him and leave him w the impression ur a lesbian???

Wendy laughed at this description of Sarah's own modus operandi. She texted, *Touché*, which her phone autocorrected to *Touched*, which was not what she'd meant at all.

Or was it? She thought of her shock when she saw Daniel's black eye, the damage Colton had done to him, and felt sorry for him all over again. She'd never felt sorry for him for being born with a silver spoon in his mouth, but tonight he'd looked so . . . solemn, isolated to the point of sadness, sitting there on his throne. Then he'd shown her a side of himself that she'd never seen before, ever, like he was under so much pressure that he was finally close to blowing.

She texted Sarah,

I made him laugh like an embarrassed teenage boy.

As she waited for Sarah's answer, she read her text over and considered it. She'd been a teenager, eighteen, and she assumed he'd been the same age, when they'd first met. Except she wasn't sure they'd ever met, officially. So . . . when they first became aware of each other. Or when *she* first became aware of *him*. She did hope he knew who she was, and that he'd only been pretending to have a hard time placing her. She would hate to think that after all those nights she'd agonized over whether she could beat him for the Clarkson Prize, he hadn't even known she existed.

Then came Sarah's answer.

When it's whack, it's crack.

This was one of Sarah and Wendy's mantras. They'd noticed that when they came into a meltdown situation and there didn't seem to be any overt cause for the chaos, usually the stars and all their entourage were busy covering up the fact that somebody was on crack: the star, the manager, the boyfriend, the star's mother.

Wendy snorted at the idea of Daniel Blackstone on crack, then typed,

More likely high on the casino's oxygen bar.

That was kind of funny, but not what she'd intended to share with Sarah. She typed,

I was able to make him laugh only once before the blast shields went up. Maybe I'll try again later.

Her nerves calmer now, she took a deep breath—smelled marijuana and looked around curiously, but the smoker was hiding it well—and stood to make her way across the room in search of Lorelei. She was slipping her phone into her purse when it vibrated in her hand again. Glancing at the screen, she saw Sarah had texted,

Stay away from him.

That was a very good idea, and yet as Wendy pictured herself sidestepping him until the Hot Choice

Awards in four nights, she felt a little sad. She definitely wanted to see if she could make him laugh again.

She put her phone away and scanned the crowd. She recognized Lorelei in a far corner, having a tête-à-tête with Giuliana, whose fake tan looked even stranger under the club lights. Then Wendy saw him coming toward her.

Rick. Blond and handsome and broad with muscles that he'd used to pin her by the throat against the wall when he attacked her at college.

Not Rick, she assured herself, tamping down the wave of panic. After he'd assaulted her, he'd fled New York. She hadn't seen him since. Even when she went back for her father's funeral in West Virginia, he hadn't been around. People said he'd skipped town right after she left for college, stealing his uncle's truck on his way out. He'd held her captive in her dorm room, then disappeared completely.

No, this was someone much more banal: a huge television star. Yet her heart didn't slow down as she picked out Colton Farr's differences from Rick in the dim and spinning lights: his surgically straightened nose, his younger age by ten years, his softer smile. He might not be her violent ex, but he *was* the last person she should be seen talking to before she'd even introduced herself to Lorelei. By the time she realized this, he was too close for her to escape without an awkward scene, and public relations specialists did not do awkward scenes.

She noted as he neared that he was uncharacteristically dressed like a grown man rather than a teenage skateboarder. His style might have matured, but his approach hadn't. He gave her a lopsided grin and dipped his head to say, "Hey, beautiful."

Her grin at him rapidly intensified until she was just gritting her teeth. She dressed well and paid attention to her hair and makeup so she'd be accepted into the stars' worlds—and yes, there was vanity mixed in. But her client's recent ex was handing her a line, and her looks had suddenly become a liability. The Darkness Fallz singer's ire over being forced to quit drugs would be nothing compared with Lorelei's complaint to Stargazer that Wendy had flirted with her ex.

Wendy gave Sarah a hard time about dressing like a women's basketball coach on the job, but now she was seeing a certain logic in that mode of fashion. She dodged around Colton. "Hey yourself," she shouted over the music. "Excuse me."

"Excuse *me*," he countered, moving with her. "Where are you going in such a hurry? I'll buy you a drink."

She took a long, calming breath through her nose. Colton was not Rick, and if she couldn't shake the feeling that she'd fallen into a bottomless pit when she *had not*, she was going to screw up this case and lose her job for real. She managed to say smoothly, "I've had a drink, thanks."

"Let me introduce myself. I'm Colton Farr."

She extended her hand for him to shake, to move their conversation from pickup line back to business.

"Yes, I've heard! Emcee of televised awards shows. Puncher of public relations specialists. Landmark fountain pisser. Congratulations."

As he took her hand, he turned his head and looked at her with one eye. "And you are?"

"Wendy Mann."

He dropped her hand and stepped back dramatically. "Oh, *you're* Wendy Mann!" He looked her up and down. "Nice."

She raised her eyebrows. "Do we know each other?" He must have talked to Lorelei about her. But that didn't make any sense. Lorelei and Colton weren't on speaking terms.

"Sure we do," Colton said. "I was at the Little Lingerie fashion show in L.A. a few weeks ago. You were one of the models. Good work up there."

Gross. This guy had plenty of money. He could be persuaded to spend it on things that would be useful to him, such as a ghostwriter to come up with better pickup lines. If she were on good terms with Daniel, she might suggest this. But she nodded seriously at Colton. "Yes. I was the one dressed as the whooping crane."

He stared at her for a moment, then relaxed. "I'm kidding with you, Wendy. You're doing PR for Lorelei."

She gasped as if he'd made the best. Joke. Ever! "That's right. How did you know?"

"Daniel Blackstone suspected you might be coming."

Wendy nodded slowly. "Did he."

"Yes. And listen. I'm not sure things are going to work out between Daniel and me. Would you come to work for me?"

She widened her eyes at him in innocent horror. "After you came on to me?"

"I was kidding, I said."

"You said that the *third* time. Anyway, hiring and firing Daniel and me is a little more complicated than that. It's not like we're doing PR out of the trunks of our cars. You sign a contract with his firm or mine, and the firm sends us."

"Please, Wendy. Daniel was talking about you like you could really whip me into shape."

"You need whipping?"

"Yes!" he said more vehemently than she would have liked.

"No, I'm sorry. Daniel will whip you into shape, too. You'll see." Also, *go away.*

Colton grinned at her. "If we're not going to work together, there's no reason we can't play together. I'm coming on to you again. You seem like the kind of lady who'd enjoy a walk on the wild side."

Oh *God.* What *had* Daniel said to Colton about her? The way people in PR talked about Daniel, someone going up against him might as well forfeit. He was that good. But nobody had ever detailed to her exactly how he worked. Maybe he really did convince his clients to proposition the PR specialists representing his clients' jealous exes. Divide and conquer. Wendy had engaged in some questionable business practices herself to get her clients out of trouble, but nothing like this. Could Daniel possibly be that sneaky?

Two could play at that game.

She threw her hands in the air, as if she were giving up. "You pegged me!" she told Colton. "But I can't walk on the wild side with *you*. I'm already with somebody."

"Who? Daniel? I saw you talking to him." Colton's eyes narrowed, as if for the first time he'd been presented with a serious obstacle to getting up Wendy's skirt. Her rejection of him didn't matter, but the threat of Daniel did.

Bingo.

"When did you see me talking to him?" she asked suspiciously.

"When you were in the outer room, at a booth near the door. I came out of the club for a minute."

"To do what? Piss on the bar?"

To his credit, he looked a little ill. "No, I was talking to the bouncer to see whether he'd throw Lorelei out if I could get her to hit me."

"Get *her* to hit *you*? You're the only one hitting people."

"You mean Daniel? That was an accident," Colton insisted. "So, are you with Daniel or not? Because if you're not . . ." He slid his hand up her arm.

"That's right," she said without missing a beat, covering his hand with her hand and sliding it back down and off her skin. "I'm with Daniel Blackstone." She couldn't have Colton coming on to her. She shouldn't even be standing next to him. Somebody was going to report it to Lorelei, and then Wendy would have even more problems.

"I could take that guy," Colton said stubbornly.

"Because he didn't hit you back?" Wendy asked archly. "As a general rule, we public relations specialists try not to strike our clients. If it weren't for professional decorum, I'm pretty sure he'd kick your ass. But let's not go there, okay? Daniel and I work for rival PR firms, and I would get in a lot of trouble if my bosses found out he and I are together."

"Really? What if you were together with the star represented by the rival firm instead? Maybe that would work out better for you."

"Ha ha ha! You're funny." Wendy giggled, then patted Colton on the cheek and slid past him. Looking up, she caught Lorelei staring right at them over the heads of the crowd. That girl was way too tall and willowy.

No. This could not be happening. Just what Wendy had been struggling to avoid. Her new client could *not* think Wendy was trying to steal the ex-boyfriend she obviously still had feelings for.

Wendy's purse vibrated against her hip. She stopped right there in the middle of the dance floor, mentally daring any of the flailing dancers around her to whack her with a stray arm. She would make this ecstasy trip one they didn't forget. Pulling out her phone, she saw she had another text from Sarah.

Have you found Lorelei? I think she just posted that you are a twat.

Horrified, Wendy scrolled through the pages on her phone to Lorelei's feed. Sure enough, there it was. Lorelei couldn't mean anyone but her.

Asscrack Colton Farr has taken up with some Repunzil twat.

"That is not even how you spell Rapunzel," Wendy grumbled to herself. She dared not look to her left again, where she could see out of the corner of her eye that Lorelei was commiserating with Giuliana. She'd gathered a few more ladies to listen to the tale, too: Lorelei's celebrity hairdresser, whom Wendy knew by sight. The producer of Lorelei's album, who was too old for a party like this but had been fighting middle age diligently with exercise and plastic surgery. Lorelei's best friend from the canceled teen show, who had gotten even more famous in the past few months for faking a heroin addiction in order to be cast on a rehab reality show. In Wendy's opinion, step one of her job was to get Lorelei some more impressive friends.

Make that step two. As she hazarded a glance to her right, she saw Colton and a point guard for the L.A. Lakers conversing behind their hands while they watched her. At any second, Colton would make another pass at her in full view of Lorelei et al.

In front of Wendy, a door opened in the dark velvet wall as the bouncer admitted someone from the outer club. Against the backdrop of the crowd pressing around him, Daniel was tall and dark, face chiseled into stone, black hair styled perfectly as if she'd never tousled it. He sauntered along the soft wall, scoping out the joint. Then he looked down at his cell phone. The screen lit his face in the black room, highlighting the sharp lines of his high cheekbones and his narrowed eyes. He glanced up at her. Realized he'd been busted looking at her. Glanced back down.

Not so fast. Wendy rushed across the club before he could escape, only slowing as she stepped around the last dancer so Daniel might not notice he was being ambushed. Wrong. He watched her unabashedly now with a look that said both of them knew exactly what was going on but neither was ready to admit it. She grinned brilliantly and stepped right up to his shoulder. He leaned down. She said in her most innocent bimbo tone, "Hi! I'm glad you got into the party after all."

"I'm so excited," he said, sounding ironically bored. "I've never been to a celebrity party before."

His voice in her ear sent electricity straight through her. They smiled at each other again, his expression visibly forced, hers genuine. She wanted to laugh out loud at his joke, but showing her appreciation would give him an advantage over her. She wished she could take her phone out right there and text

Sarah, *Daniel Blackstone makes me feel all funny inside,* because making fun of herself would take some of the edge off.

As it was, she just inched a bit closer to him against the padded velvet and pretended to watch the crowd with him in companionable silence. She longed to make him laugh again. Then they'd definitely look like they were together. She was pretty sure Daniel didn't go around laughing in his daily conversations with Colton Farr and his ilk.

However, with Daniel standing so close to her, impeccably dressed, dark eyes casually roving across the dancers in front of them like he owned the place, her sense of humor failed her. She felt like she was in ninth grade and a hot senior stood next to her in the lunchroom line. Between arms and legs flailing in the strobe lights, she spotted Colton staring at them, and she went cold in the sweaty room. Now was the time to look like she was flirting with Daniel, *now now now,* and her brain was a blank. She did the next best thing. She put her hand down by her side, slightly behind Daniel. Then she brought her hand closer to him, closer.

Daniel looked over at her. Her heart skipped a beat as he leaned down and cupped his hand around her ear. "Why are you touching my ass?" He backed away from her to let her respond, but he was watching her reproachfully.

Damn it! But whispering to each other also made it look like they were lovers. She stood on her tiptoes and said, "I beg your pardon. I was hoping you wouldn't notice. You have a very sensitive ass."

He stared at her. She'd let him off the hook a few minutes before when he hadn't wanted to acknowledge his black eye, but he wasn't going to give her the same courtesy.

She decided to come clean with him, since he saw through every tactic she tried anyway. She took him lightly by the elbow and turned him until they both faced the wall and could talk privately in their own bubble.

She kept one hand down, though. Ideally Colton across the room would think she was touching Daniel intimately as she spoke in his ear. "Here's the thing. I know you said you're here on vacation, but I've begun to suspect you're working with Colton Farr."

"Why would you think that?" Daniel asked without bothering to feign surprise.

"Lorelei Vogel is telling the whole world that Colton gave his PR guy a black eye."

"What black eye?" Daniel asked flatly.

"Don't worry. It's not noticeable at *all*. I detected it only because of my super-honed senses as a trained PR professional."

Daniel nodded. "Why are you keeping tabs on Lorelei Vogel?"

Wendy batted her eyes at him. "Wouldn't this conversation be easier if we both let our guards down and talked like we're not insane? Ready? One, two, three." She took a deep breath and let it out slowly. She noted that he glanced at her cleavage as her breasts rose and fell. His expression never changed.

"Is this what you look like when your guard is down?" she asked him.

"Yes. Does this have something to do with why you're still touching my ass?"

She scowled at him. He raised his eyebrows in response. He was going to make this as difficult as possible for her. She needed to go into a longer explanation than she could manage while they shouted into each other's ears, standing against the quilted wall.

"Come with me." Holding his gaze, she reached for his hand. There was a chance he would jerk it away, even make a production of rejecting her in public. They were enemies, after all. But she counted on the importance he laid on decorum. He wouldn't pull away from her, for the same reason he hadn't mauled Colton when Colton hit him.

Without looking—instinctively, it seemed—Daniel put out his hand to connect with hers. She felt a shock of awareness at his warm touch. She couldn't see his pupils in the shadowy room, and doubted if she could have seen them anyway because his eyes were so dark, but her heart sped up at the idea that his pupils dilated as his body reacted to her touch. She stared into his black eyes and lost herself.

Nonsense. She jerked him into motion a little harder than necessary and led him between and around dancers, back to the corner bench where she'd found privacy and relative quiet to text Sarah before.

As he slid around the far end of the cocktail table in front of them, she quickly sat and adjusted herself so that her skirt rode higher on her thighs than usual, the neckline of her blouse was pulled low, and her long hair fluffed around her shoulders. This way, Lorelei or Colton, glancing over, would assume she was having a sexy confab with her lover Daniel, whether Daniel played along or not.

It seemed that he would not. Eyeing her warily, he said, "Spill it, Mann. You've changed your tack in the last half hour. What happened?"

She glanced out at the crowd and saw nobody watching them. But she turned her chin toward the wall just in case, so her lips couldn't be read. "Colton is coming on to me," she said. "I can't have that."

"Why didn't you tell him to fuck off?" Daniel spoke so forcefully and looked so concerned that she felt a rush of the same fight-or-flight reaction she'd had when she first saw Colton here in the club, as if she really *should* consider this threat to be serious.

She swallowed her explanation: her job security was dicey, and she couldn't afford more trouble. Daniel wouldn't understand that. He was about to own the Blackstone Firm.

She said simply, "I can't state my case that forcefully right now. Colton was impervious to all my normal attempts at being obnoxious and repulsive. So I used the tools that were presented to me. He assumed you and I were together, and I jumped on it."

Daniel's mouth opened. He wasn't gaping at her in shock, exactly. He never gaped. She was beginning to question whether an easily labeled emotion ever passed across his face at all. But his lips parted and his jaw shifted to one side, which she read as outrage. She wasn't sure whether he was more outraged at Colton for coming on to her, or at her for dragging Daniel into it.

The next thing he said didn't make his feelings any clearer. "You need to state in no uncertain terms to Colton that, for reasons of professionalism, you're not interested."

Wendy nodded. "He's an actor who pisses in fountains. He understands all about professionalism. I think you got me into this mess, anyway. Did you mention me to Colton before I got here?"

"I'd heard Stargazer was sending someone to help Lorelei," Daniel admitted. "I discussed you as one of several possibilities. Why?"

"Did you describe me as some sort of dominatrix?"

He blinked at her. "Maybe."

She laughed. "Really? Is that my reputation?"

He gave her the smallest smile. "Yes."

"I guess that's kind of cool."

"If you say so."

"I guess that's Colton's type. Lorelei is a dominatrix in training, like a fluffy kitten with a Taser."

There! She thought she saw it for a split second: Daniel laughing. Almost laughing, but as soon as one corner of his mouth turned up, he regained control and turned his face impassive again.

Disappointed, she went on, "You don't really want me hooking up with your client, do you? I would totally pervert him. Besides, it would be bad PR. That cougar story only sells to one demographic: the cougars themselves. The rest of the public just thinks it's gross."

"You're—" Daniel said on a laugh. He cleared his throat, collected himself, and started again. "You're twenty-eight years old, aren't you? Not a cougar by any stretch of the imagination. But it doesn't matter. I'll tell him to stop hounding you."

"You don't know yet whether he'll follow your orders. I can't take that chance. Besides, you've already opened the can of worms. In Lorelei's mind, without you, I'm available and therefore a threat. Dating you is the only way I can take the can of worms off the shelf. I'm really sorry, Daniel, but I'm going to have to insist that you help me. You got me into this mess. You have to get me out."

"By acting like your boyfriend?" Daniel's face was utterly blank.

She acknowledged him with a grim nod. "Here where Colton and Lorelei can see."

His eyes slid away from her to the crowd undulating before them in the lush darkness. He seemed to be looking for Colton and considering his options.

And Wendy was fed up. She was out of options, because of Daniel. "I don't think you quite understand," she said. "I'm not asking you. I'm telling you."

This tactic worked on a lot of people. It had even worked on the lead singer of Darkness Fallz up until he nearly had her fired. It didn't seem to work on Daniel. He simply stared at her coldly.

She tried to hold on to her own steely gaze. But inside she was cowering. She was that eighteen-year-old girl all over again, daring to leave her home state and her controlling boyfriend behind to pursue her dream, only to have him track her down and hurt her.

"Do you still have that crick in your neck from the flight?" Daniel asked. "Turn around." He put his hands on her shoulders and started to turn her.

Maybe he was going to help her after all—although a neck rub wasn't quite what she'd had in mind. She wasn't sure how convinced Colton and Lorelei would be that Daniel and Wendy were lovers just because he worked the kink out of her neck, but it was better than nothing. She turned away from him, bent her head, and pulled her hair forward.

He smoothed his hands along her skin and across the shoulders of her blouse. Then his lips were at her ear. "My God, why are you so tense?"

She gave the smallest shrug. She'd nearly been fired today, she had an impossible job to do or else she would be fired tomorrow, and the hottest guy on earth was touching her. No stress there.

"Relax, Wendy," he whispered. "It won't look like we're lovers if you don't let go."

With a shiver of pleasure at his voice, she took a deep breath, exhaled slowly, and softened under his hands, as instructed.

She tried to suppress her gasp of surprise and pleasure as his hot fingers pressed into her shoulder muscles. Now she wasn't so worried that they wouldn't look like lovers. For her at least, this was the sexiest event of the past six months, since her last night with an on-again, off-again boyfriend. She felt self-consciously like a neglected dog rolling over happily for anyone who would rub his belly. The longer Daniel's hands deftly moved up and down her spine and along her shoulders, the more boneless she became.

"Better?" he growled as he took his hands away.

She nodded a little, so sorry the session was over, but hopeful it had been enough to stave off Colton for a few days. Though a kiss would have been better . . .

She was just telling herself not to go there, not to entertain the possibility, because she was going to be disappointed. But as she faced Daniel, he was looking at her mouth.

The beat of the music, the volume, the frenzy of it, seemed to escalate with her heartbeat as he bent toward her. But he advanced lazily, like a hot southern afternoon. They were a special effect in a film, moving in slow motion, just the two of them, while their surroundings whirled.

She wouldn't falter. She wouldn't look away shyly. She'd asked him for this. She held his gaze as his hand moved down her back and underneath her blouse. It was all she could do to keep from shuddering with anticipation now that the silk didn't separate them. His skin met her skin as he bent closer over her. His lips touched hers.

She froze against him, simultaneously telling herself she shouldn't be freezing. That was something she would do if she thought he was unattractive. She didn't want him to get that impression. It wasn't true at all. Or, it was something she would do if she found him extremely attractive and was afraid of letting him know. That was true, and she didn't want to give him that impression, either.

These panicked thoughts flashed through her brain in about two seconds, and then hormones took over as his tongue swept inside her mouth. She forgot what impression she was trying to give him or why as she responded to his kiss, opening for him. She pressed her hands against his crisp white shirt.

He shifted his solid arm up her back, holding her there, and wove the fingers of his other hand into her hair. His tongue slipped past her teeth and massaged inside her mouth.

Tingles rushed up and down her arms, through her chest, down to her thighs, making her legs weak. She felt herself sliding closer to him on the velvet bench, placing one shoe between both of his so that her thigh grazed his and his knee brushed her crotch.

His lips left hers, but his face hovered near. He looked into her eyes and brushed his lips against hers once more. Then he lifted his middle finger to stroke a long blond lock away from her face. "Good enough?" he murmured. "Colton was watching."

Oh. Of course. He hadn't kissed her because he'd wanted to. He'd done it because she'd asked him to, for the sake of her job. *Oh.*

WITTY COMEBACK. She should make a WITTY COMEBACK now, but her mind was empty of words again. It was full of pleasure, an insane lust for him, and disappointment that he didn't feel the same.

Then, thankfully, she produced the comeback after all. She hadn't held this job for six years for nothing. She grinned at him and quipped, "Now *that* is how you do PR."

"Good." With one hand he stroked her bare back. With the other he twisted a lock of her hair into a rope and wound it around his finger, reminding her that she'd allowed herself to be caught. "Because now *I* need a favor from *you.*"

5

Wendy gazed up at Daniel, her blue eyes dark with the kiss they'd just shared, her jaw set against the favor he was calling in.

He had no idea what *he* must look like to *her*, but he *felt* like he'd gotten high and lost his mind.

Reluctantly he let go of her silky hair and slipped his hand out from under her blouse. He wished he could have explored her mouth with his until they were both wild with want. Without exchanging a word, they would escape from this crowd and make their way up to his room or hers, where he would zip her out of that sexy skirt. But she wouldn't have allowed it. She'd been clear from the beginning that she was only using him. He might protest for show, but he was very, very happy for Wendy Mann to use him all she wanted. However, he kept in mind that in the end, they were both here for one thing, and it wasn't a lay.

Unfortunately.

"What kind of favor?" she asked.

Daniel smiled. He could feel that the smile didn't quite make it to his eyes—which was good, because the bruise on his cheekbone had begun to ache all over again when Wendy got his blood pumping with that kiss. He said stiffly, "I have a proposition for you."

Wendy raised her golden brows. "Do you, now."

He let his eyes dart briefly to the inebriated dancers crowding their table. Colton wasn't watching anymore—he and the Lakers player had followed the famous mistress of a shamed governor across the bar—but Daniel let Wendy think he was surveying his client as he covered her hand with his. "It's great that we've gotten together like this. We'll keep playing it up and serve as a good example. As you know, the public loves it when star couples reconcile. All we have to do to fix Colton *and* Lorelei's PR is get them back together before the awards show on Friday."

"No!" Wendy exclaimed, jerking her hand out from under his.

Momentarily stunned by her quick refusal, he gathered himself and said, "You haven't even let me explain what I had in m—"

"Absolutely not," Wendy said. "He's violent. *He hit you.*"

"He hit me by accident."

"That's what battered women say, too. Every bruise on their bodies was an accident." Her voice rose. He was very thankful that he was the only one who could hear her over the loud music as she said, "I'm not letting Lorelei near him, and if you were any kind of man, you wouldn't, either."

That blow stunned him more than Colton's had. "Colton swung at the paparazzi," Daniel said. "I got in the way. You think I would let him hit me on purpose?"

"No," she admitted. She watched the crowd for a few moments, reconsidering. "You want them to get back together for real? Or should we just release it to the public that they hooked up?"

Daniel shrugged. "Does it matter?"

"Yes, it matters," Wendy said. "Lorelei is in a fragile state right now."

"Not too fragile to sniff coke off her dead mother's Stratocaster," Daniel pointed out.

"That was three years ago, and it was a *rumor*," Wendy said sternly. "I don't want to tell Lorelei what to do. She's free to make her own choices."

Daniel was astounded. "What *planet* are you from?"

Wendy lifted her chin. "Lorelei has loved and lost. The last thing she needs right now is to get involved again with your client, who publicly demeans her."

"Wendy," Daniel said reprovingly. "You got kicked off the Darkness Fallz case this morning. You must be in hot water at Stargazer. If Lorelei loses her concert tour because she won't stop tweeting photos of her underwear, you're done in this business. How are you going to repair her reputation so quickly without my help? You need me."

Wendy frowned. She was still beautiful when she frowned—but she doubted him. He wasn't concerned about Lorelei's bodily safety in a relationship with Colton, but Wendy truly was. She was playing Daniel straight, at least on that point.

He needed her to agree to this plan. Getting Colton and Lorelei back together, or simply putting out the word that they'd made up and forcing them to play along, would assuage the awards ceremony and do wonders for this pivotal week of their careers. But he knew that even if Wendy did say yes, and even if they did continue to play at this game of being lovers, Vegas would be no fun for either of them. They wouldn't be riding the roller coaster at the New York casino, or hiking the Red Rock Canyon, or falling into bed together. All their fun was over.

"I just got here," she murmured. "I haven't even introduced myself to Lorelei yet. I haven't had time to assess the situation with her. I don't think it's a good idea, and this is definitely not the place to discuss it."

He leaned forward with his elbow on the table and his chin in his hand. "Then let's discuss it tomorrow."

She sank back exactly as far as he'd moved toward her, shaking her head no. "Avoiding each other, and having Lorelei and Colton avoid each other, would be a better course of action."

He raised his eyebrows. "Oh, you're going to avoid me? Don't expect me to make out with you anymore, then."

"We weren't exactly making out," she grumbled.

"Don't expect me to pretend we're together, either," he said lightly. "Your choice. I'm not the one with the problems at work."

She opened her mouth to respond—and he was really looking forward to what she would say—when a commotion distracted them both. All the dancers had stopped and faced the center of the room as if a dance-off were going down for cash. The disturbance was so intriguing that someone notified the DJ, who lowered the volume on the electro-garbage until they could hear the beat of different music in the outer room, and above it all, very close by, Colton bellowing.

Daniel and Wendy recognized his voice and jumped up at the same time. While Wendy pushed through the dancers and disappeared in the direction of the disturbance, Daniel walked around the edge of the crowd, toward the bar, until he spotted Colton's bodyguard in the shadows against the far wall, deep in conversation with Colton's driver. Daniel waved to get the bodyguard's attention, then opened his hands toward the crowd. The bodyguard looked surprised and hustled his big body in that direction. Either he'd been the only person in the bar not to realize that Colton was involved in an altercation, or he'd thought Colton getting in an argument in public didn't break the threshold of occasions when he should intervene. Daniel mentally added lecturing the bodyguard to his long to-do list for tomorrow.

He didn't stick around to watch the bodyguard pull Colton from the crowd. Instead, he rounded to the other side of the room, where he'd seen Wendy disappear into the fray. His pulse quickened as he heard a woman's shrieks. Pushing through the bodies, he could see when he was still several rows from the center that Lorelei, a tall, slender blonde in a designer top and six-hundred-dollar jeans, was screaming at Colton with her finger in his face and an empty martini glass in her other hand. The bodyguard had reached Colton and pinned his arms behind his back and was attempting to tug him away. Colton's eyes blazed fire at Lorelei, and his face dripped what appeared to be a pink girly drink. A plastic monkey hung in his hair.

Camera phones flashed.

Daniel suppressed the urge to snatch all the phones away from their owners. There were too many. And that would be bordering on illegal, since these people weren't paparazzi. The last thing Colton needed, on top of the barroom-brawl/drink-in-the-face headline, was an assault on a fan by a member of his public relations team.

No, Daniel's best bet now was to work Lorelei's side of the equation. Rather, Wendy's side. He snuck up behind her at the edge of the circle around Colton and Lorelei. Over Lorelei's screeching, Wendy was talking to Lorelei's enormous bodyguard.

"Do something," Wendy said.

Eyes never leaving Lorelei, the bodyguard shook his head. "She's told me not to, unless somebody's about to get shot. She likes to be free to express her emotions."

"Oh, is *that* what she calls it? Get her and follow me. Otherwise, she's going to scream her way out of a concert tour. Whoops, there goes your salary and your raison d'être."

Daniel would not have used the term *raison d'être* when issuing orders to a bodyguard, but Wendy obviously knew best. The bodyguard stepped forward, looped Lorelei around the waist with one arm, and dragged her out of the center of attention. Lorelei hardly seemed to notice, still hollering at Colton even as the spectators melted away and the music cranked up.

Wendy hurried back to the table she and Daniel had just vacated. She nodded to the plush seat she and Daniel had shared before. The bodyguard plopped Lorelei down on the bench and eased his huge frame around the table to sit next to her. Wendy pulled up a seat and crossed her legs. Daniel grabbed a seat, too.

She stared at him. Her face was a blank, but he understood her meaning: *What are you doing? Why are you here? Go away.* He grinned back at her. She couldn't send him away if she also wanted to keep up the facade that they were lovers. While that nonsense was going on, any business she chose to discuss with Lorelei was his business, too. That was his price.

Seeming to understand his message, she leaned across the table and told Lorelei, "I'm Wendy Mann. Your new PR specialist?"

Lorelei's eyes widened at her. "No. Not you!" She jumped up too fast and put one hand on the bodyguard's shoulder to steady her drunken sway. At her full height on heels, she pointed down at Wendy. "Chicks let their people take advantage of them all the time, but I am not having a 'helper'"—she made finger quotes—"who tries to steal my boyfriend. See ya!" She stepped around the table. Daniel and Wendy both watched her over their shoulders as she bounded away on her long legs, disappearing into the silk and sequins of the other party guests.

Daniel had seen what Lorelei posted online from the club, but he hadn't put it together with Colton coming on to Wendy until now. No wonder Wendy had been so desperate to make it look like she was with Daniel instead.

He was careful to make his face a blank, with no hint of triumph, as he turned back to Wendy and said, "That went well."

She glared at him. But he detected the hint of a smile on her lips, as if to say, *Watch this.*

She leaned across the cocktail table to the bodyguard. "Franklin, I'll give Lorelei a talking-to tomorrow morning, when she's sober. Right now we need to keep her out of trouble. Tell her to grab some of her girlfriends. Take them to the fifties beauty shop bar on Fremont where they can get an appletini and a pedicure."

Franklin grumbled, "I ain't getting no pedicure."

She allowed him a few seconds to think it through.

"Yes, ma'am," he said.

Wendy was turning Daniel on.

"She can even take pictures and post them," Wendy said. "But not of her boobs. I'll call the owner of the bar and ask him to send their VIP limo for you. I'll follow you and stay out of her sight, but I'll make sure nothing goes wrong. Or *more* wrong. I'm going out of the bar to the casino floor now, where I can hear and call for the limo. Give me a couple of minutes and then collect Lorelei and her chicas and bring them out, okay?"

As she stood, Daniel expected her to give him an extra-special good-bye—some acknowledgment of what had passed between them in the last hour, and what they'd pretended. But she only crossed her eyes at him before walking away.

Franklin chuckled. "You look like a man who's been had."

"Yeah." Daniel turned to watch Wendy maneuver around the drunks on the dance floor and finally swing through the doorway to the outer club. He felt disoriented. *He* was the one who was supposed to decide when the major players came and went, and *he* was the one with the contacts.

He stood. "I'm sure I'll see you around," he told Franklin. Ideally, sooner rather than later. Franklin nodded. Daniel dodged dancers and a waitress wearing little more than pasties to step through the doorway to the outer bar.

There in front of him, near the glass wall onto the casino where he'd originally sat with Wendy, women were screaming and falling into each other. Wendy would have been walking through there at just that moment. He dashed forward to pull her out of danger.

He couldn't get past the security guards running in from the casino floor. They spread their arms in front of the crowd to hold them off. At least this gave Daniel a clear view of the young women in sequined clubwear and the bouncers piled on top of them. Wendy was nowhere in sight.

"What happened?" Daniel yelled to the man next to him.

"These crazy ladies were screaming that they'd found Colton Farr," the man said. "You know, the washed-up actor in the online war with his girlfriend? They were trying to tear his clothes off. Probably wanted to sell them online. The Internet has made us all into animals."

"But . . ." Daniel silenced himself. It hadn't really been Colton. Daniel would have seen him leave the inner room and stopped him.

The man verified what Daniel had been thinking. "It wasn't even him. I got a good look at the guy. Strong resemblance, though. This guy could impersonate Colton Farr and make a killing."

The bouncers stood the women up and cuffed them. The security guards lowered their arms, and the crowd flowed in to fill the empty space. Daniel looked around for the Colton Farr lookalike. It might be the same guy he'd seen at the blackjack table with Colton earlier, the one who'd disappeared so quickly when the guards arrived. Even if it was, Daniel had no real reason to think the guy was paparazzi.

He made his way through the club and stepped from the crowded, noisy bar into the quiet of the casino. After a slow survey, he spotted Wendy leaning against an enormous Roman column, laughing into her phone, where a drunken Lorelei wouldn't notice her when she exited the club.

He stopped. Standing in the middle of the passageway was awkward, but interrupting her phone conversation would be rude. The ringing in his ear from the dance music began to fade, and the happy noise of the slot machines grew. The casino hadn't been quiet at all. Everything was relative.

Finally she slipped her phone into her handbag, looked up, and spotted him. "Hey, lovah," she called.

He walked over. "All set with your limo?"

"Yep."

"Maybe Colton and I will come with you."

Her smile never faltered as she calmly said, "Nope."

"We'll just happen to show up there."

"We're getting *away* from you." Wendy yawned. "I'm really just trying to get her to bed. The bar we're headed to closes at two, so Franklin will have a good reason to make her call it a night. My God, it must be *so late* already, and I haven't even begun to adjust to Pacific time. What time is it in New York?" She opened her purse to pull out her phone again, then thought better of it and waved the whole problem away as impossible. "I'm really not adjusted to Eastern, either, though. I just spent weeks in Seattle and then eight hours in New York. I'm so confused."

"Eighteen or nineteen o'clock," he said.

She pointed at him and grinned. "That is *exactly* how I feel."

"Or negative five," he said. "I've been up since I got the call about Colton pissing in the fountain at the Bellagio at four a.m."

"Oh, you poor baby!" she exclaimed.

Daniel eyed her dubiously. She sounded sincere, just as she had earlier when she told him to take care. His heart warmed strangely.

He must be coming down with something. Funny—after so much world travel in the past six years, he thought he'd become immune to everything.

The moment passed. Her gaze shifted over his shoulder. "Here come my peeps. Good night, Daniel." She stuck out her hand.

He looked down at her perfect pink nails. "A handshake?" he asked. "Really?"

With a small smile, she leaned forward and wrapped her slender arms around him.

He'd only been joking. Ribbing her about the fact that she needed him. Reminding her how intimately they'd explored the matter earlier. Now he wished he hadn't teased her. As her body settled perfectly against him and his hands touched her hair, he wanted her— wanted to bury his face in her neck and sniff her perfume until he'd had enough, wanted to take her back to his room and unzip that goddamn skirt—but he would never have her.

He didn't like this game anymore.

Suddenly, he drew back in surprise. "You're missing a hunk of hair." He turned her around to make sure he'd felt what he thought he'd felt under his hand. Sure enough, one long golden curl was missing, with a jagged edge in its place, as if the lock had been cut quickly. He took her hand and put it to the ends left over.

Her lips parted in horror, and her blue eyes flashed toward the club. "I *thought* I felt a little pull." With hair that long, she must be very attached to her crowning glory. He watched with admiration as she switched gears and made light of the situation in the space of two seconds. "This is what happens when you come to Vegas, right? I was half expecting to cut something sticky out of my hair anyway while I'm here."

"But someone cutting your hair . . . well. I was going to say I've never seen anything that bizarre even in Vegas, but come to think of it, I have."

"Me, too." She laughed, belying her uneasiness. She still pressed her hair with one hand. "I'd better tail Lorelei before she loses me."

Daniel glanced at Lorelei, Franklin, and two giggling women tottering through the archway that led to the hotel lobby. "We weren't through talking about Lorelei and Colton," he reminded Wendy.

"Call me tomorrow," she sang over her shoulder, already power walking across the casino floor. Daniel watched her until she disappeared through the archway after her star.

Reluctantly he turned back to the club, where dancers thrashed like the damned in hell. He wished he'd been able to talk Wendy into letting him and Colton tag along. Now his night looked grim. He would find Colton inebriated and covered in Lorelei's drink. He hoped not too many pictures of Colton's humiliation had been snapped and posted online. It might take a couple of hours to talk Colton into calling it a night, but the faster Daniel could pull it off, the faster he could get to bed himself. Tomorrow was a new day. He would call Wendy, convince her to work with him, and solve the problem.

The music in the bar was so loud that nobody heard him shout, "Damn!" as he realized he didn't have Wendy's number. She'd purposefully neglected to give it to him. And he had no way to get it, because her New York office would know better than to hand it over. If she'd wanted him to have it, he would have it. The night had given him a high he hadn't felt in forever, but right now he was as low as he'd been in a while, feeling positively bereft of her. Muttering to himself, he gave the bouncer a surly wave and stepped back into the reality star's party.

But the next morning, Daniel got lucky.

6

Daniel had finished his free weight reps and was pounding out his fourth mile on the treadmill when Wendy jerked open the door of the hotel fitness center. The entire gym was one long room overlooking the Strip from a high floor. Except for the attendant behind the desk, they were the only occupants in the dead calm of late morning. Wendy's eyes went straight to him.

He saw all of it flash across her face: recognition. An instinct to back out the door before he saw her. A realization that it was too late. An attempt to act like she'd never even thought about leaving just because he was there. Who, her?

Her steps slowed on the way to the desk as she wondered whether she should confront Daniel first thing and get it over with. He let her off the hook. Without breaking stride, he held up one hand in greeting, as if they were strangers who saw each other every day at the deli on his corner in Chelsea.

She waved back just as casually, signed in, and crossed to the abdominal machine. She did a few sets of reps on each machine, obviously finding them familiar, and didn't look up at him a single time. That was the giveaway that she was very aware of him.

Because she never glanced up, he felt free to stare at her as she went through her workout. Unlike the occasional slob wearing a cotton tee who'd happened in and left again while Daniel was jogging, she wore workout gear in the latest style that fit her perfectly—just like he did, because he never knew whom he might run into even during his downtime. She'd tied up her long hair with studied sloppiness, trying to look like she wasn't trying at all, because that was the fashion. Tendrils stuck to her face with perspiration as she pumped through her exercises in perfect rhythm, never pausing long, because she thought he might be watching.

Not that he was above that kind of self-consciousness himself. He ran faster. He ran so fast that his lungs burned. She wasn't looking, but he knew she could hear his footsteps.

Finally the machine shut down. He slowed to a walk and inched through gathering his towel and bag, giving himself time to catch his breath. When he was reasonably certain he wouldn't trip over his own feet and pass out in front of her, he sauntered over. Uninvited, he sat down on the machine next to the one where she was working her biceps.

He pulled his phone from his bag and—ignoring six calls from his father—scrolled through to add a new contact. "What's your number?"

Through three more reps, she studied him silently. She knew he was trying to hammer a wedge into her door.

"I'll call you so you'll have my number," he persisted. "That way, anytime today's hottest stars make you feel uncomfortable, you can phone me for a booty call."

Her pealing laugh mixed with a *slam* as she lost her grip on the weights. Giggling, she recited her number. He plugged it into his phone. He did his best not to grin back. He'd figured her out. He could get her to do just about anything by making her laugh.

Or by kissing her.

He affected a Brooklyn accent, not a very good one. "You work out a lot?"

Whether the impression was good or not, it was funny. Wendy giggled uncontrollably. Finally she forced herself to say, "I actually do work out a lot, just to keep Sarah Seville off my case. I know you have trouble remembering me from college, but maybe you remember her."

He knew Sarah by reputation. He didn't remember much about her from class. She'd been competent but reserved. She'd dressed way down in workout wear, even for business presentations. What he did remember about her, clear as day, was a glimpse he'd caught of her junior year, a very poignant glimpse.

Wendy had been pulled out of the middle of marketing class. While waiting for advertising class to start, he'd noticed she still hadn't returned to the crowd. And then he overheard a couple of guys saying her father had died.

What made Daniel do it, he wasn't sure. He wasn't dating this girl. He wasn't friends with this girl. He didn't even like this girl. But he'd walked back down the hall, toward the entrance of the building, and glanced through the glass wall of the business dean's office. Wendy stood facing Daniel with glistening trails of tears down her cheeks. Sarah stood on one side, holding her hand and talking to her. A couple of cops stood awkwardly on the other side, dwarfing the girls. Wendy stared out at Daniel, not seeing him, not turning her head as he passed.

He was fascinated by her. It had only been a few years since his brother's death, and when he had died, his father had made sure Daniel didn't feel anything at all. Wendy looked now like he'd been supposed to feel then. And with a kick in the gut, he felt it.

He'd never skipped class before. His father would have hit the roof if Daniel had blown class off and let his grades slip. But this day he kept walking down the hall, out the door, across the sunny lawn, as far away from Wendy as he could get.

"Sarah Seville?" he asked. "Yes, I remember her vaguely."

"She's ultra-fit," Wendy said. "Runs marathons."

"And she makes you run them, too?"

"Let's not go *that* far. But I let her hound me into exercising, so I have an excuse to hound her about other stuff. And honestly, I do feel better after I work out. When I'm traveling, I try to snag some exercise whenever I can, because I might not get another chance for a while. Also vegetables."

He chuckled. Strange, but traveling did deprive one of vegetables. Fruits. Friends. Normalcy. He knew what she meant.

"So," he ventured, "about getting Colton and Lorelei back together."

Her smile vanished. "I told you no."

"You told me you would speak with Lorelei and we could revisit it."

"I just said that to get rid of you. Colton is obviously a loose cannon. The farther Lorelei stays from him, the better."

In annoyance, Daniel tapped one finger on the bench of the workout machine, then realized he was doing it and stopped. "Honestly, Wendy, when he punched me, it was an accident. I've never heard of any violence between Colton and Lorelei. Have you?"

"Maybe not," Wendy said, "but he's calling her a whore to anyone who will listen, including— whoopsie—the *entire world*. Naming her a criminal who sells sex is the first step in dehumanizing and objectifying her, so that when he does hit her, in his mind, she'll deserve it."

"I see your point, but—"

"Kind of like sitting way above everyone else so they have to climb a mountain to greet you. Or pretending you don't remember a rival when you meet her again. If you put everyone on a lower footing than yourself, you can do anything you want to them and feel just fine about it."

He felt a twinge of guilt, but he couldn't let her see it. "Come back to the table." He patted the bench hard enough to get her attention. "You're not talking about our clients anymore."

As she eyed him suspiciously, he studied her in the bright light of morning. She'd dressed for her workout as if she might run into someone important, but her vanity hadn't extended to makeup, as it would have for a lot of women he encountered in this business. Her face was scrubbed clean. She looked pretty and young, like an English country lass in a commercial for milk or apples, except the look in her eye said she had some sharp farm implements she would like to stab him with back in the barn.

"I'm sorry I made you feel that way," he said sincerely.

She shrugged. "It's your modus operandi."

"Speaking of which," he said, jumping on the chance to change the subject from himself back to work. "I want you to consider my offer seriously. It's Tuesday, the awards show is on Friday, and Colton and Lorelei both seem hell-bent on continuing along the path that led them to this mess in the first place. If we don't make positive progress in the next twenty-four hours, I have no doubt that the show will drop both of them. Getting them together—or faking it, if that's what you prefer—is the fastest, best way to regain the public's interest and support."

Wendy shifted uncomfortably on her bench. "It just seems like a lot of trouble to fake their relationship. I suspect all the time that Hollywood couplings are faked, but I don't imagine a PR person engineering it. There are too many factors to control, too many mouths to shut up. It's not worth the effort."

"It depends on what's at stake. Sometimes it can be the perfect solution for both parties."

"Like whom?"

He hesitated. *Like whom* was his greatest triumph and his most closely guarded secret. If he told her, he'd be taking a huge risk. If he didn't tell her, he doubted he could convince her to go along with his plan.

She prompted him, "You talk like you've done this before. Do you want me to work with you or not? Spill it."

He looked over his shoulder to make sure the gym was still empty save for the attendant, whose desk was far enough away that she couldn't overhear. Satisfied, he turned back to Wendy and confided, "Olivia Query and Victor Moore."

Wendy stared at him a moment without comprehending. "Yeah. I'd heard you repped both of them. Did you introduce them and they fell in love?" Then she understood what he was telling her. "You *engineered* that marriage?"

"Shhh. Yes."

Wendy was astonished into silence. When she regained speech, she lowered her voice to match his. "But . . . Olivia is pregnant with Victor's baby!"

"It's not his baby," Daniel said.

"But . . . they had five hundred guests at their wedding."

"Right."

"But . . . they rented an island."

Daniel smiled enough to show her his smugness, but not enough to make the bruise under his eye hurt. "You don't believe me?"

"Um." She squinted at him, unsure whether to believe him or not.

"You don't *want* to believe me," he said. "You're caught up in the same romance that every other noncelebrity gets caught up in, looking on with admiration and longing at this rich, famous, talented couple in love." He cocked his head at her. "But you *do* believe me, don't you, Wendy? You don't know me very well, but you know me by reputation. I can do anything I set out to do in this business. Make a star. Ruin a star. Fabricate two stars' entire lives."

She didn't deny it. "But why?" she murmured.

"Olivia got pregnant with her hometown sweetheart's baby and insisted on keeping it. He absolutely refused to live a celebrity life with her. He's got some secrets he can't have exposed right now if the media dig into his past. And Victor is gay."

"What!" Wendy exclaimed so sharply that even she

looked over Daniel's shoulder to make sure the attendant wasn't listening to their conversation. She inched closer to Daniel on her bench and lowered her voice again. "Victor Moore is *gay*? He's the heterosexual hunk of the century! That would be a scandal of Rock Hudson proportions!"

"Correct," Daniel said.

"But . . . why doesn't he just come out? The stigma isn't there anymore."

"The stigma's still there," Daniel said. "It's not a career-ending stigma, but it's a career-changing one. You're disappointed to hear that he's gay, right?"

"Disappointed?" Wendy echoed in confusion. "No, I'm not *disappointed* at his sexual orientation—"

"Yes, you are," Daniel interrupted. "When you watch his movies, you fantasize about yourself with him. Before, there was the remotest possibility it would happen. He would have to leave his wife and baby and somehow find you and fall in love. Now, there's *no* possibility, and you've lost interest."

"That's not true," she said confusedly. "That's not how fantasy works."

"That's *exactly* how fantasy works," Daniel told her, "and that's why Victor hasn't come out. He could still get cast as the gay guy or the lovable sidekick, even the hero of a movie in which his sexuality wasn't front and center. But he would never get cast as the swashbuckling, hard-loving straight hero again. He's signed five contracts to play that part over the next three years. After that, he's divorcing Olivia."

Wendy gasped. "Does she know?"

"Of course she knows," Daniel said impatiently—
and maybe a tad let down that Wendy wasn't keeping
up. Or jealous that she really had swooned over Victor Moore. That was a totally stupid thought on his
part. He shrugged it away and went on, "Victor and
Olivia are Hollywood's golden couple right now. They
generate a lot more public interest together than they
would apart. He'll milk the prime of his career for all
it's worth. She'll do the same in her career. The divorce
date is already set. I have the press releases on file. I'll
just need to tweak them a bit to match their future
movie titles and charities. A year after that, Victor will
quietly start dating the boyfriend he's secretly been
with for years already. His agent will move him toward
those quirky sidekick parts, Best Supporting Actor
material. Olivia will move from leading lady parts to
motherly parts. With the spotlight off her, she'll marry
her boyfriend."

Wendy's blond brows knitted as she worked through
what Daniel had said. "So you've saved two careers by
putting two romances on hold."

"I guess. But we're not talking careers in account-
ing. As you know, we're talking multimillion-dollar
movie careers."

"Still, they're careers these stars don't really want in
their heart of hearts, right? Victor is gay. Is it really his
heart's desire to play heterosexual hunks? Is that career
worth putting off being with his soul mate?"

"He said it was."

"Ah, and that's where you and I approach the prob-lem differently," Wendy said. "You get stars what they say they want. But if it seems to me that the stars don't genuinely want that, I say, 'You don't really want that.' It's making more work for myself, but I think my long-term results are better."

Daniel nodded. "Unless you're trying to convince the lead singer of Darkness Fallz to kick meth."

Wendy glared at him. "Touché."

"And I guess you didn't even broach getting him to go out in public without the rubber devil costume."

"He has an eczema problem that he's sensitive about," Wendy said stiffly.

"Ah. But in your world, he gets what he really wants, which is to stay on meth."

"That's not fair," Wendy said.

Daniel knew it wasn't fair, and that she was getting pissed at him. But he'd been right about his plan for Victor and Olivia, and he would make sure Wendy knew it. "In my world, maybe Olivia and Victor delay what they really want, true. But in the end, everyone lives happily ever after."

"Until someone talks," Wendy said. "If one florist or dog walker leaks the story to the tabloids, your stars' careers will never recover."

"Nobody talks," Daniel insisted. "I made sure of that. The only people who know are the key players."

"And me," Wendy said.

"You won't talk," Daniel said. "You know how easy it would be for me to ruin you. So here's what we'll do.

After you discuss the plan with Lorelei, we'll sit down and coordinate her schedule with Colton's. Make sure they're seen together at events. Arrange some encounters that appear to be impromptu. The tabloids will start asking whether they're back together. When the time is right, we'll announce jointly that they *are* together. The public will forgive all their behavior up to now. The two of them won't look like ill-bred young adults behaving badly anymore. They'll look like they've finally learned that the ones you truly love are the ones you hurt the most. They will have moved through that dark stage in their relationship and emerged into the light on the other side. Viewers will tune in for that triumphant story on Friday night."

Wendy stared past Daniel's shoulder and said nothing. At first he thought she was staring into space so she could process all the information he was giving her. But as he neared the end of his plan, he got the distinct impression she was tuning him out. "Wendy," he prompted her. "Are you listening to me?"

"No." She grabbed the handles of the weight machine and swung herself up to standing. As she stalked away across the gym, she tossed over her shoulder at him, "You lost me when you threatened to ruin me. You and your client need to work on your lines."

7

Wendy marched to the treadmill Daniel had vacated and took it over as her territory. She leaped onto it, set it to a higher speed than she was used to, and hoped to God he would leave soon, before she hacked up a lung.

On the other hand . . . she would miss the scenery if he left. He was so handsome slouched on a weight machine, long legs bent, biceps and muscled chest straining against his tight shirt, glaring at her. He was gorgeous when he was angry. At least, she *thought* he was angry. She still had a hard time telling his emotions apart, unless he was laughing.

And then he was gone, as she knew he would be. He wasn't one to hang around and sulk, or to beg her. In a few swift steps he left the gym, tossing his balled-up towel over his shoulder and ringing the hamper with it after the door was already closing. He'd tried with her. He'd failed. He would move on to plan B for revitalizing Colton's career. If it were up to him, he wouldn't talk to her again while they were in Vegas. Their relationship was over.

That was fine with her. She'd agreed that telling the public Lorelei and Colton were back together would be a great way to repair their images before the awards show. Maybe the only way. She'd also agreed that if she didn't succeed with Lorelei, her career in PR was done. But she absolutely would not let Daniel bully her.

Her anger at him pushed her through a more exhausting workout than she'd thought possible. She returned to her room, half hoping to pass him somewhere along the way so she could pointedly ignore him. After a shower—a longer shower than she intended, because she kept getting lost in little fantasies about an apologetic Daniel joining her after his own hearty workout, and making up to her for being heavy-handed—she took the elevator to the penthouse level and knocked on Lorelei's door. The wardrobe mistress let her in, saying Lorelei was always slow to get up in the morning.

Wendy took the opportunity to step straight into the huge closet. In a whisper, she asked the wardrobe mistress to show her the outfits she'd planned for Lorelei's next few public appearances. Wendy could work as hard as possible and drag Lorelei along with her, but all their efforts could easily be negated with one slipped bra cup and an unplanned nipple calling hello to the world. Judging from Lorelei's past run-ins with the paparazzi, Wendy thought this was unlikely. Lorelei had done and said many stupid things in public, but none of them involved wardrobe malfunctions. If unseemly parts of her were showing in pictures, that's because she'd taken the photos herself.

Lorelei's clothes were beautifully made and edgy without being trashy. Wendy complimented the wardrobe mistress with the truth: "I've got my work cut out for me, as you know, but I've never worried about her wardrobe. You always make her look like a million bucks." The wardrobe mistress replied with a brilliant smile and protestations that she only helped. Lorelei herself had a terrific eye.

And ear, Wendy thought, as the strum of an acoustic guitar and pitch-perfect humming meandered down the hall and into the closet. Lorelei was awake.

Replacing a gorgeous sequined skirt on the rack, Wendy slipped past the wardrobe mistress and tiptoed into the bedroom. Lorelei sat at the head of the bed, leaning back against the pillows, eyes closed, singing one of her mother's hard-rocking classics. Lorelei was tall and thin, but that only added to the impression that she was young and hadn't yet grown into her long limbs. The sun rendered her linen nightshirt and shorts translucent but not tawdry on her slender frame. She strummed the guitar. Her long fingers worked a complicated countermelody on the strings. Her high voice warbled half a lovely tune with nonsense words. Wendy was transfixed.

The morning sun backlit Lorelei's messy curls and shone in a halo around her face. She wasn't a stereotypical beauty—her eyes were narrow and wide-spaced, her nose long, and of course there were the diminutive boobies—but she was pretty enough for girls to want to be her, and not so pretty that they hated her. Wendy had always thought Loralei's offbeat looks added to her appeal—back when she had appeal, that is.

Her song ended. She kept her eyes closed, basking in the warm sun streaming through the window, listening to her last guitar chord ring through the room. Finally she opened her eyes, saw Wendy leaning against the wall, and flared her nostrils. "No, bitch," she said firmly. "I told you to take your weave and your cheap ass home."

Wendy had lots of experience with West Virginia schoolgirls taunting her. And with bratty young stars who possessed all the eloquence and sophistication of those schoolgirls. In either case, Wendy's usual response would be to let herself get angry and to dish it out just as well as she could take it.

This time she had her career to worry about. She needed to shut Lorelei down in a way that made Lorelei want to thank her for it later. Being nice was doubly difficult when Lorelei had punched her in her soft spots: insulting her hair and calling her cheap.

Reaching deep inside herself, she came up with this: "Hey, pretty girl." She didn't remember much about her mom, but she remembered *pretty girl* was what her mom had called her in a quiet, loving moment.

Lorelei stared uneasily at Wendy.

Exactly what Wendy wanted. She continued in a chipper tone, "You hired me to get you *out* of this little PR scrape. I'm certainly not going to let you fire me. That's just going to get you deeper *in* trouble, especially when you're accusing me of . . . what are you accusing me of, again? Having long hair?"

Lorelei let her guitar slide down to her lap and crossed her arms. "Stealing my boyfriend."

"Colton's not your boyfriend anymore," Wendy said firmly. "But in any event, you don't need to worry about me and him, because I'm with Daniel."

Lorelei squinted at Wendy. "Who?"

"Daniel!" Wendy repeated in an exasperated tone, as if her relationship with Daniel Blackstone were the most obvious thing in the world. "He was sitting right next to me in the club last night."

"Wait a minute!" Lorelei exclaimed, pointing at Wendy. "Isn't he Colton's new PR guy? No way! You're sleeping with the enemy."

Wendy shrugged. "I fell in love with him before he was the enemy. I promise we'll be able to keep our personal and professional lives separate. So . . ."

Lorelei still stared at her as if stunned. Wendy had the advantages of surprise and a confident delivery. As long as she could keep Colton off her and Daniel *on* her, she doubted she'd personally have any more trouble from Lorelei.

She needed to keep going, capitalizing on her momentum. But here she lost her train of thought, distracted by the fantasy that she and Daniel had fallen in love.

Forget it. She pressed on, "We need some ground rules for getting you out of this mess. First, no throwing drinks in anyone's face."

"But Colton called me—" Lorelei started.

"Sticks and stones," Wendy interrupted. "Throwing anything at anybody could be construed as assault. Do you want to go to jail? Again?"

Lorelei's slim shoulders sagged. "No."

"No posting pictures of your lady parts online," Wendy persisted. "Your pics from the beauty shop bar last night were adorable. They were of you and your friends and your nightlife and your fingernails. Judging from the responses, the fans seemed to love them. We need more of that. Okay?"

"Okay," Lorelei said reluctantly.

"No calling your new PR specialist a twat."

Lorelei looked up sharply at Wendy, suspicious again.

"You hate it when people judge *you* without meeting you," Wendy pointed out, "or knowing the facts, or giving you a chance."

"Okay," Lorelei grumbled, looking out the bright window.

Wendy had won the battle, it seemed. Lorelei had accepted her authority. But they couldn't win the war with an absence of negative publicity. They'd have to generate the positive, too. The sunlight glowing in Lorelei's curls gave Wendy an idea.

"We need to get you on TV," she burst out. Lorelei's TV performance wouldn't be nearly as special as the song Wendy had just witnessed, snatched from thin air. The sunlight wouldn't stream in behind Lorelei. She would insist on wearing her usual heavy makeup. She would be wearing leather and sequins instead of soft clothes to sleep in. Belatedly Wendy realized she wanted Lorelei to look like she'd just gotten out of bed, and that was kind of perverted.

But even without these details, Lorelei's real talent and her easygoing, sweet nature—when she didn't feel threatened—would come through on the small screen, possibly for the first time ever.

"TV!" Lorelei drawled. "TV and I don't agree with each other."

"You'll like this kind," Wendy said. "Let's see. You've got the awards show on Friday night. So at lunch on Thursday, between your rehearsals for the show, we'll get you into a local news studio to play a few songs. I know it doesn't sound like much, but they'll post the video of your performance to their web page. We'll link to it and make sure it goes viral before the awards show."

Lorelei tilted her head, confused. "How can you make sure it goes viral?"

"We're Stargazer PR. We have our ways," Wendy said mysteriously. Daniel Blackstone might be able to engineer a wedding on a private island and convince megastars to maintain a fake relationship for a span of years, but Wendy could make a video go viral with a few phone calls. So there.

"Even if it does, how will that help?" Lorelei asked.

"Trust me," Wendy said. "It will help that people see you being yourself. Except don't tell the anchors or the audience to fuck off."

Lorelei laughed. "I was about to say, *that's* me being myself—"

"Yeah," Wendy said. "Don't do that. It might even be okay not to talk much. Sometimes you tell people to fuck off, or you say something else to them that seems inappropriate and too harsh in retrospect, because you couldn't think of anything else to say, right?"

Lorelei looked shocked.

"You're actually kind of shy, right? And you think you can't be shy in this business. You have to be ballsy and strong. You may be right about that when it comes to, say, contract negotiations. But when you're a guest on somebody else's TV show, no matter how big a star you are, maybe it's okay, or even better, to act shy and polite, especially if that's how you actually feel."

Lorelei stared at her and nodded slowly.

Wendy prompted her, "Do you think you could do that?"

"Yeah." Lorelei smiled at Wendy. "I think I could do that."

"Another thing. Don't talk to the reporters about your best friend the choreographer or your homie the housecleaner. If you do have relationships like that, we need to hide them as well as we can."

"Why?" Lorelei pouted.

"The public wants to see you as larger than life. Even royals are just real people with lucky bloodlines, but commoners are sheep. They love to look up to somebody. They don't want you consorting with them, because that makes you seem more like them. They want to hear about rock stars who are best friends with Oscar-winning actresses, and singers who are dating the governor of California."

"You mean, I got it right with Colton, and now I've lost it," Lorelei said dejectedly.

"Colton was great for your career." Wendy thought for the millionth time that morning that she shouldn't have turned Daniel's offer down. But he shouldn't have threatened her, and it was too late now. "I am *not* saying go back to Colton. I'm not saying fake a glamorous relationship. I'm saying hide the unglamorous ones."

"But that's just not how I am." Hugging the guitar, Lorelei flopped over on the bed and lay on her side in the fluff. "I don't think I'm better than other people. I'm not going to test each person when I meet them to see if they're worthy of being friends with me or whatever. One of my best friends in the world is my limo driver back in L.A. I've spent Christmas with him and his wife and kids before, when I didn't have my own place yet and my dad spent the holidays on his yacht in the Mediterranean with some stripper. I'm not going to drop that guy or pretend we've never met just because 'my public' doesn't want to see that." She

let go of her guitar to make finger quotes. "'My public'
can bite me."

"I'm not telling you to lie if the TV station asks you
about that," Wendy said. "I'm telling you to withhold
information and become a more private person. You
can have relationships the public doesn't know about.
Just because somebody asks you a question doesn't
mean you have to answer. Especially if it comes from
the paparazzi."

"Oh." Lorelei's whole lithe body sank into the cloud
of padding around her. "I can't dis the paparazzi. A lot
of those guys are my friends."

And that was exactly why the public had known so
much about Lorelei's snockered coming of age. Lorelei
had invited the paparazzi into her parties on occasion.
Wendy was guessing that Lorelei was very lonely.

"We'll work on this," Wendy assured her. "It's a process. We're not changing you into a different person.
We're presenting a different side of you. It'll be fun."
She hopped on Lorelei's plush king bed like they were
at a slumber party and opened her laptop.

She asked Lorelei to recite every rehearsal and appearance she'd planned for the week. Lorelei seemed to
know where she was going. That was good. She remembered the events out of order, as they popped into her
obviously scatterbrained head. That was bad. Wendy
made a mental note to double-check the schedule with
Lorelei's wardrobe mistress and her agent.

"The biggest deal is probably the party I'm throwing Thursday night for my twenty-first-and-a-half

birthday," Lorelei said. "It's here at the casino, but in the club on the roof, Wet Dream."

"Good Lord," Wendy blurted. "These club names were all made up by fourteen-year-old boys. Are you serving food? Is that even sanitary?"

Lorelei laughed, and Wendy realized she was lucky this star wasn't as easily offended as the lead singer of Darkness Fallz. She needed to dial down. And despite the untoward name of the club, it was one of the hottest spots in Vegas right now. She wished the party weren't so close to the awards show, but it had already been planned and she would work with it. "Will there be a cake shaped like a penis?"

"You are so funny!" Lorelei exclaimed. "Of course not. It's a guitar."

Lorelei sounded too cavalier for Wendy's liking. She made a note on her laptop to check personally for penis cake. Stars ruined themselves being photographed with penis cake with almost the same frequency that they were arrested with their pants down in public parks.

Then Lorelei said, "Tonight there's a party at the wax museum because they're unveiling a statue of my mother."

"What?" Wendy exclaimed, going back over what she'd already typed. Some of these shindigs had been forwarded to her by Lorelei's agent. Not this one. "That's a terrific public relations opportunity, but I haven't heard a peep about it in the media."

Wendy could picture it already. Lorelei's kick-ass,

rock star, heroin-chic mother in her ethereal and wasted blond glory standing next to her musical prodigy daughter, who, for all her faults, would look positively angelic in comparison. If Wendy didn't keep tabs on Lorelei during the party after the unveiling of the statue, the night could go badly. The tabloids could run a drunken photo and say Lorelei was following in her mother's staggering footsteps. But if Lorelei kept herself together, the public would see only that she'd inherited her mother's talent and, despite a difficult childhood, had turned out okay, considering.

But it would all be for nothing if nobody showed up to the party. In fact, a tabloid report that Lorelei threw a party and nobody came would be worse PR than anything Lorelei had come up with yet.

Lorelei shrugged. "The museum said at first they were going to make a big deal out of it. I guess they decided not to, with all the shit that's gone down."

Wendy gripped the sides of her laptop. Any other day, she would have launched a tirade at Lorelei. The *shit* had not *gone down*, unattached to anyone, a misfortune Lorelei had unsuspectingly walked into. Lorelei and Colton had been the manufacturers of said shit.

Today Wendy did not yell. She was not that person anymore. She grimaced, swallowed, and said, "I'll call the museum and get the announcements to the media outlets so plenty of paparazzi are there to watch you walk in. I'll contact the publicity people for all the guests to make sure they'll be there. I'll fix it." She typed a few notes on her computer, omitting the curse words she normally would have included, because Lorelei beside her on the bed might catch a glimpse of the screen. "Who's on the guest list?"

"Oh, anybody who was going to be in Vegas. Lots more people are coming in for the awards show rehearsals today." Bored with serious conversation, Lorelei plucked the strings of her guitar and wiggled her fingers on them to make funny noises.

"Colton?" Wendy asked.

Lorelei plucked a string so hard that Wendy thought it might break. "Yeah."

Wendy waited for Lorelei to ask if they could have Colton taken off the list. Lorelei didn't say a word. She went back to fingering her guitar, more thoughtfully now.

Daniel had been right about this, too. Lorelei was still interested enough in Colton that she wanted him at her party, even if they were at each other's throats. Daniel and Wendy might well be able to get them back together. But Wendy had said no to this.

Jet lag was catching up with her. Taking a deep breath with her eyes closed, she pondered the possibility of excluding Colton from Lorelei's party to avoid another altercation. If she called Daniel ahead of time to warn him they were blackballing Colton, Daniel might stage repercussions. If she *didn't* warn him and Colton found out the hard way, standing in the street outside the wax museum while pedestrians wandered by and stared curiously, the repercussions would be worse. The tabloids would say—and Daniel might even feed them this line—that Lorelei had invited Colton, then maliciously reneged on the invitation and humiliated him.

Bitch.

"Sit up and look at me, sweetie," Wendy said.

Obediently Lorelei crawled toward the headboard like an overgrown toddler. She propped herself up against the pillows and held her guitar in front of her for protection, sensing she was about to be scolded.

"You can't have another run-in with Colton tonight," Wendy said. "Everybody understands there are hard feelings between you, but beyond that, you have to take the high road. You can't keep posting pictures of your private parts and telling him to suck it."

Lorelei ran one freshly manicured finger along the glowing wood grain of her guitar. "I just want to show him I don't need him to have a good time."

Wendy nodded. "Like you're in middle school. Totally. Listen, pretty girl, there is more at stake here than your battle with Colton. There's your performance on the awards show. Your concert tour. Your album. Your whole career. All of that depends on your PR, and that's what you're paying me to repair. Yes?"

"Yes," Lorelei said earnestly.

"In PR, we have tools to track your ratings," Wendy said. "We contract with companies that conduct surveys and ask people if they've heard of you and what they think of you. Your name recognition is extremely high, but people say you're as likable as that executive in New York who swindled her company out of a hundred million dollars, abandoned her husband and children, and escaped with her lover to Papua New Guinea."

"Oh," Lorelei said dejectedly. Now she was getting it.

"We want to rebuild your image as America's sweetheart."

"No, wait!" Lorelei exclaimed. "Why do I have to be that? There are plenty of girls who have a badass image. Why can't I be a badass chick that people like better than the cheater lady?"

"You're not a badass at heart," Wendy said. "When you try, like in this war you're having with Colton, you just end up sounding insecure. To be a real badass, you have to *be* one, and those girls are a special breed. You could, however, be America's sweetheart."

"I could?"

"You totally could, but you have a deep hole to crawl out of. I can picture people in a few years saying, 'Remember when Lorelei Vogel went through her difficult period?' and other people will be unable to recall this at all. But you would need to start today to build that image. Definitely don't do anything else to make it worse."

"But I just posted last night that you were a twat. If I suddenly turn nice, won't it seem like I had a talk with my PR expert and she told me what to do? I mean, *that's* not going to play well."

"You're a fast learner," Wendy said. "Yes, we may have a clean break here from your past behavior, and people may comment on its suddenness. The alternative is worse. Let me explain something to you. It's wonderful publicity for you to hang out in Las Vegas. There are bars here that your average chick would kill to get into. You can get into them. You need to go wearing your shortest skirt and your highest heels, *but* you have to look good in the dress, and you have to be able to walk in the heels. Don't pull a Björk on me, or a Gerald Ford."

"Who?" Lorelei asked.

"Inside the club," Wendy went on, "sure, you can drink. That's what you went for, and it would be weird if you didn't imbibe. But you can't get too drunk, Lorelei."

"I can't? I thought *that's* what I went to the bar for."

"Maybe so, but the public can't know that. You need to drink but not get drunk. You need to eat but not look fat. You need to wear high heels without getting blisters and wear short skirts when it's cold out without getting goose bumps. You have to be a superhero, because that's what the public expects. *I* don't expect that. Maybe the awards show doesn't, either. But we expect you to make every effort to hide that you're human. And so far, you are doing a terrible job of it. You're acting like a senior on spring break from a West Virginia high school.

"Keep your eyes on the prize, pretty girl. I have trouble with this, too. We want our dream careers, but we have to battle against our own natures to get and keep those careers. If you want it badly enough, sometimes you just have to swallow things you were going to say. Like this." Wendy swallowed, closing one eye as if everything she shouldn't have said to Darkness Fallz was very hard to get down. "Ah, it tastes good and makes you feel so much better afterward. Try it."

Lorelei performed her own swallowing act, then asked, "Can I make a blow job joke about this?"

"A lady should never make a blow job joke in public. Let someone else make the blow job joke. You may giggle good-naturedly."

"Tee-hee!" Lorelei played along.

"Very good." Wendy patted Lorelei's knee, then consulted the notes on her laptop. "Prepare me for the unveiling of your mother's statue. You feel okay posing for the magazines with this likeness of your mom?"

"Sure." Lorelei nodded. "The photographers will get some cool shots I can use in my tour."

Exactly what Wendy had been thinking. "You're not going to do anything to her statue, though." Wendy didn't want to approach this touchy subject, but Lorelei was so unpredictable that she felt it was her duty to make sure. "You're not going to be photographed picking your mom's nose? You don't harbor any ill will toward her?"

"Oh, gosh, no," Lorelei said. "I was so little when she died, you know? I hardly remember her. All my dad ever said about her was how much she loved me."

"Really." Wendy's very low estimation of Lorelei's ne'er-do-well father rose several notches.

"Yeah. It was only later that I learned all the other stuff. What she was into and how she died." Lorelei turned away from Wendy, toward the window onto the sunny Strip. She was clearly used to the idea of her mom being gone. It was more a part of her than her mom herself. But it still made her sad, and she liked distraction. Wendy knew the feeling.

"My mom died when I was three," Wendy said.

Lorelei turned back to her in surprise. "I'm so sorry. How'd she die?"

This question would have been rude coming from anyone else. Coming from another motherless girl, Wendy didn't mind it.

"She had cancer," Wendy said. "My dad was between jobs. We didn't have insurance. When you don't have insurance, they do stuff to try to save you, but they don't do everything." Unlike Lorelei, Wendy had always known the details of her mother's death. Her father had described it like the losing end of a cash transaction.

Lorelei opened her hand on the duvet. Wendy put her hand inside Lorelei's. They held hands for a few moments while something passed between them. Wendy wasn't sure what it was, and for once she didn't try to analyze it. It wasn't part of her job.

She drew her hand away and placed her fingertips on her laptop keyboard again. "So. Tonight. Do you have any really good friends coming to the museum?" Lorelei named a few who passed muster. Wendy would call their PR folks and invite them to go with her and Lorelei to a braid bar before the party. Lorelei would get a stylish, dreamy updo to go with tonight's bohemian outfit, which the wardrobe mistress had showed Wendy. Lorelei would be photographed having comparatively innocent fun with her friends: a first. And Wendy's own braid would hide the jagged ends where her hair had gone missing.

8

"Let Colton in." Even over the phone, even when Daniel's tone was stern, his voice in Wendy's ear gave her a jolt of excitement.

She stood at the edge of the soiree in the spacious lobby of the wax museum. In the center of the room crouched the lifelike replica of Lorelei's mother, mid-stroke on her electric guitar, mouth open, hair somehow suspended in air, head-banging to her own beat. The press had been fascinated by the amazing work of art. Lorelei had behaved perfectly, thanking her mom's fans for honoring her memory over the years by enjoying her music. The speech hadn't even sounded staged—because it hadn't been. Lorelei had ad-libbed from the heart.

After the unveiling, hors d'oeuvres were served along the museum ticket counter. A tribute band had started their run-through of Lorelei's mom's song catalog. They were good. Not as good as Lorelei—but Wendy wanted her to save her voice for the TV miniconcert she'd scored for Thursday, and of course the awards show Friday.

Wendy's roundup of the movers and shakers in town had been a success. Several hundred guests, most of them famous, laughed and danced, assisted by leather-clad waiters passing around shots of Lorelei's mom's notoriously favorite gin. Lorelei was getting a little drunk already, but Wendy figured the night had been hard on Lorelei, despite the brave face she'd worn. Wendy was willing to cut Lorelei a little slack as long as nobody wheeled out a box of syringes and Lorelei's mom's favorite opiate.

Now Wendy was trying to calculate how unhappy her arch-rival was on the other end of the phone call. His careful control made it impossible to tell. "Lorelei went out of her way to say something kind to Colton at rehearsals in the afternoon," Daniel said, "and now this? She was just baiting him, and you directed her to do that."

"Absolutely not. We're not keeping Colton out of this party." Though Daniel hadn't raised his voice, she felt like shouting back at him in defense. She reminded herself that she was innocent—this time, at least—and she kept her tone friendly. "He should be on the list to get in. The bouncer must have gotten confused. Serves you right for being fashionably late." In truth, several times she'd caught Lorelei scanning the room—for Colton, she suspected. And despite herself, Wendy felt the same way. She was still angry at Daniel for making the comment about ruining her, but that didn't mean she didn't want to see him. The night felt empty without him.

"He *is* on the list," Daniel said, "but your people are telling me his name is crossed off because he's already inside. If this is your trick to embarrass him, Wendy—"

"No trick," she said quickly. "Put the bouncer on the phone."

She didn't find out why Colton's name had been crossed off the list. The bouncer seemed confused on this point. But two minutes later, Colton's bodyguard opened the lobby door, followed by Colton's driver, Colton, and Daniel. In his slim suit, with his black eye, Daniel looked like the height of gentlemen's fashion on his way to a fight club. He caught Wendy's gaze briefly and then, frowning, backed against the opposite wall and surveyed the party from his end of the room.

Which, unfortunately, gave Colton the leisure to make a beeline for her. She saw him coming and thought of a lie to tell him about checking in on the caterer, but he was shameless. He actually jogged across the dance floor to catch her before she could escape behind the ticket counter and into the make-shift kitchen.

"Hey, Wendy," he said knowingly.

"Hey, Colton!" She tried to sound as innocent as he sounded guilty. "I almost didn't recognize you without a plastic monkey in your hair."

He grimaced at her, then snatched her hand. "Ha ha. Lorelei and I are over, obvs. What are *you* doing later?"

"Handling the shutdown of a major public relations event." Wendy tried to pull her hand from his, but he was really gripping her. He was trying to be funny, she assured herself. He knew she wouldn't want to be seen with him, and he was making fun of her by forcing her. He didn't understand the panic he was sending her into. He wasn't the spitting image of Rick. It was only the blond, looming, muscular threat of him that had her backing up and pulling her hand until it hurt. "Let go."

He stepped closer. "What's the problem? Daniel said the two of you broke up."

Damn Daniel! Heart beating like she was a frightened rabbit, she couldn't even work out the logic of the situation now that her fake boyfriend had thrown her to the wolves. "Lovers' quarrel," she said quickly. "And I know you're just doing this to make Lorelei mad. I'm not playing. Don't make a scene."

"Problem?" Daniel was beside them, taller than both of them and looking down at them. She was getting used to her heart speeding up every time she encountered Daniel. But her heart couldn't have beat any faster. Now it slowed down. She was so relieved to see him.

Colton glared at Daniel. "You *said* the two of you were over. Why should you care if I move in?"

"I'm not a condo," Wendy muttered.

Daniel told Colton, "I'm over her exactly like you're over Lorelei. Back off."

Colton looked surprised. He released Wendy's hand so suddenly that she was still pulling, and she fell backward.

Daniel caught her by the elbow without even looking in her direction. He remained focused on Colton. "One of the movie producers interested in you is standing by the statue of Richard Nixon. Why don't you quit hitting on my ex-girlfriend and go save your chance at an audition?"

Colton rolled his eyes, but he walked away in the direction of the president.

Daniel stepped into the space Colton had relinquished, boxing Wendy in against the wall. One hand slipped onto the hip of her sequined minidress as he bent to whisper in her ear, "Sorry. I didn't know he was going to come after you again."

She hoped he couldn't feel that she was trembling at the touch of his hand and his deep, soft voice in her ear. Colton or no Colton, she should duck away from Daniel rather than letting him body-block her. He'd threatened to ruin her twelve hours before.

But as she stared into the open collar of his crisp white shirt, inhaling his musky cologne, loving the feeling of his breath in her ear, she was seriously thinking he hadn't meant what he'd said to her that morning.

Right! *It would be easy to ruin you* was a term of endearment around the Blackstone Firm, just as *I hope you die and rot in hell* was an invitation to a birthday party. No, Daniel was only using her. There were no genuine friendships in this business. She felt sick, but this was her life. This was the life she'd wanted.

Ignoring the chill bumps breaking out over her bare arms, she teased him in a tone of mock innocence, "Why did you break up with me?"

He looked down into her eyes. "I thought *you* broke up with *me*."

"Oh, no!" she exclaimed. "It's all been a terrible misunderstanding."

"Miss Mann," he said in a perfect British accent straight out of *Masterpiece Theatre*, "we should endeavor never to be drawn apart again."

Her jaw dropped. "Daniel. Do *not* talk to anybody else like that, unless you want these girls sexting you."

He beamed at her. "I'm sure. Back to work." He stole a kiss from the corner of her mouth, then turned and followed Colton across the room.

Wendy pulled the phone out of her purse and checked Lorelei's accounts. She'd posted only polite compliments so far. Colton had posted nothing. A few entertainment and tabloid sites already showed photos of Lorelei and other stars on the red carpet outside the museum, with begrudgingly positive stories about the party. Wendy concentrated on this very, very important activity so her eyes wouldn't trace Daniel as he talked with beautiful celebrities. Any of them would be glad to have this devastatingly handsome man. Several of them appeared to be working on it.

Half an hour later, an argument near the hors d'oeuvres drew her attention. Lorelei and Colton were shouting at each other. Oh *no*. The party would be closing down soon, and they'd *almost* made it to the other side unscathed.

She put her phone away and pushed through the milling crowd, hurrying for Franklin, who was lounging in a corner. He was easy to spot because he was head and shoulders above everyone else there except other bodyguards, professional athletes, and Daniel. "Can you go corral her?" she pleaded.

As she said this, Lorelei stepped up onto a stool beside the museum ticket counter, then onto the counter itself, straddling a plate of finger sandwiches with her back to the room. As Wendy watched in horror, Lorelei shoved down her skirt and undies and bent over. Half the crowd, oblivious, kept dancing. The other half turned to watch and cheer her on.

No.

Wendy started forward, but it was too late. Brilliant light flashed and disappeared. Wendy blinked blindly. As her vision cleared, she saw Colton moving away and a fully clothed Lorelei stepping down from the ticket counter. She couldn't be sure, but she thought that Lorelei had just mooned Colton from above, and Colton had snapped a picture.

Anger boiled up in Wendy. She wondered whether Daniel had put Colton up to this in retaliation because Wendy had refused to go along with Daniel's plan.

Of course, nobody had made Lorelei pull her skirt and undies down. Wendy asked Franklin, "Did you see booty?"

"Yep."

"Did Colton take a picture? This party has a strict no-picture rule."

"Colton's bodyguard is bigger than me. Besides, Lorelei likes to show her stuff."

"On the Internet?"

"Sure!"

"Look—how could you let her get that drunk?"

"Oh, she doesn't need to be drunk to moon somebody, believe me."

The crowd dispersed along with the altercation. Lorelei put her arm around a girlfriend and disappeared into the darkness behind the counter she'd been standing on. Or mooning on. Colton, still gripping his phone, turned to greet a fellow actor from his canceled teen TV show. They embraced drunkenly, then did some kind of immature hand-slapping greeting that would have made Wendy roll her eyes if she hadn't been a supernice person. Speaking of which, she saw her chance.

She rushed up. "Hey, Colton!" she exclaimed as if she hadn't seen him in months.

"Uh-oh." He tipped his chin down and looked up at her with puppy dog eyes. "You're probably mad at me for taking that picture of Lorelei's ass."

"Fine, tight ass, though," the other actor said. The two of them high-fived.

Pigs. "I'm not mad at *all*," Wendy said. "Hey, let me take a picture for you guys!" She held out her hand for Colton's phone.

And he gave it over! She squealed with triumph inside. *Finally,* something was going right for her. "Smile!" She held the camera in front of her and centered the men's embrace in the frame. She snapped a picture, then said, "Hold on," and pretended to examine the photo. "The flash is messed up. Try again." They put their arms around each other. She snapped another picture and pretended to be looking at it.

The second they got bored and turned away from her, continuing their macho catching-up, she fled across the room. All she needed was a head start to get away from Colton and a few seconds to find the photo of Lorelei and delete it.

She didn't look back. She imagined a heavy hand clapping her on the shoulder at any second. No one stopped her. She slid past the velvet rope across the entrance to the museum exhibits. In a murky room lit only by the exit sign overhead, she stopped between statues of Babe Ruth and Cher and thumbed backward through Colton's photo gallery to the picture of Lorelei's naked butt cheeks. She hit the menu to bring up the command to delete the picture.

Out of the darkness, the phone was grabbed away from her so fast that her fingers stung.

That was the last thing she remembered.

*   *   *

Daniel spent a long time talking with the movie producer on the sidewalk outside the museum, far enough away from the paparazzi gathered at the entrance that he and the producer wouldn't be overheard. Surprisingly, Colton had made a good impression when he'd talked with the man. Daniel skirted the subject, building rapport as he and the producer discussed mutual colleagues such as Victor Moore. By the time they wrapped up their talk, Daniel felt confident that the producer would be calling Colton in the next few weeks for a reading to be cast in a blockbuster movie.

They said good-bye, and Daniel was very thankful the producer headed for his car. Colton had been mostly sober when Daniel left the party, but that might not still be the case, the way the gin had been flowing.

The night was dark, but as Daniel reentered the party, the museum was darker. The spotlit statue of Lorelei's dead mother seemed to suck all the light out of the rest of the room. As his eyes adjusted to the darkness, movement was the first thing he detected. The tiny figure edging past the barrier into the exhibit rooms was Wendy, the front of her long hair swept into a braid that hid the space where her missing lock should have been, the back cascading in loose curls around her shoulders. Her curve-hugging sequined dress caught one sweeping strobe light, and then she disappeared.

Colton was harder to find. And it was harder to move around the room looking for him now that the partiers were drunker. Some people wanted to stop Daniel to ask him about Victor and Olivia's wedding of the century. Others wanted to discuss whether Lorelei was really on coke after all, the way she'd pulled her skirt down. *What?* Daniel became alarmed as more people told him parts of this story. He suspected Colton had something to do with it.

He finally found Colton coming out of the restroom. Daniel asked, "Did you take a picture of Lorelei mooning you?"

"Yes!" Colton laughed.

"What did you do with the picture?" He prayed Colton hadn't posted it online. If Lorelei wanted to self-destruct, that was Wendy's problem. But if Colton posted a picture of that self-destruction and helped it along, the public would associate him with it, even blame him.

Colton opened his hands. "I didn't do anything with it. I lost my phone."

"You lost your—" Daniel stopped himself before the top of his head blew off. Colton eyed him sheepishly. Daniel stepped out of the way of another man entering the restroom, then started again. "How could you lose your phone? Do you realize what the paparazzi could do with your photos and your contacts?"

Colton nodded. "I know. I think Wendy may have it. I hope she does, but I haven't seen her since I gave it to her."

Daniel pressed his lips together and counted to five. "Why did you give Wendy Mann your phone? She's the enemy."

"She was doing me a favor, taking a pic of me and my home slice," Colton protested. "Since when is she the enemy? I thought you were back to tapping that ass."

Daniel uttered the filthiest rebuke he had ever delivered to a client in his six years of representing the Blackstone Firm. Colton looked outraged. Daniel thought for a moment that if his father found out, this could be the end of his career. He didn't care. Colton was not going to talk that way about Wendy. He turned on his heel and stalked toward the forbidden exhibit where Wendy had disappeared.

As he went, he tried to calm himself down. He was afraid he was falling for Wendy. Nothing could be more horrible when he needed to manipulate her to get Colton out of hot water.

She had the upper hand.

And now she had Colton's phone. Daniel had no idea what she planned to do with the information she found on it. Possibly pure evil. Tomorrow he would get another ten calls from his father telling him that his inability to control Colton was a disgrace to the firm. His brother, had he been alive and in charge, would not have allowed this to happen. Daniel plowed around the velvet rope.

In the shadows, Wendy's body was a pink and blond spill across the floor.

He skidded to his knees in front of her, grabbing her wrist so he could take her pulse, which was still there, thank God. He kept his fingers on her artery and counted her heartbeats. With the other hand he found his phone and dialed 911, quickly explaining the situation to the dispatcher.

"Daniel," Wendy murmured. "I'm up. I think some-body hit me." She reached for the back of her head.

"Don't move." He leaped up, hurried to the edge of the lobby, and waved Colton's bodyguard over. Daniel gave the bodyguard his phone with 911 on the line and told him to bring the paramedics through the back of the building so the paparazzi wouldn't report that someone had been injured at the party.

On second thought, Colton might be in danger if Wendy's attacker was still in the building. Lorelei, too.

On third thought, why had he left Wendy alone?

He barked instructions for the bodyguard to find Franklin, and for both of them to close the party down and take Colton and Lorelei to the hotel, pronto. He dashed back to Wendy, who was trying to sit up, brac-ing herself against Cher's knee-high boot.

"Hey. No." Daniel settled on the floor and pulled Wendy's head into his lap, blond hair everywhere. He ran his hands over her arms, down her legs. "What else is hurt?"

"Just my head, ow."

Gently he moved his fingers through her thick hair to the back of her scalp. He felt the gash, then parted her hair to look at the bloody wound and cringed. He pulled out the handkerchief he always carried—an old-fashioned habit that had served him well, because he'd used one for many things in PR over the years.

But never for this. He pressed it to her head. "I'll bet it hurts. You may need a stitch or two. And . . ." He went cold with the realization. He didn't want to tell her, but she needed to know. "You're missing more hair."

"Where?" she squeaked.

Gently he picked up her hand from her lap and placed it over the chopped-off lock, on the other side of her head from the first.

"Daniel," she wailed. "He had his hands on me. Where is my hair? He has my hair, like a trophy."

"What else? Do you think he . . ." Daniel's voice trailed off. He couldn't bring himself to finish. Something seemed to catch in his throat.

Wendy finished for him, ". . . touched me in a way that made me feel all funny? No."

He sighed with relief at her answer. If her sense of humor was coming back, maybe she didn't have a concussion. "Have yourself checked out, though, okay? The ambulance and the police will be here soon."

"Daniel!" She was trying to sit up again. "What did you call them for? Are you trying to get me fired?"

He pressed her back down into his lap. "Why would you get fired for being attacked?"

"Not for being attacked," she said to the black ceiling. "For the headline LORELEI VOGEL'S PUBLIC RELATIONS MANAGER ASSAULTED IN VEGAS CLUB running the same day as the picture of Lorelei mooning her own musical career good-bye. It all sounds like one big drunken brawl. Oh shit. Oh, Daniel." She looked at him so sadly, like she was sorry she'd just killed his cat. "That's what whoever hit me must have been after. Colton's phone is gone."

The possible consequences were astounding. And Daniel couldn't think about any of that right now. Not with Wendy bleeding and devastated in his lap. He said soothingly, "Maybe it's around here on the floor. I'll look for it after the ambulance comes." He cast a glance around the dark room. He might even catch a glimpse of the glow from the phone's screen.

As he did this, he realized for the first time how vulnerable they were. The exit sign over the doorway behind him and a faint glow around the corner from the lobby were the only lights preventing the room from plunging into blackness. The legs of the statues around them were visible. Beyond them, anyone might be lurking.

A new surge of adrenaline rushed through him. He should get her out of there, but he was afraid to move her. He would protect her if anyone came at them from the shadows.

"I think the phone is long gone," Wendy said dismally. "That's what the guy wanted. He took it from me before he hit me."

"Well, if what he's after is to sell the picture of Lorelei, that might be hard for him. I'm sure Colton has security on his phone, so someone would have to enter a numeric code to access his files." Daniel was not actually sure of this at all. Colton was turning out to be *that* kind of celebrity.

"He probably does," Wendy acknowledged, "but

the security block hadn't kicked in when I came back here to delete the photo. That's why I was in such a hurry. If the guy who hit me e-mailed the picture to himself right away, it's his. It'll be on the tabloid websites by tomorrow night." She gave a shuddering sigh, bolstering herself. "Maybe that won't happen."

"Maybe not," Daniel lied. "Maybe it was just a robbery. If the guy stole your wallet, he probably doesn't even know whose pictures he has on the phone." He reached way out to retrieve Wendy's purse by the strap.

Wendy's eyes widened. As Daniel held her purse for her and she fished inside, she muttered, "Just what I need, for some jackass to be passing himself off as Wendy Mann and charging a hundred thousand casino chips on my Stargazer credit card. Archie would send someone to break my legs." She opened her wallet and fumbled with the contents. Daniel noticed that her fingers shook as she slid out one card after another and slid them back. "Driver's license, Stargazer card, my card. I wouldn't vouch for my shoe store card and stuff like that, but the important stuff is here."

"Money?" Daniel asked.

"I didn't have much cash. I've bribed a lot of people in the past twenty-four hours." She peeked in the long compartment for her bills. "Still here. Oh—nope, my phone's still here, too, thank God."

"Then just relax." He moved her purse aside. "Don't think about it anymore. The ambulance will be here soon, and I'll go with you."

"No!" she tried to struggle up again.

Daniel held her down. "Stop."

"Daniel, seriously, please. You have to stay here and make sure everything gets taken care of."

"I already sent Colton and Lorelei to bed."

"Not together," Wendy insisted.

"Not together," Daniel agreed. "And I can't let you go alone to the hospital."

"Yes, you can."

"What if that guy comes after you?"

She hesitated as if thinking of that herself. But then she said, "He won't. He got what he wanted."

"If all he wanted was Colton's phone, yeah. That sounds like business. But he's cut your hair twice. That sounds personal. And he could be anybody. Let me go with you until we figure it out."

"I need you to stay here and protect my job, not me. I would rather get attacked again than lose my job."

He eyed her. "Seriously? That's some job."

She closed her eyes and rolled her head to one side on his thigh. He caught her wrist again. Her pulse had sped up.

Her soft voice sent a vibration through his thigh as she said, "Remember that last paper for Dr. Benson, the one that won you the Clarkson Prize?"

He remembered, but he said nothing. He didn't want to upset her more.

"Of course you don't remember," she grumbled. "It was just another victory for you. I worked forty hours on that one paper, Daniel, making sure all my research was bulletproof. I didn't sleep for the last two nights and probably suffered brain damage just to turn a perfect paper in."

Daniel had worked sixty hours on that paper, even traveling by train to Philadelphia one afternoon to interview the president of an image management firm, a friend of his father's, because he was so terrified that Wendy would beat him out for the Clarkson Prize and his father would be ashamed of him.

"You still beat me," Wendy went on, "and you were the celebrated graduate at the top of the class. But since you didn't want a job at Stargazer anyway, I lucked out and snagged it. I'm not giving up that job now. Not after six years of a ridiculous workload. Not just because of a bump on the head. Please, Daniel, please stay here."

She was getting so agitated that he really did think it would be better for her to go alone. The decision would torture him, though. In his mind he would be with her in those bright, cold rooms. "If they let you out of the hospital tonight," he said, "can I stay in your room with you? Or you stay with me. I have a suite. You can sleep on the bed. I'll sleep on the couch."

She hesitated. "You don't have to take care of me."

"If something like this happened to me when I was out on assignment, I would want a friend," he said truthfully.

She sighed a long sigh. "Okay. Thank you. I'll take

your couch. But I'm going to remind you that you said this if you get hit in the head."

"Fair enough." He wrote his room number on her palm and slipped his extra key into her purse. "Do you want me to get some things from your room and bring them up?"

"Oh, man, would you? Yes, take my extra key. Promise you won't look at the mess. I guess that's impossible." She closed her eyes and groaned softly. "You can't let Lorelei know anything about this, okay? If she asks, some random woman was attacked in the back hall, not me."

"Why not? Don't you think she's going to find out?"

"Not if you don't tell her. She's got a lot of important performances on her mind right now, and I'm supposed to be her rock. Nothing can happen to me."

He wished that were true. Gently he stroked her hair away from her eyes. He felt the warmth of her body through his slacks. Every instinct told him to pull her closer and never let her go.

But he did let her go. At first he braced himself, thinking the noises from the depths of the exhibit might be the bad guy coming back, but it was only the paramedics weaving with a gurney around the wax statues. Reluctantly he moved out from under her. The paramedics worked over her on the floor, then lifted her onto a stretcher. He felt another wave of misgiving as they hovered over her. Now that he wasn't touching her, she seemed to go limp. She didn't look at him again. Though there was nothing for him to do, he stood there watching until they wheeled her out and disappeared behind the statues.

As he walked back into the party, Daniel gazed around at the drunken stars and hangers-on, laughing or arguing, wondering if any of them had hurt Wendy. But he suspected the guy was long gone. And the party was closing down. On Wendy's behalf, he made sure there were no issues with the caterer or the museum. The museum's administrators didn't mind the notoriety that the mooning incident might bring them. To their credit, they seemed more concerned that someone had been attacked in an exhibit room. Daniel stayed to tell the police what he knew, simultaneously wrangling calls between Colton and his phone company to shut down access to his electronic files.

Finally Daniel hailed a taxi in the deserted street. After a quick call to Colton's bodyguard to make sure Colton and Lorelei had been deposited safely, he texted Wendy:

They're in bed. I'm coming to the hospital.

A minute later he got a response:

No, I'm on the way to the hotel. I'll see you there. No concussion.

He breathed a huge sigh of relief at that news. His mind had been spinning with his plan of attack, offensive moves he could make to head off Lorelei's photo going viral and the inevitable backlash against Colton. But as soon as he saw Wendy's text, he stopped caring about work. He couldn't concentrate on anything but his last glimpse at her being wheeled out between the replicas of stars.

At the hotel, he went straight to her room to gather her things for the night. His first horrified thought was that the place had been ransacked, possibly by the same person who'd hit her. It looked like several fashionable women had exploded. But as he carefully stepped around the outer edges of the piles, he realized there was some bizarre order to it all, and this was Wendy's notion of unpacking. It rather resembled her logic. It seemed rude to rifle through it—though it was rifled already—so he just repacked everything, wishing he had more time to examine the bunny ears and cottontail, and headed for his own room.

As he exited the elevator, he spotted her in the hall in front of him. "Wendy," he called softly, because, though Vegas, it was three in the morning.

She turned and stopped to wait for him. She was a small woman, but she'd never looked smaller than in this endless corridor with high ceilings. Her face was pale as paper.

When he reached her, he let go of the handle of her suitcase and encircled her in his arms.

She didn't protest. It was only after he'd initiated the hug that he wondered what it meant, and what she must think of him now.

He didn't have a clear view of the wound on the back of her head, but he could see a new pink streak down the middle of her hair.

He let her go and gently pressed her toward his room. "Did they give you good painkillers?"

"Not even." She sounded bone-tired. "They gave me over-the-counter stuff. They said anything stronger could mask symptoms that come up later. You're supposed to watch me, and if I forget what year it is or I fall down, you're supposed to take me back to the hospital."

"I can do that." He unlocked the door and held it open for her while she ducked around his arm and walked inside.

"Wow, what's up with all the booze?" she asked, gesturing to the bar. "Do you ask the hotel for this just because it looks cool?"

"Yes," he admitted.

She nodded. "I always wondered about PR folks with that setup. I've wanted to do it myself, but I don't have the budget. I guess you have any budget you want, since you own the place."

"Almost," he acknowledged.

Her lips parted, and she watched him. She probably was trying to think of another probing question for him with a joke at the end, but her brain wasn't cooperating.

"Give up," he said. "Here's your bag." He set it down inside the bathroom door. "I didn't know what you would want, so I brought it all."

"Thanks," she said on a sigh of relief, trudging past him. "You're not going to ask me about the bunny ears?"

"And the bunny tail? No, I didn't see those." As she was closing the door behind her, he warned her, "Don't lock it."

She stared at him blankly, like she suspected him of something but didn't have enough evidence to accuse him.

"I'm worried about you," he explained. "You seem a little unsteady."

"I am completely steady," she said, but she gripped the doorjamb so hard that her knuckles turned white. "Okay." She disappeared back into the bathroom. He listened, but he didn't hear the lock turn.

He moved some of the bottles aside on the bar and set water heating in the coffeepot. After he changed clothes, he poured water over a teabag for her. Then he walked to the window and stared out at the blackness shot through with all the colors of the rainbow, glowing to entice tourists toward their own destruction. For the millionth time in the day and a half he'd been here, he wished he were one of these tourists. The only sounds that penetrated the window were the occasional siren or an especially insistent horn, but the Strip *looked* like it should be noisy, even through the glass.

He heard the bathroom door open. She padded out in bare feet, boxer shorts, and a threadbare T-shirt, weaving a bit.

"You take the bed," he said. "I'll sleep on the couch."

She shook her head. "No, Daniel—"

"I'm so tired of arguing. Please."

She slipped under the covers on one side of the bed and propped herself up against the pillows. He brought her the cup of tea.

"Thank you," she said, taking the mug with both hands. "What is it?"

Sitting down in the desk chair on her side of the bed and propping his feet up near the mound of her feet under the covers, he said, "It's tea. What did you think it was?"

She took a sip, then said with her eyes closed, "I have no idea what you've got at the Blackstone Firm bar over there. Beverages made of ground souls and topped with fallen stars."

"I think you're tasting the rose hips."

She snorted, which turned into a short whine. "Don't make me laugh. It hurts my head."

"Did a detective interview you at the hospital?" he asked.

"Yes. His name was Detective Butkus. I asked him if he made that up so people who'd been hit in the head would remember it later. He laughed uncomfortably."

"You don't say."

"Yeah, but I couldn't tell him anything helpful. I felt like a dork."

"I talked to the police when they came to the museum," Daniel said. "They didn't find Colton's phone, but they did find what they think the guy used to hit you. It was the butt of a long-barreled Colt .45 from a statue of Wyatt Earp. They didn't seem optimistic about catching the guy, though. I told them he'd taken a hunk of your hair, and that he'd done the same thing at the casino bar. They said he's probably an overzealous photographer who took a shine to you.

"Somehow he snuck past security at the museum. He saw the opportunity to steal the phone from you, and he took it. He kept going through the exhibits and escaped through a back entrance. Apparently you can't get into the museum from the back, but you can get out without an alarm sounding. And they're not big on security cameras."

"I guess they're not too concerned about a patron making off with a wax statue of John Denver." She set the mug on the bedside table. With no ceremony, she snuggled down in the covers. Her blond brow furrowed. Her soft-looking hand, perfectly manicured in an understated pink, lay next to her cheek.

Sensing that he still watched her, she murmured, "I'm okay. Don't worry about me. I hurt, and the hospital was torture because I wanted so badly to go to sleep. All I dreamed of doing was getting here and finally lying down and letting go, and now I'm being stared down by the winner of the Clarkson Prize."

He grimaced. "Sorry."

"No." Her hand flailed blindly until it settled on his hand. "I didn't mean it. I'm relieved to lie down, but I feel so safe with you. Thank you."

She dropped off to sleep seconds after that, it seemed. She stopped talking—a first—and her breathing turned deep and even. Rising, he turned off the lamp.

Then he bent over her body and gently kissed her forehead. When she half smiled, he couldn't resist touching his lips to the corner of her mouth.

He stood up straight in horror. Just as he'd feared in the museum, he was falling for her, hard—this brazen, complex strategist, the enemy of his firm, the worst possible woman for him to want.

With a long last look at her pretty face—deceptively angelic when she was unconscious—and a wistful sigh, he eased a pillow from the other side of the bed and a blanket from the top of the closet. He settled on the sofa, facing the Strip, and stared at the view for a long time, mind spinning like the lights in the signs, wondering who had hurt her. And resolving not to let it happen again.

9

The next morning, Daniel sat in a chair, surfing the news on his laptop, like pretty much every morning when he was traveling. Wendy still slept in his bed, which was unlike any morning ever.

Sometime in the night, she'd rolled to face him. The late morning sun kissed her face and made her seem to glow with gold and blush. Her breasts looked large and soft underneath her T-shirt. He thought one of her nipples strained against the fabric, but he couldn't be sure. It might have been a wrinkle. After considering this for a while, he turned back to his computer screen. He'd been staring at her breast so long that the screen saver had turned on.

"Ow," she finally mumbled with her eyes still closed, reaching for the back of her head with one hand. "Zounds."

"Hold on." He crossed the room, found her pain-killers in the bathroom, and brought her a glass of water.

"Thank you," she said blearily. She eased upright long enough to swallow the pills and down the water, then sank into the sheets again. She didn't move.

Daniel settled back down with his computer and tried not to think about her. And failed. The shock of finding her on the floor last night played over and over like a tape in his head.

After another quarter hour, she rolled off the bed, stood unsteadily, and disappeared into the bath-room. He expected she would take a long time in there. But seconds later, she emerged in sweatpants and flip-flops, dragging her suitcase behind her. "Daniel, I really appreciate everything you've done for me, and I—"

"Whoa." The sharpness of his tone surprised him, but she looked like she felt terrible. "Can you drop the professional courtesy, just until you feel better?"

She shook her head carefully. "Stargazer expects a bill for my room. I can't tell them I've been sleeping with the enemy, like Lorelei thinks. Even though, I mean, you know what I mean. That we're not really doing that. There would be no way to explain what's actually going on without also admitting to them that I've complicated matters by acquiring a hair-stealing stalker."

"Keep the room," he said. "Stay with me anyway."

She set her suitcase upright on its wheeled bottom and crossed her arms over her T-shirt, which pushed her breasts up against the fabric. "Oh, suddenly you're not asking me. You're telling me. Are you genuinely worried for my safety? Or are you simply trying to keep your friends close and your enemies closer?"

His reasons for wanting her in his room had everything to do with her safety and nothing to do with strategy. And unexpectedly, her suggestion that he was still manipulating her smarted like a kick in the gut.

"Wait." She unfolded her arms. "Was that a hurt look I saw cross your face just now?"

"Indignation, maybe," he muttered.

"No, I'm sure it was. Daniel, I didn't mean to hurt your feelings. I didn't think you had any." She rolled her eyes. "That didn't come out right, either."

Watching her squirm made him feel a little better.

"I'm really sorry," she gushed. "I have no idea what to do now that you're sitting there looking hurt. I didn't think that was possible. I'm in shock."

"Stop talking," he said.

"Okay," she said sheepishly.

"You look ill."

"I do?" She sighed.

"Come sit down. I've already ordered breakfast."

She pulled her own laptop from her bag, kicked off her flip-flops, and sat on the sofa. Still feeling insulted, he tried to ignore her and concentrate on his computer screen. She did a better job of this than he did. Surfing bright pink tabloid sites, she didn't even seem to notice when room service knocked and wheeled in a steaming cart. She only blinked at Daniel when he handed her a slice of orange and told her to eat it.

After that, she set aside her computer. They ate together in companionable silence, only asking each other in low tones to pass the salt and the butter. He felt a lot better with something in his stomach. She looked less pale, too. He thought the meal had broken the ice between them, until his bare foot accidentally touched hers and she flinched.

When his phone buzzed with the ringtone for his father, he figured he'd better take it, since he'd been avoiding these calls for almost forty-eight hours. He clicked the phone on. "Hello?" he said as if he wasn't sure who was calling, just to make his father angrier.

His father immediately started yelling so loudly that Daniel was afraid Wendy a few feet away would overhear and be horrified. He watched her out of the corner of his eye, but she didn't look at him. He used the calmest tones he could muster while getting an earful of abuse.

Finally it was over. He clicked the phone off and placed it far away on the coffee table in distaste, then pulled his computer back onto his knees. He surfed to another of his regular sites and tried to concentrate on the news of a couple of bills making their way through the state legislature in Albany. The longer the silence stretched, the worse he felt, culminating in his realization that he wanted to explain the call to Wendy.

He popped a knuckle. "My dad makes me feel like killing someone."

"My dad made me feel that way."

He recalled that college girl again, standing in the dean's office receiving the news about the death of her father, eyes hollow. She'd been back in class the following Monday, he'd noted at the time. This was what she'd made of herself, out of nothing. The same thing he'd made of himself, when he'd had every possible advantage.

"Your British accent kicks in when you talk to him," she said.

He shrugged. "I've tried to get rid of it. I guess . . ." He rubbed the bruise under his eye, which had begun to throb. ". . . I sound like him when I'm stressed."

"What's he mad about?" she asked gently. "The picture of Colton in the tabloids with strawberry daiquiri on his face?"

"That, and the rumor he badgered Lorelei so badly at the unveiling of her deceased mother's wax likeness that she mooned him. I can't wait to hear what my dad says when the picture of Lorelei surfaces."

"Maybe that won't happen."

"You keep saying that."

She looked surprised. "Really?"

"Yes."

"Hmm. My dad used to tell me that when I worried about him working in the coal mine. Of course, he died in the mine, so . . ." Daniel could tell she was struggling to find a way to end this comment with a joke, but the punch line escaped her completely. She mumbled something inaudible. Then she started over, gesturing to her computer. "Have you actually seen the headline or the photo of Colton?"

"I don't have to. Why?"

"Just curious," she said. "I've been surfing every gossip site for stories on Lorelei and Colton, like I would every morning for any star I was representing. I'm looking for events we could use to promote Lorelei in the future, or contacts I might find helpful. I'm examining the bylines on pictures in the tabloids to see who's buying, and which paparazzi are getting the shots and how. While I've been watching you, you've looked at the political news. That's it."

"I don't have to look at that other garbage. People in my office in New York keep track of it and alert me when there's a problem. I have to do this job, but I don't have to enjoy it."

"Really!" Wendy was aghast.

"Well, yeah." He'd thought this was obvious, that all PR people felt the same way. "Stars hire me to come here and tell them what to do. I present them with the key to unlock the box and fix all their problems. And then they don't do what I say. They're paying me for nothing. If they're alcoholics or drug addicts, that's its own problem. But if they're just obstinate? I don't understand how they've worked so hard to get to this level, or at least lucked their way into it, and now they're going to throw it all away purely out of stubbornness. I'm Sisyphus for dummies." He expected to edge further back into her good graces with this joke.

She didn't laugh. "Look at it from their side. They may be famous, they may be especially talented, but they're all real people. They get tired. They get frustrated. They want to have fun and do their own thing. It's hard being a brand name all the time. You should know that better than anybody."

He looked sharply at her. "What's that supposed to mean?"

She gave him an innocent smile. "What do you do for fun? Or, to narrow it down, what have you done for fun since you've been in Vegas?"

"I got punched the first day. You got hit on the head last night. It hasn't been fun."

"You could look at it that way. On the other hand, I let myself enjoy dressing up last night and having my hair done. I get tired sometimes of being the dull workhorse tagging along while my clients enjoy all the glamour. I can have some glamour, too. And the night before, I enjoyed an appletini and got a mani-pedi a few booths away from Lorelei, where she wouldn't see me. I found a way to have fun despite everything that's happened. Have you done *anything* since you've been here that wasn't by the book?"

He gestured to his computer. "I'm having fun surfing the news. I'm interested in politics."

She gazed at him blankly. "For fun. That's your fun."

"Well, for a job. A job I can't have. You know how they say that if you love your job, you'll never work a day in your life?"

She gave him a bemused smile like she thought he was kidding. "So what's this job you can't have? You want to run for office?"

"Oh, God, no. I want to be behind the scenes, doing basically this same PR job but for politicians whom I actually support." He paused. "You know, I was class president."

"I remember."

"That was just on a whim. My dad was furious because it took so much time away from my class work."

"Well, your whim got you elected leader of a class of five thousand at a prestigious university, and you still managed to win the Clarkson Prize. I'd say you balanced everything okay."

He hadn't told anyone this. He took a breath to speak. Then paused. How could he trust her? This secret wouldn't ruin him, but it would certainly embarrass his family.

She arched her brows expectantly. And he realized he *wanted* rather desperately to tell her. She was a colleague in the same industry, a classmate from college. Though she wasn't an old friend, he was seriously beginning to wonder why not.

"Senator Rowling offered me a job," he said.

Wendy's blue eyes widened. "No shit! Doing what?"

"Press secretary for her New York office."

"Dude!" Wendy leaned across the coffee table between them and shoved his shoulder. "That would be perfect for you! I can see you now, holding a press conference, batting those pesky *Times* reporters down like flies. Are you going to take it?"

"Nah," he said with even more reluctance than he'd felt before, now that someone was seconding what a great idea it was.

"You're *not*?" she exclaimed. "Then why'd you apply?"

"I didn't apply. I worked on her campaign when I was in college. They offered me a job then, too, but I couldn't take it because I had to work for my dad. I still know some people there, and they've kept tabs on my work. They came asking for me. I haven't officially turned them down, because I guess it's a little . . ." He opened his hands.

"Heartbreaking," Wendy finished for him.

"I was going to say 'disappointing,' but if you want me to feel even worse about it . . ."

She laughed halfheartedly. "Why don't you accept it?"

He shook his head. "I can't. My dad expects me to take over the firm next month so he can retire."

"That sounds like his problem, not yours."

"No, I have to run the place because my sister really wants to work there. She's still in college."

"That sounds like *her* problem."

"And my brother . . ." He looked up at the ceiling, unable to go on. It was impossible to explain his brother, who'd been the only member of the firm killed that morning because he went to work so early to impress their father. Daniel's voice cracked a little as he said, "You don't understand."

"Explain it to me," she persisted.

"Like . . ." He was talking with his hands, fingers splayed in front of him, and he'd opened with *like*—two things his father had constantly belittled him for when he was young. He put his hands down. "Before my brother died, I was interested in history and rhetoric and politics and progress and forward thinking. Nobody told me I couldn't pursue that, because my brother was there to take over the firm. And then after he died . . ." Daniel forced himself to put his hands down again. "There was this double whammy. He died, *and* I couldn't do what I wanted anymore. But somehow that second lesson never quite sank in."

"Or," Wendy said, "you still want that dream career for yourself, and the career you have now is for everybody except yourself."

He shook his head. "You don't get it." She had no idea about that feeling he had sometimes, that he'd had since he was sixteen, of shoring up his whole family so the world didn't cave in on them.

"Okay," Wendy said evenly.

He looked over at her. There was absolutely no judgment in her face. She'd been grilling him a few seconds before, but now her expression was devoid of blame.

Absently he flicked his finger across his trackpad. The screen saver blinked off, and five new headlines scrolled up.

"When my dad started the firm," he said, "things were different. It was a lot easier to keep a secret. There were no social media sites, for one thing. There was no Internet and a lot less television. There were fewer paparazzi because there were fewer outlets for selling a photo. But even more importantly, stars were genuinely stars. There was a reason they were famous—looks, family, occasionally even talent. They didn't become stars overnight. They didn't expect to ride the train for a few weeks and lose everything just as quickly. Today's reality shows have interjected this strange influx of bums, ingrates, and no-talent sons of bitches into the mix, and sometimes you can't tell who's who at an Oscars after-party.

"Nowadays it just doesn't matter, you know? I wanted to work in PR for something that really matters, like politics, like getting someone into office who can make a difference, and keeping that person there no matter what mud the other side slings. But whether the public likes or dislikes Colton Farr for pissing in the fountain at the Bellagio, and whether he's able to land his blockbuster movie and pull his career out of the gutter . . . I don't care, and nobody else should, either."

"*I* care," Wendy spoke up. "I mean, not about Colton. But if you're a little girl living in the middle of nowhere and your life is basically nothing, it can really give you hope to idolize a glamorous star." She pointed to her pink computer screen. "I have *always* read the tabloids."

Daniel leaned closer, gazing dubiously at a montage of overdressed starlets and their ratlike dogs.

"Even reality stars have talent," Wendy said. "They have a larger-than-life personality that people want to watch, even if it's just strange or grating."

"You should know," Daniel said.

Wendy's brow furrowed in protest, but then her expression relaxed, backing away from his challenge. "I guess I walked into that one."

"I meant the larger-than-life personality," Daniel clarified, "not the other."

She sniffed. "Right."

Daniel huffed out frustration. He really hadn't meant to insult her, but he'd been putting his foot in his mouth constantly around her, which wasn't like him at all. If he didn't know better, he'd say she made him flustered. "I'm not telling you anything you haven't heard already," he said. "Isn't that why you got kicked off the Darkness Fallz case? Isn't that why you got called into the dean's office a couple of times in college? I know that's why nobody could take their eyes off you."

"I think that was the hair. That's what it usually is." She grabbed a lock falling over her shoulder and examined the ends. The front of her hair was still bound in a braid, but tendrils had come loose and framed her face in soft gold. The back hung in big curls. Yes, it was the hair.

"Maybe," Daniel said.

She looked over at him. "Do you need to get in the bathroom? Because I'm going to be a while. I need to wash my hair, which is an undertaking. I used it to mop the floor of that exhibit room. It's three shades darker than normal."

"Only at the roots," Daniel said diplomatically. "It looks like your darker roots are growing out."

"That's grease."

"There's blood in it, too." He nodded toward the bathroom. "Go ahead."

She felt the back of her head for the blood. Then she walked toward the bathroom, slowing once and listing a bit to one side as if she weren't quite steady on her feet. After she'd disappeared and he could hear the door start to swing shut, he called sharply, "Wendy."

She stuck her head back out to look at him.

"Don't lock the door."

She didn't protest this time. "'Kay." The door clicked shut.

Reluctantly he navigated away from his news feeds so he could address his father's concerns with a few well-placed press releases on Colton's stability and his excitement about the upcoming awards show. But he found himself listening very hard for noises through the bathroom door: The whisper of Wendy pulling the cotton T-shirt across her bare breasts and up over her head. A cascade that sounded like relief as she pushed the material of her sweatpants to the floor.

The vent moaned, and shortly afterward, the shower hissed. The striptease in his head was over. He tried to go back to his work.

But the sound of the shower danced with Wendy underneath it. The droplets drummed against the shower walls, paused as her body blocked the spray, and resumed their beat as she moved. He couldn't get her out of his head. He pictured her naked with the hot water streaming over her creamy body, turning her bright hair slick and dark.

He turned away from his computer, toward her. He peered down the hallway to the bathroom. He couldn't go down it. Or, he could, but he wouldn't.

Just for a moment, though, he put his chin in his hands, staring at the laptop but not seeing it, and allowed himself the fantasy of Wendy. He'd done this before, in college. Back then the fantasy had turned physical. He'd returned to the dorm after class, closed himself in his room, and pleasured himself with the thought of her, this saucy girl from Appalachia who thought she would get the better of him.

The fantasy had involved Dr. Abbott's class. He'd bent her over Dr. Abbott's desk, with or without Dr. Abbott still behind it, with or without the whole class watching. He'd wrapped her golden hair around his fist, holding her down and motionless as he entered her.

Now he was still thinking about her hair—how could he not?—but he didn't need an audience. He'd grown out of that urge for public sex. The new fantasy had him walking down that hall. Turning the knob on that unlocked door. Walking through the mist and raking back the white curtain, slowly so he wouldn't startle her, to be greeted by that brilliant smile, those sparkling blue eyes. Her long, wet hair would be streaming over her shoulders and down her front. He would reach forward and slick it away from her breasts—

"Daniel?"

He started in surprise and nearly lost hold of his laptop.

Shaking off his shock, he realized she'd called to him from the bathroom. She was in trouble.

He leaped up and reached the bathroom door in two steps. It was open a few inches, the light golden beyond it. He swung it open.

Wendy stood there with a white towel wrapped around her, gripping the terry cloth closed with both fists. Surprisingly, her hair was dry, with the same golden glow he'd always known, hanging in strange waves now that her braid was undone, but her face was wet. Her eyelashes were wet and dark, and he couldn't tell from her expression whether she'd just washed her face or she was in tears.

Her shaky voice gave him the answer. "I am so sorry," she sobbed. "I need your help."

"Okay."

"Because I'm not supposed to get the stitches wet. But I have to wash my hair. In this business it's important that the smell of your hair doesn't repulse people. You understand this."

"Right."

"And I tried but I'm not going to have enough hands. I'm going to get the stitches wet and then I'm going to have to go back to the hospital and while I'm gone Lorelei is going to have a threesome with a showgirl and a taxi driver and tweet the pictures and I'm going to get fired."

He'd thought she was incredibly strong, seeming to shrug off the attack on her body last night. Turned out she just hid things well. Almost as well as he did.

"Hey." He put out one hand, but hesitated to place it on her shoulder, which was wet and bare. He put it down. "I'll help you. I would help you even if you weren't naked."

"Oh." She heaved a deep sigh. "You just looked so . . . I didn't think you were going to help me. You looked mean."

"I didn't feel mean."

She tilted her head, considering him, and her long hair inched even farther down her bare arm. "Someone could make a poster with captions for all of your emotions and use the same photo for each one. Meanness. Anger. Happiness. Hunger. Giddiness. Lust."

He raised his eyebrows.

She swallowed. "Embarrassment."

"Charitableness," he said. "What do you need me to do?"

She handed him a small plastic bag. "Hold this over my stitches while I wash my hair. If you think that's gross, I have latex gloves, too."

"I have my own latex gloves, but I don't think it's gross."

"You have your own latex gloves? I thought I was being weird to pack mine."

"You never know what you'll encounter in this job. Especially in Vegas." He took the plastic bag from her.

She slid another towel from the rack as she turned, then dropped it on the tile floor beside the shower. She glanced back at him. "To kneel on, so you don't hurt your knees."

"Do I look that fragile?"

She shrugged, which made her towel slip a little. She tightened it around herself, blushing. "I just . . . okay." She kneeled on the towel herself and pushed back the shower curtain to reveal the still-gushing faucet. A cloud of steam escaped.

"Just a sec." Daniel stepped into the hall, pulled off his T-shirt, and tossed it in the direction of the bed, thinking as he did so that reality was verging closer and closer to his fantasy of Wendy. He stepped back inside.

Wendy was watching the door for him, looking small and so sexy with the towel barely covering her breasts. When she saw him, her eyes widened. He expected her to comment on his naked upper body, but she didn't. She turned back to the tub.

He kneeled behind her on the towel. Parting her hair, he found the stitches in the back and held the plastic bag over them, cupping his hand to protect the wound without using too much pressure and hurting her. "Okay, go."

She leaned forward to wet the front of her hair. His hand didn't follow, and her head slipped out from under the plastic bag.

"Wait a minute," he said. "You know what? I'm afraid I'm going to hurt you. Let's switch jobs." He brought her hand back and placed it over the plastic bag. "You hold it. Now lean forward."

Obediently she held the front of her head under the stream again. Her long hair seemed to become part of the water, glinting golden and pooling on the bottom of the white tub. He reached behind him to the sink for the ice bucket, then filled that with hot water and poured it on her hair around the wound, carefully avoiding the stitches. He squirted out a handful of her shampoo, rubbed his hands together to spread it, and worked his palms through one side of her hair, then the other, massaging her scalp with his fingertips and lingering over the job way longer than he needed to. He was getting hard.

To steer himself away from the fantasy again, he joked, "You have a lot of hair."

"Sorry."

"Don't be sorry. It wasn't an insult, just an observation. If you could see the expression on my face, you would know that. I'm grinning ear to ear."

"I don't believe it." She moved as if she would turn to look at him.

He put his wet hand on her bare back. "No, don't look. I'm almost done." And he needed to get rid of this hard-on before she noticed. He filled the bucket with water again and carefully poured it around the wound, then over the rest of her hair. The suds slid away and vanished.

Finally he'd rinsed all of her hair. He should turn off the water and end this now. He was loath to do that. His bare chest was inches from her bare back, and steam transformed the bathroom into a sexy cloud.

This had to stop. He'd always prided himself on his professionalism. He wasn't about to come on to a business rival. She thought he was okay to partner with up to a point. This was that point, and there was no need to give her a weapon to use against him later. Abruptly he reached over her and turned off the water.

He carefully patted the surface of her hair with a towel. "Lean back," he commanded her. As she eased backward out of the tub, he caught her hair between the sides of the towel and scrubbed it. Now he stroked the towel closer to her wound. "There. Not completely dry, but your stitches aren't soaked, either." He gently moved her hand away from the back of her head. Lifting her under the arms, he set her on the side of the tub.

She looked down at him dully. Her face was stark white.

"Hurts?" he asked her.

She started to nod, but moving her head seemed to hurt worse. She swallowed.

"Maybe you should go home." He didn't want her to leave. The two of them had circled each other in New York for years, never crossing paths. He was afraid it would happen for another six years if he let her go. But she wasn't well. She had a stalker in Vegas. "Let Stargazer send Sarah or one of your other agents to take over. I'll fill her in and work with her like I've been working with you."

"Ha!" Wendy said. "I don't think so. Her husband might have something to say about that."

He blinked. "I didn't mean—"

"I'm kidding. Come to think about it, he probably wouldn't say a thing. I hate that guy." A rivulet of water formed at her hairline and snaked down one side of her face. "Besides, I have a deal with Stargazer. They're firing me for losing Darkness Fallz unless I save Lorelei."

"Oh." That didn't sound like a good deal to him. Her chances of repairing Lorelei's career looked slimmer every time Lorelei pulled her skirt down. He couldn't imagine how much pressure Wendy must be under. He'd thought *he* was in a pressure cooker, and he wasn't threatened with losing his job if he failed a client. The worst that waited for him back in New York was shame.

"When I was surfing online, I didn't see a sign of anyone posting the photo of Lorelei," she ventured. "Maybe that won't happen."

"Maybe not," he agreed, doubtful.

"But the possibility is so horrible that I'm ready to work with you to make it seem like she and Colton are back together, if you still want to."

Looking into her blue eyes, he nodded solemnly rather than pumping his fist in the air.

"I do think if that picture comes out and we're claiming they're back together," she said, "we can brush it off and say Lorelei mooned Colton as a result of flirtation and youthful exuberance."

He cracked a smile. "When in actuality it was a result of spite and gin."

She laughed, then winced and reached for the back of her head. "But even if they don't really get together, we're putting them in proximity. I don't feel comfortable doing that unless we sit down with them." She reached for his hand—his adrenaline spiked—and turned his wrist over so she could read his watch. "If we hurry, we'll have time before their afternoon rehearsal. We need to explain what we're doing. But we also need to talk to them about what went wrong between them, and try to defuse the situation before they blow up at each other again."

"Agreed. I'll get them both down here pronto." He stood. "In the meantime, I'll give you some privacy. Let me know if you need me." As he slipped out of the bathroom, his heart felt heavy with worry for her, and with unrequited desire. He couldn't let that cloud his judgment. They were working together now to save the reputations of both their clients. The best way to keep the air clear between Wendy and himself, he was learning, was to make a joke. He called back into the bathroom, "Especially if you're still naked."

10

An hour later, breakfast had been cleared away, Wendy was dry, Daniel was dressed, and he'd asked her to hang her clothes in the wardrobe alongside his instead of leaving trails of exploding women all over the suite, which she thought was pretty funny but also pretty insulting. She was glad he would never see the inside of her apartment in New York.

Lorelei and Colton would arrive any second. Wendy stood in the center of the spotless seating area, drumming her fingers together, mentally preparing for this meeting. Daniel lounged in a corner with his arms crossed, watching her, impassive as ever.

"When we grill them about their behavior," she said, "you be the bad cop. I'll be the good cop."

"*You're* going to be the good cop?" he asked in disbelief.

"Are *you* going to be the good cop?" she challenged him.

"No," he said.

She held open her hands, meaning, *Duh.* "We can't do bad cop/bad cop. It's not a technique."

A knock sounded at the door. As Wendy crossed the room to answer it, Daniel called softly, "What about you and me? We need to be on the same page. Do we tell them you stayed here last night? Are we supposed to be dating again?"

He might genuinely be asking so they got their stories straight before they confronted Lorelei and Colton. Or he might be teasing her right before this important, job-saving meeting. That ticked her off. She turned and mouthed to him, "We are *fucking* like *rabbits.*" She opened the door.

"Hi, sweetie!" She gave Lorelei a big hug and greeted Colton less enthusiastically. She expected Daniel to come forward and seat them, but he was doing his sullen bad cop thing, alternately scowling at everyone and staring out the window at the Strip. Okay.

Colton nodded toward the bar. "How about a drink? I have a feeling I'm going to need it."

Wendy had the same feeling. She grinned stiffly. "Not before your five-hour-long rehearsal, sorry." She ushered the stars onto the sofa, then took a chair beside them and leaned in earnestly. "We asked you here because we've got a big problem. Colton knows this, but I'm not sure you do, Lorelei. When you mooned him last night, he took a picture, and someone snatched the phone from me."

"I don't see why we get called in and, like, reprimanded for that," Colton complained. "You're the one who took my phone, and it got stolen from *you*." Wendy noted he might be defiant, but he was again dressed in duds a few steps up from his usual redneck-casual ratty shorts and hat. Daniel must have threatened him. And Colton had listened. That meant he did care about salvaging his career. Wendy had an in.

"We wouldn't be here talking about this if you hadn't taken the picture," Wendy told him gently. She turned to Lorelei. "And there wouldn't be a picture if you hadn't pulled your skirt down. We need to be prepared for that photo to appear on the front page of every tabloid magazine with a black rectangle over your butt cheeks, and all over the web without the black rectangle." She paused for Lorelei's horrified realization. Lorelei only furrowed her brow as if trying to remember which pair of killer heels she'd been wearing in the picture.

Sure, that could be useful information—what Lorelei had looked like in the photo. "Let's just pause here for a moment," Wendy said. "I don't want to make you feel uncomfortable, pretty girl, but if you don't mind, let's run to the restroom. I want you to show me what you did so I'll have a better idea of what we're working with."

"You mean, if my ass is nasty, we're in worse trouble," Lorelei said flatly.

"Of course!" Wendy exclaimed. "Don't you read the tabloids?"

"No."

Wendy couldn't imagine this. The tabloids were her life. But it was probably best that Lorelei didn't read them. That way, Wendy could interpret them for her and tell her when to worry and when not to worry. Though Lorelei didn't seem like much of a worrier.

Wendy explained, "If your ass looks good, the photo will run with an article about how out-of-control you are. That's exactly what we don't want when the awards show is watching you and thinking about firing you because they don't trust you, and concertgoers are weighing the probability that you'll go into a tailspin and cancel your tour after they've already bought a ticket. However, if your ass looks bad, the photo will run with lots of other photos of stars' asses and an article about cellulite. That would be worse."

Lorelei nodded. "You want me to moon you guys? Hell, I don't have to go to the bathroom and moon you in private. I'm not ashamed of my body." She stepped up on the coffee table and unfastened her jeans.

"That isn't necessary," Wendy said, to no effect. "It's better if you're elevated, is it?"

Sarcasm was no deterrent. Lorelei wiggled to loosen the waistband of her jeans, then shoved them down, bending over. Daniel sauntered from his corner and crossed behind the sofa for the view.

"See?" Colton said. "This is how she is."

It certainly was. Lorelei had a dragon tattooed on her ass. Not a dragon in profile that started on one ass cheek and extended to the other, either. It was the head of a dragon with its snout coming forward, one nostril on each buttock. She had gone full dragon.

"Satisfied?" Lorelei called between her legs.

"Yep," Wendy, Daniel, and Colton all said at once.

Daniel bent to speak in Wendy's ear. "We're toast," he understated. He took up his post at the window again as Lorelei buttoned her jeans and plopped down on the sofa beside Colton.

"So . . ." Wendy wasn't often at a loss for words, but it was hard to find a segue after what they'd all seen. The plan she'd been about to explain melted away. Lorelei's rump kept marching across her vision, clad only in its imaginary serpent. Maybe it really would be better if Wendy lost her job, because this did not qualify as actual work.

She felt the dark mountains of West Virginia crouching over her.

"What's the matter, Wendy?" Lorelei asked. "You look sick all of a sudden. You've never seen a tattoo on somebody's naked booty before?"

"Excuse me just a minute," Wendy said to the tunnel vision infiltrating the afterimage of Lorelei's bottom. She stood up too fast, forgetting her head injury. Dizziness rushed upward. She stood very still, pretending to look out on the vista of Las Vegas but actually waiting to regain her balance.

Daniel was at her side, holding her up by the elbow. "Are you okay?"

"Yes. Just give me a minute." She swayed on her way to the restroom, where she leaned heavily on the door as she closed it, then felt her way to the toilet and collapsed on the shut lid with her head between her knees.

She thought about her father, always talking about escaping work at the coal mine, and then, when he broke free because he was laid off, utterly unable to hold a job doing anything else. He finally took the first coal mining job he could find and died there a week later in a massive tunnel collapse, no air pockets, no saving grace, no lives spared.

She wiped her hair away from her clammy forehead before remembering with a start that the ink in her palm, Daniel's room number, hadn't disappeared during her bath. She didn't want his number smeared across her forehead. She did want to keep it in her hand. The 7 had a horizontal line through the middle as the Europeans wrote it, something he must have picked up from his father.

Out in the suite she heard him say almost apologetically, "She's missed a lot of sleep."

"Maybe you should leave her alone at night," Colton said.

"Maybe you should shut the fuck up," Daniel said.

It was Daniel's voice that propelled her up from the toilet with a final shake of her head. The talk with Lorelei and Colton had been going well. She needed to get back out there before male egos ruined everything. She glanced in the mirror and wished she hadn't—she looked ashen and ill, which would not help her save her job—and went back out into the suite.

Daniel was waiting for her at the bar. He handed her a glass of ice water. "Want me to be good cop for a while?" he whispered.

She glanced dubiously at his expressionless face. "I don't think that's possible."

"Me neither."

"I'm better. I just needed a moment. Let's do this thing." She swept back into the room on her high-heeled boots and settled on the chair again like she'd taken a phone call instead of nearly passing out on the toilet.

"Lorelei," she began again, "I'm here because you asked for me. Colton, Daniel is here because you'd driven your talent agent to the brink of suicide. We've told you both to stop slandering each other online. You haven't complied, and this morning Daniel and I got calls from the awards show, wanting you replaced. We've talked them down, for now. But the photo is out there." She turned to Colton. "And the tabloids are reporting that you upset Lorelei so much that she mooned you. Daniel and I can't work magic, but we've thought of a way to mitigate the damage. You two need to get back together."

"No way!" Lorelei yelled.

"Screw that." Colton's words were harsher than Lorelei's, but his tone lacked her conviction.

Wendy explained that Colton and Lorelei wouldn't *really* get back together. They would only fake it, and fake it well, at least through the awards show Friday night, and possibly until after Colton had snagged his movie audition and Lorelei had started her concert tour.

"But here's the thing," Wendy said. "We told you two to lay off each other and mind your manners, and you didn't do it. This time you *must* do it. Daniel and I are releasing to the press that you're together. If you prove us wrong, you're not just threatening your own careers anymore. You're threatening our professional reputations."

"You tell the press lies about the stars all the time," Lorelei protested. "Don't you?"

"Yes," Wendy acknowledged, "but we don't *admit* it. Now, to ensure that we don't have another public meltdown, I want us to have a conversation about your relationship." She made her voice soothing, which was something of a stretch, especially since her head was aching. "You dated for three years. You both enjoyed the height of your popularity during that time. You never once broke up. What happened last month?"

"She cheated on me!" Colton burst, voice breaking.

"I did *not*," Lorelei said.

Wendy held up her hand toward Lorelei and looked to Colton. "Let's take turns. Tell us your side of the story."

"She . . ." He jumped at the chance to start. After that first word, though, he sat blinking at the Strip, the sunlight reflecting in his eyes.

For the first time Wendy felt bad for him. Unless he really *was* a good actor, which she doubted after viewing a few of his TV episodes, he felt so strongly about Lorelei that he didn't know where to begin.

He finally said, "She went behind my back with her drummer."

"I did not." Lorelei rolled her eyes.

Wendy put up her hand to stop Lorelei again. She asked Colton, "What evidence do you have?"

"I don't have any *evidence*," he spat. "I don't need any. I just knew. Everything was fine when we were on the show together. Then she decides she's going to start a band. She handpicks the players herself. All dudes. She can't go out with me like she used to because they practice *all the time.* She tells me she's going on a world tour with these guys and I'm not going to see her for months. And then I find texts from the drummer on her phone!"

"Because we're friends!" Lorelei hollered with her hands open.

Wendy turned to Lorelei. "And what's your side of the story?"

"Yeah, I picked my own band," Lorelei said. "That's what musicians do. Yeah, we practice. Yeah, we're going on tour. Yeah, I'm friends with my own bandmates!"

Wendy nodded solemnly. She turned to Colton. "And then you called her names online."

"Because she deserved it," he said.

Wendy resisted the urge to throw her tumbler at him. She turned back to Lorelei. "And then you started posting photos of your lady parts, and everything went downhill from there."

"Basically."

Wendy glanced over her shoulder at Daniel, who was gazing out the window like he couldn't care less about these ridiculous people and the argument they'd been having online with millions of witnesses. The usual hard lines of his brow and mouth relaxed. He seemed ten years younger. In fact, the longer she looked at him, the more he seemed like a tourist on vacation, watching the Strip with interest as if planning what he would do with his delicious free day.

Then he surprised Wendy by shoving off from the corner and taking a few steps toward the sofa. "Lorelei is telling you the truth," he said to Colton. "She's a free spirit. She does what she wants and says what she thinks. She's also honest to a fault. There is no way she would cheat on you and not admit it. If she didn't want you anymore, she would tell you."

"How do you know?" Colton asked angrily, but sounding a lot less confident than he had a few minutes before.

"I've been in this business for too long," Daniel said.

"But she never came to me and said she *wasn't* cheating on me," Colton said, looking at Lorelei now.

"Because you were already calling her names," Daniel said, "and she made an executive decision not to beg when you were in the wrong."

Lorelei raised her brows at Colton. Colton looked pensive. The conversation was going in the right direction.

But then . . . something changed for Wendy. The sunlight caught Colton just right. Now that he was dressing better, he didn't look as much like Rick as he had in some of his previous tabloid photos. But with the light glinting in the blond stubble on his cheeks, he looked a lot like Rick had looked whenever he blew up at her, *blew the fuck up at her*, and came back the next day to tell her he was sorry. And then blew up at her again.

Wendy fought hard to shake off that memory. "Here's what I think," she told Colton. "I think you were comfortable with your relationship with Lorelei when you were the TV star first, and she was invited to be on *your* show. It was precisely when she formed her own band, picked her own musicians, decided on her own tour, and made her own decisions that you got uncomfortable. But instead of stating what the problem was, as in, 'I am too insecure to trust this talented girl full of gumption,' you did the worst thing you can do to a female in society right now, which was to accuse her of being a fallen woman!"

The room was carpeted and filled with plush furniture that should have absorbed noise, yet her words echoed against the ceiling. She hadn't realized she'd stood up at some point and stuck her finger in Colton's face.

Daniel put his arm around Wendy's shoulders, easing her away from Colton. "Wendy, can I speak with you in the hall for just a minute?" As he guided her toward the door, he called back into the room, "Why don't you make yourselves that drink now?"

He closed the door behind them. The long, vast hallway with insanely patterned carpet was empty, but he whispered anyway. "I thought *I* was supposed to be the bad cop." He reached for her hand and—didn't hold it, exactly, but wrapped his hand around her cold fingertips. "You're shaking. We're working together now. You have to tell me what's going on. Did Colton say something to you I didn't know about?"

"No."

Daniel let her go and stepped back. "Come on, Wendy. Colton is my client. If he said something inappropriate to you, I need to have a talk with him. And then kill him."

"It's not that at all, I promise. Reluctant as I am to jump to Colton's defense, he didn't do anything."

"What is it, then?"

She raked her hands back through her hair, stopping suddenly when her fingertips encountered soreness on her scalp. "I promise I'll tell you later."

He eyed her warily, then opened his arms. "Come here."

She couldn't resist that invitation. She stepped forward willingly. He wrapped his arms around her, hugging her close. His hands rubbed up and down her back with enough pressure to warm her and wake her up. She sighed into his shoulder.

"Need to take ten?" he asked. With her ear pressed to his chest, she heard his voice as a rumble.

"Already did," she said.

After a few more seconds of rubbing the life back into her, he set her upright, holding her by the shoulders. He looked into her eyes as if to make sure she was stable. Then he dropped her hands, took his key card out of his wallet, and slipped it through the lock. "Back to the grind."

"I wish," she said under her breath.

He glanced back at her and gave her his rare, brilliant smile.

She was behind him so she couldn't see his expression, but she was sure he'd wiped away his smile before they rounded the sofa to face Lorelei and Colton again. In the end, it didn't matter. His face contorted with the same fury Wendy felt when they saw Lorelei and Colton tangled together, making out.

Wendy couldn't shout at Lorelei. Her job was at stake. She cleared her throat and said, "This is not what I had in mind."

Colton released his lip-lock with Lorelei to turn around and glare at Wendy. "Could you give us some privacy?"

"Get off her," Daniel said.

Colton and Lorelei reluctantly rolled away from each other.

Wendy told them, "These new feelings you've experienced toward each other while we've sat in this conference have been *emotions* rather than *physical sensations*. Let's just stay on this for, oh, at least a couple of hours."

Lorelei nodded and turned to Colton. "She's right. I'm glad we talked, and I want to forgive you, but you accused me of sleeping around. You broke up with me. You called me dirty names to the whole world. You may be sorry, but it's not like you didn't do it."

"That sounds like you *don't* want to get back together," Colton complained.

Lorelei started to say that she hadn't decided—at least, that's what Wendy *hoped* she was going to say—but Daniel broke in. "Colton, as I've told you, I'm not a high-priced relationship counselor. Neither is Wendy. You and Lorelei brought us here—"

"*I* didn't bring you here," Colton said testily.

Daniel was correcting himself even before Colton was through interrupting. "Your very smart agent brought me here to save the career that you have been so diligently attempting to flush down the toilet. That's what you're paying us for, and that's what we're going to do until the awards show on Friday. Repairing a real relationship takes time and work. You have neither to spare for the next forty-eight hours. But we've helped you to the point that you can treat each other like decent human beings. After Friday night, when you're back in Hollywood, you could work on this further and see if Lorelei chooses to respond favorably. I would suggest groveling."

Wendy bit her tongue. She was glad Daniel was putting the quietus on a hookup, but she wished he wasn't so accepting of Lorelei and Colton's future together. She was thinking of her relationship with Lorelei after the awards show, and whether Lorelei would hate her. True, the immediate problem was to get Lorelei through the show and drum up sales for her floundering concert tour. But Lorelei would still need PR after that. Wendy would be the likely candidate to give that to her—provided Lorelei hadn't grown to despise her for facilitating her reconciliation with Colton. On the other hand, if Lorelei had a horrible breakup with Colton, perhaps she would run to Wendy for comfort, and Wendy would have a better chance of keeping her job long-term.

The thought of this made Wendy's stomach hurt. She wanted to keep her job. She didn't want to do it through the ruination of someone else's life. Even worse than a bad breakup between Lorelei and Colton, in her opinion, would be if they stayed together. Lorelei and Colton had both heard her harangue, but maybe they hadn't really been listening. Colton would pursue his career and ask Lorelei not to pursue hers. Lorelei would acquiesce. She would be pregnant with their third child when the tabloid photos appeared of him naked in a hot tub with two prostitutes and a discount store tycoon. He would lose his upcoming movie roles and sink into oblivion. He would make a small comeback as a wisecracking pimp in an Oscar winner's pet indie project before sinking into his meth addiction. Lorelei would retreat to a bungalow in Burbank, raise her children, and marry a tax accountant. Occasionally she would appear at a red carpet premiere and the tabloids would post photos of how old and fat she had grown, a final indignity. She would never play guitar again.

"Wendy," Daniel said.

"What?" she asked. All three of them were watching her expectantly. She'd missed part of the conversation. Both her hands were cupped over the back of her throbbing head.

"I am so sorry," she murmured. "I am really out of it this morning."

"Sit down," Daniel said gently.

Suddenly fatigued, she thought sitting down sounded like a great idea. She sank into the chair. Daniel came up behind her and applied pressure to the crick in her neck. It hadn't been hurting much—especially not in comparison with her head—but his firm fingers felt so good massaging her muscles that she let out an involuntary, "Oh."

A consummate multitasker, Daniel kept right on rubbing her as he issued orders to Lorelei and Colton. "Go to rehearsal this afternoon. Don't make it obvious yet that you're getting back together. Flirt with each other. Post some polite, vague comments about each other. Tonight, you'll go out separately with friends, but you'll post comments that indicate you want to join each other. We'll be specific about the meeting place so the paparazzi will be sure to follow us there, taking photos."

"And then we'll pretend to be together?" Colton asked.

"You'll pretend to be moving in that direction," Daniel said.

Colton looked pointedly at Wendy. She wasn't sure what he was trying to convey to her. But as his glance moved to Daniel, she wondered whether Colton was telling her he knew her relationship with Daniel was a scam.

She closed her eyes, listening to Daniel's voice, enjoying the hard rub he was giving her, and hoping the expression on her face told Colton everything he needed to know. Her hookup with Daniel might be fake, but her feelings for him were real.

He ushered Colton and Lorelei out the door while Wendy stared at the coffee table in front of her, head throbbing, so happy not to be moving. Or talking. Then Daniel was standing in front of her, holding out his hand. She took it and let him pull her up and guide her across the floor to the bed. Gratefully she sank down on it and rolled onto her side.

She was surprised, though, when she felt the weight of him lying down behind her. Surprised and—she had to face it—thrilled. He spooned her, draping his arm across her waist. She snuggled backward into him before she realized she was rubbing her rump against his pelvis. She doubted he was looking for that kind of trouble. She teased him, singing, "You're going to get wrin-kled," but her voice came out weak and pitiful.

"For some reason," he growled in her ear, "around you, I'm as wrinkled as I've ever been. Metaphorically."

"I metaphorically wrinkle you," she puzzled with her eyes closed. It wasn't exactly a compliment, but an acknowledgment that she affected him in a fraction of the way he affected her—

—and then his hand moved from her waist down to her hip and rubbed there, the same hard strokes he'd used on her neck, lending her comfort at the same time he lit her on fire.

"Now tell me why Colton bothers you," he coaxed her. "You promised."

She didn't want to go back there. But she felt so comfortable under Daniel's hands that she almost didn't mind telling him. Almost. She sighed, "In high school, I had this boyfriend. He was the reason I left West Virginia. Colton reminds me of him, though I understand that makes no sense. It is *so annoying* to turn human and have normal, illogical emotions right in the middle of a case." She laughed nervously. "You wouldn't know about that."

His hand never stopped rubbing her hip. "Tell me what happened," he said.

"I was eighteen. Rick was twenty-one. He had a friend who ran a club in town and gave me a gig strip-ping, even though I was underage."

"*What?*" Daniel asked sharply. His hand gripped her waist.

"I know." She didn't like admitting any of this, especially to Daniel. But he deserved to know why Colton made her crazy. And she *had* promised. Besides, it was easier to talk when she faced away from Daniel, staring at the far wall. And easier still when his hand moved along her hip again.

She explained, "I always wanted to be part of Hollywood. So did Rick. He told me I was beautiful. He wanted me to try stripping. From there I would get discovered. I would be the next Anna Nicole Smith. This was after she was a model, but way before she died. She was kind of staggering around her reality show, and I pointed out to him that she wasn't the best role model. But I danced for a week and we made more money than we'd ever seen before."

"We," Daniel repeated.

"Right. I'd gotten a scholarship to college in New York. Rick didn't want me to go. He wanted me to strip for a while longer and see how it went."

Daniel interrupted her, disgust in his voice. "That is—"

"I know," she stopped him. "You don't have to tell me. It seems ridiculous to me now. But I can remember how I felt then, like it was yesterday. My dad was always either at work or drunk. When he didn't have a job, he was just drunk. Rick paid attention to me. I thought he listened to me. He said he loved me.

And stripping wasn't so bad. I didn't mind dancing or taking my clothes off. I guess I've always been a little Lorelei-esque. Not ashamed of my own body. I did mind that men called me names while they were stuffing dollar bills in my garter. Maybe I believed them a little bit. And when Rick said that I couldn't handle New York, that I wouldn't stay in school, that I was too much like my daddy and I wouldn't be able to keep a job, that I'd just end up stripping there anyway but it would be darker and dirtier and soon I'd be dead . . . I almost believed him, too."

Daniel let out a pained sigh, his warm breath blowing chills down Wendy's neck. Wendy's heart broke. He was acting like a concerned friend, ready to talk her out of self-destruction. But that friend hadn't existed for her back then, when she'd needed him.

"You left, though," he said.

"I did. Despite our heady week of profits, I took the bus to New York the next day. I guess I was thinking in the back of my mind that he might follow me, but after a few days at college, I felt safer and more at home than I'd ever felt."

"And then he followed you?"

Suddenly Daniel's body was too hot against her back. Sweat pricked her forehead, and the air in the room was suffocating. She rolled away to face him, then sat up on the bed. Blinking at her, he sat up more slowly.

She took a deep breath. "He was standing outside my dorm room when Sarah and I came back from our first dinner together at the caf. He said he wanted to talk with me in private. I said no, of course, and Sarah and I tried to slip into the room without him, but he pushed her out and dragged me in and chained the door. He put his forearm on my throat." She balled her fist and reached up to put her arm near Daniel's neck, not touching him, just showing him, as full of rage as Rick had been. "He told me I was only good for one thing, and I would fail at everything else, because I couldn't keep my mouth shut. That I was a worthless slut and I deserved to be raped and left to die. I mean, he—" She squeezed her fist tightly because she couldn't press down on Daniel's neck as hard as Rick had pressed hers. He'd choked her until her legs collapsed beneath her. His body had been a blur as sirens sounded outside the dorm and he ran out of her room.

Beyond her arm, Daniel stared at her, steady and unmoved as ever. The room was bright with desert sunlight. She was safe.

"Sorry," she said, putting her hands in the air near his chest, not quite touching him. "I didn't mean to—" She swallowed. "And I'm sorry about the way I acted toward Colton. He looks so much like Rick that I didn't want the Lorelei gig in the first place. I knew I'd be dealing with him sooner or later. I wouldn't have taken this account if my job hadn't been on the line."

"Why didn't you tell me?" Daniel seethed.

Wendy frowned at him. She'd felt she owed him an apology for blowing up at Colton, but she hadn't thought he would be *this* angry. "Why would I tell you

Colton looked like my boyfriend from ten years ago? I didn't think I would have that much of a problem with it until—"

"I saw that guy," Daniel insisted.

"Who?" she breathed.

"Your boyfriend. Rick. He was in the casino playing blackjack at the same table as Colton when I got here Monday."

"No," she protested. "That doesn't make sense."

"It makes perfect sense," Daniel said grimly. "There was a disturbance in the Big O on Monday night because fans thought they'd seen Colton, but it wasn't him. Right after that, a lock of your hair went missing." He reached out to touch the side of her head where one of her curls was gone, even though she'd trimmed the jagged ends and tucked them into the rest of her hair. "Last night, the bouncer at the museum wouldn't let Colton in because he was allegedly already inside. That must have been Rick, too, making his way in before Colton did. Another lock of your hair disappeared. He knocked you out and took Colton's camera."

Wendy's heart beat painfully. She didn't believe Daniel, but the story made a certain kind of sense, sort of like when she started with a new client and a lot of strange things happened and she finally figured out the star's mother must be smoking crack, which explained everything. But she didn't want this story to be true. It couldn't be. "Rick's not paparazzi," she said.

"But he's an opportunist," Daniel said. "Right?"

"Right," Wendy said faintly. "No. Why would Rick be here?"

"For you."

Her blood went cold.

"When was the last time you saw him?" Daniel persisted.

"That night at college."

"Did the police catch him?" Daniel prompted her.

"No. He'd stolen his uncle's truck to drive up there. They found it ditched in New Jersey. There was never another trace of him. A couple of years later when my dad died, I was terrified he would be waiting for me in West Virginia, but he wasn't there, and nobody had seen him."

"You said he always wanted to go to Hollywood," Daniel reminded her. "Maybe he went. He became a photographer, and now he's followed the stars here to Vegas."

A job with the paparazzi was *exactly* what Rick would be doing with his life now. But she couldn't wrap her head around it. "No, Daniel. That's too crazy. I spent a couple of years in New York staring out the front window of my dorm room, terrified that I would see him walking up the street. I'm not going to do the same thing in Vegas. I'll be careful because whoever hit me is a crazy person who's collecting for a wig, but he's not Rick."

Daniel stared at her, face hard and immobile. "Just in case," he said, "don't go out at night by yourself."

"All right."

"Call Detective Butkus. Did he give you his card? Tell him what you told me about Rick."

Wendy made a face. "He's not going to do anything about that. He's going to scoff at me."

"Maybe," Daniel said, "but they should have that information on record. Promise me."

"I promise," she grumbled.

Sinking down to lie on the bed again, he let out a long breath. "On the bright side," he said, "I doubt we have to worry anymore about Colton coming on to you."

She laughed. "I don't know. Some men like strong women."

Daniel reached out to touch a long tendril of her hair, winding it slowly around his finger. This had turned her on when he did it in the club two nights before. Now her cheeks flamed, and her heart went wild.

He said, "Yes. Some men do."

11

Late that night, Wendy was down a hundred dollars at poker in the casino. Lorelei was down two hundred. Franklin was down fifty. Two actresses from a wildly popular sitcom were down seventy-five and three hundred, respectively. Wendy wished Sarah were there. Her parents were bridge players, and she cleaned up at poker. When she played, she tried her best to give Wendy advice and drag Wendy along after her.

Wendy's phone rang, giving her an excuse to back away from the sad table. She saw it was Daniel calling, and her heart did a dance to the jaunty rhythm of the slot machines nearby. She took a moment to close her eyes and take a calming breath through her nose so she wouldn't answer the phone in the tone of an eighth grader with a crush. Then, afraid she'd waited too long and Daniel would hang up and she'd miss him completely tonight, she hurriedly answered.

"What's up, lovah?"

"Hello, Wendy," he said. "I need your help."

"This should be good."

"I'm at the Horny Gentleman."

"The strip club? Or is this a personal problem?"

He laughed for a long time, which made her suspicious, because it wasn't *that* funny.

Sensing that this conversation was going to be longer than a quick check-in to decide where Lorelei and Colton should hook up, Wendy glanced at the crowded poker tables, then headed across the floor toward a chocolatier storefront that had closed for the night, where she wouldn't be overheard. "Oh, honey," she said as she walked, "not again. What's the matter? Do you need some money to pay your tab?"

"Listen," he said. "I want you to know I did everything I could to prevent this. Judging from what you told me this morning, I figured strip clubs are not your favorite thing."

"Perspicacious."

"Colton was insistent," Daniel said. "Of course, I couldn't explain what my reservations were without telling him more about you than I would ever want him to know. And my turning down the invitation on some sort of moral grounds would not be a manly man thing to do, because duh."

It was her turn to laugh at his appropriation of her language. He was in rare form. Possibly drunk.

When she stopped laughing, she warned him, "Colton's going to get seen there at best and videoed there at worst. It's going to look like he's not interested in Lorelei at all. Obviously he needs an outlet for his misogyny."

"Actually," Daniel said, "Colton and Lorelei came here together on their first adult romp through Vegas last year. So it will be like an elderly couple retracing their steps on their first date."

Wendy shouldn't have been surprised anymore at much Lorelei and Colton did. "That's sweet."

"That's why I need you to bring Lorelei down here. Right now Colton looks like a reject at a strip club. When she comes in, it'll look like a fun, bawdy night they're enjoying together. We'll get Lorelei on the pole."

"We're *not* getting her on the pole," Wendy protested.

"I'll bet she can do it. Wasn't that a fitness craze in Hollywood recently?"

"That was before her time. Now it's *boxing*, remember? How much have you had to drink?"

"I was trying to have fun on the job, like you said. Too much fun." He paused. "Look, just bring her down here, unless you have a better idea. That's the only way I can think of to solve this right now. Reason only works with Colton when he's not drunk yet. Now that he's plastered, even if you have trouble with Lorelei, it's going to be a lot easier for you to get her in here than for me to get him out of here. We won't stay long, though. It's so late already. Just come, let the paparazzi take pictures of her arriving and the two of them leaving the club together, and we'll all call it a night."

Wendy bit her lip. Her stomach turned flips at the thought of venturing into a dark strip club again—this time through the front door.

"Wendy," Daniel said gently. "Seriously, is this going to bother you? I didn't intend to make you feel uncomfortable. Surely to God I can figure out something else, or we can start over tomorrow—"

"Tomorrow is too late," she said. "You know what? I need to get over my strip club stigma. That way I can finally go see my next-door neighbor's act."

"She's a stripper?"

"His boyfriend is a stripper. He himself is more of a burlesque performer." She glanced back at the poker table where Lorelei and company sat losing their money and looking glum. Her star crashing a strip club might not be *better* press, per se, than her star losing two hundred dollars at poker, but it would be more exciting. "Yes, we'll be there in a few. Ask Colton to commence the polite but provocative tweets."

The strip club, long and low, lingered on the outskirts of the Strip, not so close that the casinos could chase it off, but not so far away that the tourists wouldn't be tempted. The lighted walkway from the parking lot to the building was lined with paparazzi. Wendy's heart leaped. Daniel's plan was working. When the two taxis full of Lorelei's party pulled up, Daniel himself was leaning against a column at the front entrance with his arms crossed. He walked forward and opened the taxi door for Wendy.

Beside her on the seat, Lorelei said wistfully, "Such a gentleman. The best Colton can do is not slam the door in my face."

Wendy was more concerned about whether Daniel was, in fact, a horny gentleman. He'd dressed down for once, though he still looked like he'd stepped out of a men's magazine in a tight designer T-shirt, dark jeans, and expensive shoes. He didn't seem drunk—he moved smoothly as ever—but his steps and gestures weren't as big, as if he were purposefully holding himself close to counteract the alcohol. In short, he wasn't three sheets, but he was probably as loose as Wendy would ever see him.

And as much as she ached to run her hands across his perfectly defined chest, she didn't want to seduce him. No, she didn't. She would get in trouble at work, and he would dump her anyway, and it wasn't worth the heartache. But thanks to their charade, she could *act* like she wanted to seduce him. The night promised to be fun.

She stood on her tiptoes to whisper in his ear, "I missed you."

"I missed you, too." He nuzzled her ear and gently bit her earlobe.

She sucked in a breath, and her eyes darted around the paparazzi as if she'd done something deliciously guilty. But they were focused on Lorelei as she stepped out of the cab, long legs first. She stopped and talked to the photographers, even hugging one she hadn't seen in a while. Wendy shook her head. This was the reality of Lorelei. At least there would be gorgeous photos of her online tomorrow, giving the cameras her genuine grin.

Daniel held Wendy's hand, saluted the bouncer, and led her through the doors into the dark club, music throbbing. One woman shimmied onstage, and strippers boogied around poles throughout the room. About half the patrons were women, Wendy noted with relief. That's what Sarah had told her about the strip clubs she'd crashed sometimes with their friends in college. Wendy had always opted out. In the club where she'd worked for a week, only men had leered at her.

Daniel squeezed her hand. "Are you okay?"

She nodded. He watched her as if he expected her to elaborate, but she didn't particularly want to talk. She wanted *him* to talk to *her* again. Every time he put his voice and his breath in her ear, all her blood rushed downward.

"How's your head?" he asked.

"A lot better," she answered truthfully.

"I guess you don't want a drink," he said doubtfully.

She shook her head. She could have used one, but there was way too much over-the-counter painkiller in her bloodstream for a drink to be safe.

"I'm drinking a soda now myself," he said. "I had to cut myself off."

She laughed. "You don't seem drunk, but you seem very careful."

Oh, he treated her to that rare, open laugh she loved so much. "You're right. It really has been fun tonight. Colton and his posse have become my best buds, which tells you a *lot* about how drunk we all are. Thank you." He kissed her on the lips.

She hadn't been expecting the kiss. It was so fast that her heart opened to it after it was over.

Daniel had sat down in a huge booth scattered with shot glasses and entire bottles of liquor. He scooted over to give her room, pulling her by the hand. Obediently she sat beside him. He let go of her hand and sandwiched his fingers between her crossed thighs. It was a signal of possession that was not allowed in polite settings and was barely socially acceptable even in a strip club. Wendy felt like the presence of his hand was a hot rock sinking and melting through the ice of her body. They were fully clothed. They were *not* really together. And she had never been so turned on.

"Where is everybody?" she asked, looking around. Except for them, the booth was empty.

Daniel nodded toward the nearest pole, where a stripper talked with Colton. They didn't look like they were in intimate conversation. They looked like she was giving him instructions. Colton reached up, braced his hands wide apart on the pole, and pulled himself close to it. He was able to hold his body up for several seconds before collapsing to the floor. Lorelei and her friends clapped for him as they approached the table. Colton stood and bowed to them, grinning goofily.

"This has been going on for a while," Daniel said, nodding to Colton's driver and bodyguard, who stood to one side of the pole as if they'd already taken their turns. "It started out with everybody displaying their big guns."

He slid his fingers out from between her thighs, making her shiver. He pulled back his T-shirt sleeve to show her his thick bicep. "Go ahead. You can touch it."

Seeing him like this was hilarious. She humored him by trying and failing to wrap her hand around his upper arm. "Wow," she said dreamily.

Grinning, he put his arm down. "Then the lady here"—he gestured to the stripper, who was now laughing with both Colton and Lorelei—"came over and told us that pole dancing is the true test of upper body strength. And here we are."

"Did *you* take a turn on the pole?" Wendy asked in disbelief.

"Ha! I'm not *that* drunk." He sipped his soda, made a face, and set it down.

Wendy was very glad Lorelei was now hanging out with classy young actresses instead of the reality star and the celebrity hairdresser. These girls had spotless reputations. And they were now taking turns getting instructions from the stripper on how to tackle the pole. In their company, Lorelei wouldn't look bad when she inevitably tried it.

Sure enough, Lorelei came bounding up to the booth. She asked Wendy, "Am I allowed to pole dance?" Her face fell. "Don't look at me that way. It was a fitness craze a few years ago."

"I know," Wendy said. "Like boxing!"

Daniel pinched her.

Lorelei still stood in front of Wendy, looking unsure.

"Go ahead," Wendy said. "I think it's an okay PR move. Even I know how to pole dance."

"Yay!" Lorelei jumped up on the small stage. The men in the party gave each other knowing looks as they slid into the booth with Lorelei's friends to watch. There was an interim while the stripper offered Lorelei some pointers and the men poured Lorelei's friends some shots. Then Lorelei braced herself on the pole as Colton had. She couldn't hold herself very long at all, but her dismount was a lot more graceful. She curved her body around the bottom of the pole. The men cheered for her.

"Five point five," Daniel whispered to Wendy in his dead-on British accent, sounding exactly like an announcer in the summer Olympics. "Five point six. Five point five."

Wendy was laughing so hard that she didn't realize Lorelei was standing in front of her again until Daniel nudged her. "What?"

"Your turn!" Lorelei exclaimed. "You just said you knew how to do it."

"Immersion therapy," Daniel murmured to Wendy. "Hair of the dog. I dare you."

Wendy raised her eyebrows. "Oh, you *dare* me, do you? You just want to see me do a pole dance."

"Duh," he said.

Wendy told Lorelei, "Let us negotiate for just a second." She whispered in Daniel's ear, "We're supposed to be together. Isn't this going to ruin your reputation with these guys?"

"Ruin my reputation? You just *made* my reputation. It's every man's dream to be with a nice lady who just *happens* by accident to know her way around a stripper pole."

"Every man's dream, or every fourteen-year-old boy's dream?"

"That kind of fantasy doesn't change with age."

"Is that right?" She examined him more closely. "Are you okay?"

"Very." He grinned at her. "Why?"

"You don't seem like yourself, even taking the drunkenness into account. It's not like you to tell me what you're thinking. Suddenly I'm finding out that your mind is as dirty as mine."

He raised his brows. "You doubted this?"

"Yes."

He gave her a small, naughty smile. "Never doubt this."

She threw back her head and laughed. "You're *sure* you're okay? I just heard a little hint of British accent."

"Uh-oh." He covered his mouth with one hand.

She set her forehead against his and asked, "If I do this for you, what will you do for me?"

His eyes widened, filling her vision, black like the darkest night. Suddenly this bargain had turned serious. His lips parted, but he didn't say a word.

"Kidding," she said breathlessly, scooting away from him. "This one's gratis, in celebration of your newfound fun." She turned to Lorelei. "Get the DJ to put on some Missy Elliott."

"Um . . . kay." Lorelei scampered away.

As Wendy slipped out of the booth, Daniel slid to the seat where she'd been. "Your stripping soundtrack is Missy Elliott?"

"She was very big in 2003, and this was my small protest against the patriarchy. While stripping. I know. Shut up."

"Curiouser and curiouser," he said. "Please don't fall on your injured head."

"Don't worry about me. Though bare skin gives you traction. I think it's going to be harder to do with my clothes on—"

"Keep your clothes on," he stressed.

"I love it when a man says that to me. So sexy. Instills a lot of confidence." She laughed at the face he made at her. "Anyway, I don't think I'll have trouble. I haven't done it in ten years, but I'm sure it's like riding a bicycle, except without the carefree innocent overtones." The creepy beat of her favorite Missy groove pumped through the speakers. "That's my cue. Here I go."

The helpful stripper waited onstage for her. "I don't need any pointers, if you know what I mean," Wendy told her. The girl swept her arm toward the pole: *all yours.*

The cheers from her booth had gotten so loud that they were attracting the attention of the rest of the bar. Shadowy figures turned their backs on their own pole-dancing ladies and approached their corner of the club, curious. Wendy would have felt intimidated if she hadn't been good at this.

With a wink at Daniel, she braced herself on the pole as the losers had done, then hefted herself up, splitting her legs on either side of the pole and pointing her toes. The booth was whooping, but she couldn't pay attention to them. Pole dancing took concentration. She allowed gravity to spin her body down the pole. Then she launched herself up again and wrapped herself around the pole this time, spinning down. After a quick calculation of whether she could hold herself upside down on the pole by her ankles in these particular high-heeled boots, she took a chance on the affirmative.

The hard part was holding herself up by the arms while she balanced her body upside down in the first place. But it *looked* like the real trick was letting go with her hands and hanging there by her feet. She could tell by the slight resistance that her hair was touching the floor, which, strangely, she was beginning not to mind. All of Vegas was finding its way into her hair, and all of Vegas had taken a piece.

The applause for her was growing wild. The thought passed through her mind that if she got fired from Stargazer, maybe she really *could* go back to her first career. She could laugh at this now, almost, because she had hope of salvaging Lorelei's image.

She did a few more tricks, until her head wound began to throb from all the blood rushing to her brain. She dismounted from the pole, curtsied ironically, high-fived the stripper, and jumped down from the stage. The table went crazy. The women kept screaming "Wow!" at her and the men were agog. She focused on Daniel, who'd been laughing moments before but now looked dangerous, his face full of dark shadows, the smudge under his eye still visible.

She shouldn't come on to him. It wasn't fair to lead him on, and she couldn't risk her job by following through. But she wanted him. She breathed deeply, feeling her nipples tight against her bra, and imagined him wrapping his hands around her heavy breasts. She was twenty-eight years old, a grown woman, and so needy tonight. *Why* did the man she was falling for have to be the one she couldn't have?

Against her better judgment, she slid into his lap. He still watched her seriously, which was starting to make her nervous. She tried to lighten the mood by saying, "Boy, will I be sore tomorrow. I'm in okay shape now, thanks to Sarah's badgering, but I was so much better at eighteen. I used to be built like a truck." When he looked grim and didn't respond, she clarified, "A feminine, dainty truck. What's wrong?"

"We have to get out of here," he barked. "Now."

Heat rushed to her cheeks. Daniel wanted to leave with her. She couldn't say yes to sex with him, yet she'd never wanted anything more in her life.

But as she stared into his dark eyes, racking her brain for what she should say, she realized that wasn't what he'd meant. His tone was wrong. And then he said, "All of us need to get out of here."

"Why?" she breathed.

"Someone drugged me." He nodded to his glass, pushed to the middle of the huge table. "Someone is trying to get past me to Colton. Or the guy who's been after you is trying to get past me to you." His intense gaze dissolved into a vacant expression. He looked lost.

A chill swept over Wendy. She felt afraid for the first time. It was not in Daniel's nature to look lost.

"What?" she squeaked. "Like, a roofie?"

He nodded solemnly at her.

She hopped off his lap, jerked him up by the hand, and dragged him through the club, despite him calling, "Wait. Wendy, wait." Finally he stopped next to the main stage. Her pulling didn't budge him. When she turned to him, desperate and questioning, he said, "We have to tell the bodyguards, at least."

"I'll call them from the cab," she promised. "We can't screw with that right now. We have to get you to the hospital. People die from that stuff."

"I only drank a sip."

"You don't know how much drug was in that sip, though. Come on." She tugged at his hand.

"We can't go to the hospital by ourselves," he insisted. "We can't leave you out in the open now that I can't protect you."

"It'll be crowded," she reasoned. "Nobody would dare do anything there. We'll walk to the crowded taxi stand and take a cab to the crowded hospital. Stop arguing. Don't make me cause a scene. That's not good for PR."

She kept tugging his hand until he reluctantly took a step after her, then another, and followed her through the packed club, dancers jostling them on all sides. When Colton brushed past them, she put out her other hand to grab him so she could warn him what was going on. But he'd already hurried three deep into the crowd. She kept going, pulling Daniel out the door.

She flinched in panic as bodies moved toward them. She'd forgotten about the paparazzi lying in wait for Lorelei and Colton. She forced her heart to stand down, and the photographers, realizing she and Daniel weren't the celebrities they were after, retreated.

In the taxi, she phoned Franklin, then Colton's bodyguard. They couldn't hear their phones in the din, and she had a flash of panic that someone else would get a mouthful of tranquilizer. But on another try, Franklin answered. She told him what had happened and extracted a pledge from him to close the party down and tell the club manager—quietly—what they suspected. Then she phoned Detective Butkus and left a message. She sounded stupid to her own ears. A stolen phone, stolen hair, and a roofie. Their case would hardly be high on the priority list for the crime task force.

Frustrated, she clicked her phone off and looked over at Daniel. He stared out the window, his head bobbing strangely as the car bumped over seams in the pavement. Anxious to make some connection with him, she smoothed her hand onto his knee. Without looking at her, he placed his hand over hers.

An hour ago she would have thrilled at this intimate gesture. Now it just seemed strange, and it certified how sick he was.

At the emergency room, still dragging him by the hand, she marched up to the counter and said, "Poisoned." Four people rushed from behind the counter and led him through swinging double doors to the bustling network of examining rooms. Wendy followed, not sure whether she was allowed. After all, she was not Daniel's wife or his girlfriend or even his friend, really, but his business rival, his enemy. This would become clear as soon as they wrapped up their jobs in Vegas and returned to New York. But right now, she was determined not to leave him.

A nurse pointed her into a tiny examining room and shoved a clipboard into her hands, along with Daniel's wallet. Wendy paused a moment over the expensive black leather, then drew out his insurance card. She examined his New York driver's license and slowly, neatly copied his name onto the form: *Blackstone, Daniel, I.* The act of putting pen to paper and scratching down this representation of him tugged at her deep inside, as if helping him in this small way would heal his whole body. With difficulty she resisted the urge to dot the *i*'s with little hearts.

Soon he wandered in. He clung to the doorjamb for a moment, then pushed away from it, tripped over her feet, and managed to land in the chair beside her.

"Jesus, I'm toasted." He laughed.

"There's a whole bed for you to lie down on." She knew instinctively that he wouldn't take her suggestion. Lying down would mean he was a patient, out of control. As long as he sat beside her in a chair, he was as healthy and as free to leave as she was, theoretically.

He shook his head. Then he blinked rapidly, as if shaking his head had disoriented him.

Tentatively she reached behind him. She placed her hand on the other side of his head, fingers sliding into his coarse hair, and pressed his head down toward her shoulder. She was a lot shorter than him. She sat up straighter and squared her shoulders to give his head a place to settle.

He resisted, his head pressing up against her hand.

She whispered the words he'd said to her the night before: "Give up."

After a final sigh, he relaxed against her shoulder with more weight than she'd expected. She remained steady for him, shoulder firm, while she filled out the rest of his forms. She listed herself as his emergency contact and felt another flood of warmth in her belly.

"Now, tell me what happened," she said, setting the clipboard across her knees. "How do you know you were drugged? Did you taste it in your drink?"

"Not at first," he said. "When I thought back on it later, yeah, it had tasted salty. But I wasn't expecting it, so it didn't occur to me until my face went numb. I've felt that way before."

"All the girls give you the date rape drug?" she joked. Then she realized she shouldn't be kidding about this. "When?" She heard her own alarm as her voice pitched higher. "Here in Vegas?"

"No." He waved her panic away with one loose hand. "Back home. A long time ago. High school."

"Somebody slipped you a roofie?" she asked in disbelief.

"No." He paused so long that Wendy was about to remind him what they'd been talking about when he sat up straight and said, "It was on 9/11, when my brother died."

"Oh." He'd always seemed so aloof. Now she wasn't just seeing him loose for the first time. She was seeing him more vulnerable than ever. And she was beginning to understand how his hauteur was a protective shell for the pain underneath.

"The first few days," he said, "I had a hard time holding it together. And, you know, holding it together is everything." He took a deep breath. "My dad told the doctor to give me something. He needed to fix the situation and he couldn't help my brother anymore, so he fixed me. I did feel calmer on the surface, but underneath, the horror was still there, just weighed down with sedative where I couldn't access it, like oil floating on water."

"You were how old?" Wendy thought back to 2001 and how surreal it had felt to see images of the Twin Towers collapsing from her living room in West Virginia. "Sixteen?"

He nodded.

"And you've been trying to make it up to your dad ever since."

He looked down, black brows furrowed, lips pursed in concentration on that lost day he couldn't help. She'd known him when he was college age. It was easy to picture him younger still: thinner, in a rock band T-shirt rather than a designer one, his face more open and trusting.

As she considered the sixteen-year-old Daniel, the older one finally came into focus for her. His need for control, his perfectionism—it all made sense to her now. With that knowledge came a wave of longing. She wished she could reach out to smooth her fingertip over his dark brows and stroke away some of that pain. But she didn't dare. Whatever temporary and tenuous alliance they'd formed, that would crumble the instant he felt she was treating him like a child.

She simply turned back to the forms, placing her body at the ready, and relaxed a little when his head finally sank onto her shoulder again.

A few minutes later, he jerked away from her, as if he were embarrassed to be seen in a moment of weakness, when a doctor stepped into the room to give them the report. Daniel did have the drug in his body, but the level was low enough that, since he hadn't had respiratory failure already, he would be okay in another eight hours.

Back at the casino hotel, as they got out of the taxi, he murmured to Wendy, "Rick will see us and know I'm fucked. It's not safe for you."

His paranoia was catching. But she honestly didn't feel like they were in danger. "Nobody's going to do anything in a crowded casino," she assured him.

"I can't walk straight," he said.

"Lean on me," she said. "Act like we're lovers." She slipped her arm around his waist, and they made their way through the lobby.

Inside the elevator, he pushed away from her and backed against the wall. "I'm so sorry. I'm all over you, and I don't mean to be."

"You're not all over me," she said stoically.

"Yeah, I am, and you know why? You're hot, and I am very attracted to you."

She laughed lightly. "You're high, as we've established."

"No, seriously. I've been hot for you for a long time." He settled his shoulders against the wood-paneled wall of the elevator and gazed at her sexily through half-closed eyes. "In Dr. Abbott's class, you used to wear this blue tank top, and I would think, *Does she know how low that shirt is cut? Does she know what that looks like when I'm standing up and I pass by her desk?*"

Staring at his shadowed face, she felt herself flush. She *had* known how low that blue tank top was cut. She'd worn it to get his attention. She'd thought it hadn't worked.

They both started as the doors slid open at their floor.

"Come on." She held one arm out to him. They walked down the hall together, weaving only a little.

"I am so tired of this gargantuan hotel," he whispered. "It's like walking from my apartment to the Lower East Side."

"Where's your apartment?"

"Chelsea."

"Mine, too. Do you ever go to the Hell's Kitchen flea market?"

"All the time."

They arrived at his room. He leaned his forehead against the wall as he reached into his pocket for his wallet, drew it out, and stared at it.

"Need some help with that?"

He laughed. She loved to hear him laugh. An hour before when he'd laughed, she'd been afraid for his health and his sanity. Now that she knew he would be okay tomorrow, it moved her to see him so undone. She treasured the moment, because she knew she'd never see him like this again, unguarded with her.

Putting her head close to his, she peered into his wallet and plucked out the room key card. She swiped it through the lock. He pressed down on the handle. As he pushed the door and followed it into the room, he gave her a hard look over his shoulder, suddenly lucid. She wasn't sure whether he was wishing she would stay out or sexily urging her in. Either way, she followed him inside, because she would have felt uneasy leaving him alone like this.

He shut the door behind her, turned the dead bolt, and placed the chain in the lock with surprising dexterity. And then she got her answer about what his look had meant. He backed her against the door, slid his hands around her waist, and kissed her.

Instinctively she opened her mouth for his. He accepted her invitation and swept his tongue inside her, making her shudder with want. She couldn't do this, though. If he half remembered this later, he would hate her for letting it happen when she had control and he didn't.

She would let him kiss her only for another second. She pushed her hands back through his short hair.

He released his hold around her waist. Propping one hand on the wall behind her, he stepped even closer so that the whole length of his body lay along hers. As he massaged her mouth with his, she felt his body heat burn through his jeans, through her jeans, into her thighs. And then his other hand crept across her crotch.

"Okay," she gasped, moving her hands from his hair down to his chest. "We can't do this, Daniel."

"Seems to me we're doing a pretty good job," he murmured against her lips.

"You might not remember this tomorrow," she said softly. "I don't want to take advantage of you."

He closed his eyes and rubbed the tip of his nose against hers. She thought this was his way of acquiescing. He would back away now, and their strange, sweet night together would be over.

Instead, his hand kept moving up her jeans. He yanked the buttons of her fly open in quick succession. His fingers found their way beneath her panties and shoved the material to one side, stretching the elastic. "But it's okay if *I* take advantage of *you*, right?"

Before she could answer in the negative, his fingers plunged inside her.

She cried out in surprise and ecstasy. His mouth came down on hers again. The rest of her cries were only guttural noises in her throat as he moved his fingers out of her, then in, then out, then farther in. She tipped up her hips so he could slide his hand even farther into her.

But when his thumb rubbed her clit, she stood straighter in shock and found the strength to push his hand away. "Daniel," she said firmly, "We can't. I won't."

"Are you sure? You're so wet for me." He traced the pointer finger that had been inside her along his bottom lip.

Oh, Lord.

He was so dangerously handsome, tasting her, his dark eyes drilling into her.

As she watched, his hard gaze on her relaxed. His eyelids fluttered.

"No," she repeated firmly, "I can't."

He relented, letting his hands fall to his sides. He leaned against the wall above her.

She wrapped her arm around his waist and led him across the room to the king bed. He weighed more heavily on her than he had all night. They barely made it to the bed before he stumbled on the carpet and collapsed facedown on the luxurious white duvet. He rolled over on his back and blinked at her, struggling to stay awake.

She said, "Give up, Daniel." This time she had the courage to bend over him and run her finger across his black brows. "You're safe with me. The only way to get better now is to sleep. Give up."

His whole face relaxed, going slack. She'd come to associate him with a calculating expression and a gleam in his eye. Without these now, he didn't look like himself at all.

She glanced down his long body. He was fully clothed. After their intimate episode, she thought it would be okay to take his clothes off, but he was built solidly, and she knew from supporting him through the lobby how heavy he was. She only slipped off his shoes and stowed them in the closet next to the others in a neat row. She would have just flung hers somewhere, but Daniel's shoes deserved better. Then she found an extra blanket in the top of the closet and spread that over him. His brows went down, disturbed in sleep.

She settled on the plush carpet next to the huge window, looking down over the Strip in all its neon glory. She could have stared at it for hours. Briefly she imagined that this was her room, too, that she and Daniel were staying here together as a couple. But that would do her no good. She erased that thought from her mind. With great reluctance, she dragged her phone out of her purse and clicked through the screens to Lorelei's latest updates. She hoped to God that Franklin had gotten her out of the Horny Gentleman without any public nudity.

"Wendy," Daniel said softly behind her. He lay on his side, watching her. His sleepy eyes blinked slowly. "Did I lock the dead bolt?"

"Yes," she assured him.

"Did I lock the chain?"

"Yes."

"Don't open the door for anyone until I wake up."

He stared so earnestly at her that she asked, "Why?"

"You're missing more hair." He held out a hand toward her.

She put up her own hand where he was pointing. Another big lock had been hacked off the side.

She went cold.

When had this happened? Not playing poker at the casino. Lorelei would have noticed Wendy's hair was missing in the taxi. And not before Wendy pole danced. Someone would have seen.

She remembered pulling Daniel through the crowd. She was several steps ahead of him, and Colton pushed by her. Colton, who would have asked her why she and Daniel were leaving without everyone else.

That hadn't been Colton.

"If he breaks down the door," Daniel whispered, "send him over here and tell him to get down on my level. I'll punch him in the knees." He was making light of it through his haze, trying to put her at ease, but his eyes were worried. They fluttered closed.

Heart racing, she tried to take her mind off her stalker and put it back on her job, where it belonged. She checked the most prominent gossip sites. The photos of Lorelei and Colton going into the strip club separately or—better yet—leaving it together most likely wouldn't have been uploaded yet, but perhaps comments had been posted about the paparazzi seeing them there. That would start the rumors on the path that Wendy and Daniel wanted them to travel.

But on the very first site she visited, she came face-to-face with the photo of Lorelei's untoward dragon tattoo.

So much for *Maybe that won't happen.*

She scrolled to other sites, stomach sinking as she went. All of them had posted the picture. Each headline was more creatively insulting than the last. And the comments below the articles—oh, the comments. Accusing Lorelei of drinking, spiraling, going insane, hating her mother, turning out exactly like her.

As she read this last tidbit, Wendy realized she'd clapped one hand over her mouth. Bile rose in her throat.

She glanced over at Daniel again, sleeping now, oblivious to this new obstacle, but dreaming through so many of his own. She'd doubted she could do this job of saving Lorelei. She'd felt better about her chances when she teamed up with Daniel. But now she knew it was going to take more than the two of them to get through this ass scandal, Lorelei's TV mini-concert tomorrow, and her party tomorrow night, while convincing the public that she and Colton were a couple worth watching on Friday. And avoiding Wendy's stalker.

Who possibly was Rick.

Hoping and praying that Sarah would be awake in the wee hours of the morning, she texted her. Both hands shook as Wendy composed a couple of messages explaining the photo and the drugging. She left out Rick. She would save that until Sarah came, if she came.

She was so relieved when Sarah immediately replied:

I told you, when it's whack, it's crack

And just after that:

There's not a flight now but Tom and I will catch the 6 a.m. and be there at 9 a.m. Vegas time. Hang on.

Wendy breathed more easily knowing Sarah and Tom were coming to help. In the meantime, her body surged with adrenaline, itching to take action, but there was nothing she could do. She checked Lore-

lei's accounts and Colton's. They'd posted kind things
about each other, details of their trip to the club, and
then nothing. Eerily, nothing. She half expected Lorelei to post outraged and vulgar reactions to what her
"fans" and detractors were saying about her photo.
Nothing. She watched with increasing panic as the updates scrolled past. The trolls composing these insults
stayed up for a long, long time.

Wendy did, too.

12

⁓

Daniel woke at dawn, facing the view of the Strip. Above the casinos, the sky was strange and colorless, bathed in sunlight but still missing the sun itself. The neon lights glowed more intensely in that gray moment than they had in the black night. Against this backdrop, Wendy lay on the carpet, high-heeled boots kicked away, legs bent comfortably. One hand lay over her heart, on top of her phone.

He remembered the night before. Watching Wendy execute a pole dance like a professional had been an intense, heady fantasy laced with poison, because that's when he'd begun to realize something was wrong with him.

The longer the night had gone on and the more confused he'd become, the better he remembered it, possibly because he'd been so mortified that Wendy had seen him that way and he'd needed her help. It pained him that he'd come on to her and she'd rejected him. He'd handled the end of their night so badly that they'd ended here, with him on his bed and her on his floor.

He rolled off the bed, taking a blanket with him that she must have tucked around him. His clothes dug into him everywhere: jeans, belt. He padded to his closet, silently stripped everything off, and hung the items away. Closing the bathroom door behind him so he wouldn't wake her, he brushed his teeth and took a shower, washing away the hospital and at least half the stigma of being tricked. The doctor had told him to expect to feel terrible at least until lunchtime, but he felt great, never better.

He slipped into sweats, then returned to Wendy. Carefully he teased the phone out from under her hand. She must have been tracking Colton and Lorelei. He could have turned it over and viewed the horror himself, but he wasn't quite ready to do that. It was cool and quiet here in the dead calm of daybreak. He liked this peaceful time and space, being out of touch. He slid her phone onto the bedside table.

Then he gathered her up in his arms, rounded the bed, and placed her in the sheets. She hardly stirred, shaking her head and murmuring, "Fuck off." He pulled the covers up to her chest and slipped into bed beside her.

"How do you feel?" she asked him throatily.

"Good," he said.

"How much do you remember?" she asked.

"I remember everything." He wished he didn't.

The next second, he opened his eyes and she wasn't there.

He sat bolt upright in bed. Midmorning sun streamed through the window. The back of his neck was hot with it. Wendy was gone.

"Wendy," he called. No answer. But a scrawled note was propped on his closed laptop: *Call me as soon as you get up!*

He snagged his phone and collapsed on the bed with a throbbing in his temple and a lighter heart.

She picked up immediately. "Hey! How are you feeling?"

"Worse, actually," he admitted.

"I was worried," she said. "If you hadn't called in the next ten minutes, I was going to come check on you. You were completely dead to the world when I left. But to me, the obvious sign you weren't yourself was that the room and the bathroom were a complete wreck."

He frowned into the phone. "Are you sure that wasn't you?"

Her laughter warmed him. "Seriously, your clothes are in the bottom of the wardrobe like you meant to hang them up and missed the hanger, and there was water sloshed everywhere in the bathroom. Maybe you got up and *thought* you were okay, but you weren't. Just promise me you won't try to shave."

"Mmph," he said. "Where are you?"

"In my own room. With the door locked," she added quickly. "We're going to use this room as a conference room. I've called Stargazer for backup. Sarah and Tom will be here within the hour."

Of course she'd called them. It made perfect sense for her to ask additional Stargazer reps to come help her on this difficult case. But he felt like he'd let her down.

"Lorelei's bare ass showed up all over the Internet last night," Wendy was explaining. "With that out there, and Lorelei's TV appearance today and her party tonight, and someone attacking me and now you, I felt like we could use some extra hands today or we're going to drop this ball."

"We," he muttered.

"We're working together," she reminded him. "The job you do affects the job I do. The job I do determines whether I still *have* a job next week."

"Okay," he grumbled.

"Come down here and we'll talk about it," she said. "Don't forget what I told you about shaving."

Ten minutes later, he slid his key card through her lock and walked into her room. She sat up on her bed with her laptop open on her thighs. She looked gorgeous, more like a star herself than a professional helping one. The lopped-off ends of her hair were hidden in a stylish loose bun. She'd dressed up to greet the TV station for Lorelei's appearance in a few hours. She wore a tight tan tweed skirt that ended temptingly just above her knees. Her matching suit jacket parted for a pink silk blouse. A big necklace didn't quite hide her cleavage. She'd kicked off her expensive high-heeled sandals. He hoped she wasn't embarrassed to be seen with him today, especially if he appeared as low as he felt.

"Aw," she said when she saw him, confirming how bad he looked.

He went for the chair beside the bed, trying to control his fall, but he more collapsed than sat. He leaned forward with his elbows on his knees and steepled his fingers. "Wendy, I came on to you last night."

She nodded, her face blank and nonjudgmental, just as she'd looked when he tried to explain why he couldn't quit the family business.

With a sinking feeling that he'd ruined everything between them—if there had been anything to begin with—he said, "I wanted to tell you how sorry I am. It won't happen again."

"Daniel," she said gently. "You weren't yourself, and I understood that."

"I want you to feel safe with me."

"I *do* feel safe with you. And actually, I didn't mind."

He laughed and instantly felt better.

"See, you're still not yourself, as evidenced by the easy laughter. Come lie down." She patted the bed beside her. "You have a few minutes for another nap before Sarah gets here."

He hesitated. He wanted to get close to her again. But every time he did, he messed things up. He'd never wanted a woman so badly, and he'd never been so far away from having her.

"Don't worry about last night, Daniel. When Sarah and Tom get here, we'll grab brunch and you'll feel better. Right now, get some more sleep. Give up."

With a sigh, he kicked off his shoes, hung his jacket in the closet, and crawled across the bed to her, taking care to lie flat on his stomach so he didn't wrinkle his shirt.

"Here." She moved her laptop over onto a pillow and patted her thigh. He wasn't going to argue with this. Screw his shirt. He rolled toward her, set his head in her lap, and closed his eyes.

"Oh God," he muttered as her fingernails found their way through his hair and down to his scalp.

She chuckled. "When was the last time somebody stroked your hair?"

"I was probably . . . seven."

"Yeah, you act like you don't want your hair stroked. Your entire vibe could be summed up as, 'Don't touch my head.'"

"Which is why you messed up my hair in the bar that first night," he pointed out.

"The devil made me do it." She increased the pressure on his scalp. Other than the kisses and brief bouts of heavy petting he'd snuck from her, this was the best he'd felt in a long time. He made an effort not to push his head against her hand, encouraging, like his cat.

Without pausing in her massage, she asked him, "Do you remember telling me about your brother last night?"

"Yeah," he grunted. "It's not a secret. Just . . ." With her hand doing these things to his head, he had a hard time thinking of *what* it was. "Sad."

"What were you like before your brother died?" she asked.

He smiled. "I was in a band."

"What did you play?"

"Lead guitar. I could practice with my headphones on without my dad hearing."

"What kind of music did you play?"

"Oh, punk. We were a punk band when punk was out of style. We were very proud."

She giggled. "Did you dye your hair green and spike it?"

"I wanted to, but I had to be at the breakfast table in the morning and the dinner table at night with my hair looking completely normal, or my father would have grounded me for life. I did what I could. I really know my way around a jar of hair gel."

"Speaking of which," she said, "I'm ruining your hairdo."

"I can fix it," he said quickly, because he didn't want anything to interrupt the exquisite march of her fingernails across his scalp. "What were *you* like at sixteen?"

"I ran away a lot," she said. "My dad was between jobs then, so he was drunk most of the time. When you played a gig at a club, I would have been the girl hanging around outside, wanting to look cool but too poor to get in, with an inappropriately old boyfriend. Except it was Morgantown instead of New York, so take that girl you would have seen outside your club and make her one fourth as worldly and sophisticated."

"That girl would have been trouble," he declared.

"Yep, that was me."

"That girl would have eaten me for breakfast."

"I don't think so," she said.

He knew so. Back then, he'd given his heart to music, to friends, to girls. He'd gotten shot down a lot, but that didn't matter. He'd had deeper to dig and more to give. If he'd seen Wendy sitting with her legs crossed outside one of the dives he used to play, blond hair long, makeup heavy, stockings ripped, and then he'd heard her laugh, his resilient heart wouldn't have stood a chance.

As Wendy watched, Daniel's breathing slowed and the planes of his face went slack. He was asleep.

She returned to her laptop, typing press release salvage jobs and checking Lorelei's posts, as if Daniel weren't touching her. But he *was* touching her, and she was very aware of this. The past three days had been three of the worst of her life, and she feared the worst was not over . . . yet here, in a strange hotel room in a strange city, doing her work, she felt like she'd come home. Her face tingled with delicious awareness that Daniel was with her.

It was domestic and strange to host him on her lap. She fully realized how fleeting it was and how wrong she was to have any kind of inkling that her relationship with him would last beyond their launch of Lorelei and Colton's promo. But she couldn't deny that she felt better and more at peace in this moment than she had not just in the past three days, but in years. As she examined that thought and her fingers paused over the keyboard, she wondered whether she'd felt so at peace . . . ever.

She lightly traced one fingertip along the smooth, light skin over his cheekbone, then let it dance down through his black stubble to cradle his jaw.

He didn't stir, his breathing deep and even.

She went back to work.

After several minutes she heard a key card slide through the lock and the door open. Sarah and Tom had made incredibly good time from the airport—*too* good. Wendy's first instinct was to dump Daniel off her, but it was too late. The best course of action was to play this cool. After all, there was nothing *really* going on between her and Daniel. And it wouldn't have been at all unusual for *Sarah* to fall asleep with her head on Wendy's thigh. Daniel and Wendy were friends, just like Sarah and Wendy.

So she held her place and beamed at Sarah as she came around the corner.

With a glance at Daniel, Sarah grinned back. She sat in the upholstered chair beside the bed and pulled out her phone.

Ten seconds later, a text blinked onto Wendy's phone.

Daniel Blackstone is totally in your lap

Wendy suppressed a laugh and texted back,

I know right?

Sarah replied,

In fact his face is in your lap

Wendy knew what Sarah was implying. She bit her lip and shook her head. Sarah raised one eyebrow and texted,

Normally your response would be I WISH

While Wendy still racked her brain for how to respond, Sarah texted again,

Tom is dropping off his bags, has key to this room, will come loping in any second. Wake Daniel or he's going to be embarrassed. I'll leave.

Sarah stood just as a key card slid through the lock and the door opened. "Honey, I'm home!" Tom called.

Daniel stirred on Wendy's thigh, his face rolling down so that Wendy could feel the huff of his hot breath through her skirt and panties. She tried not to look alarmed. He shouldered himself up to sitting, blinking at the sunlight streaming through the window. Finally he saw Sarah and Tom watching him. He jumped off the bed in one motion.

"Hey," Wendy started, about to tell him they were all friends here and he didn't need to look like he'd just been caught—but immediately he had the situation under control. He rounded the bed with his hand extended to Tom. "Daniel Blackstone," he said.

"Tom Ruffner," Tom said.

Wendy should have been intervening, introducing, but the whole scene was so bizarre that she was shocked into silence. She'd feared her relationship with Daniel and her relationship with Stargazer were going to collide, but not like this.

Daniel waited until Sarah extended her hand before reaching forward with his own, a level of etiquette that Wendy had had no idea existed until Sarah had explained it in college. "Daniel Blackstone," he murmured.

"I remember," Sarah said, shaking his hand. "Sarah Seville." When he released her, she still gazed up at him, then looked at Wendy. "So, you two are together."

"No, we're not," he and Wendy said at the same time. Wendy tried to shoot daggers through Sarah with her expression. Why couldn't Sarah keep her discoveries to herself for once?

Sarah's eyes roved warily over Wendy, then Daniel, then Tom, then back to Wendy. "Yes, you are," Sarah said.

Finally Wendy said carefully, "Sarah, sweetie, you know how you always imagine things when you're off your medication."

Sarah raised one eyebrow at Wendy.

Daniel waved uncomfortably at the bed. "I don't know what that was. So. Excuse me a moment." He passed Sarah and Tom, disappearing down the hall. The bathroom door opened, the lock clicked, water ran.

A suspicious Tom and a concerned Sarah turned to Wendy for an explanation. Wendy didn't have one. Or rather, she *did*, but not one she wanted to share.

Daniel splashed water on his face and dried off. When that didn't seem to reset him, he rested his forehead against the cool door and closed his eyes. He was realizing for the first time how incredibly whipped he was.

He heard Wendy exclaim out in the bedroom, "Scruffy! Why did you have to say that and come romping in here like a golden retriever puppy?"

"Why do you care?" Tom countered. "I think *somebody* has been moonlighting with the Blackstone Firm, *if ya know what I mean.*"

"I think *somebody*—" Wendy responded, but her voice faded, as if they'd realized Daniel could hear them, lowered their voices, and moved away from him, toward the window onto the Strip.

He jumped backward as a knock sounded on the door very near his forehead. "It's Sarah. Let me in."

He'd had hardly any interaction with Sarah in college, but he knew her by reputation. She was friendly. Helpful. And very persistent. She wasn't going away until she'd said her piece. He opened the door for her, hoping she would castigate him about his relationship with Wendy, then leave.

Instead, she entered the room, forcing him back against the sink, and closed the door behind her. She focused on him with her big brown eyes. He felt like one of her clients whom she was talking down from a ledge as she coaxed him, "Tell me what's going on."

"Wendy and I aren't together," he said. "Not like you're implying. I don't know where you get that idea. Last night was rough, and this morning I just fell asleep while we were waiting for you. I thought you would be longer—"

"It wasn't that you were in her lap," Sarah interrupted. "It was the way you both acted about it. Alarmed that anybody else would see you, but reluctant to let each other see that you were alarmed. There's clearly something you two need to talk about."

At the moment he was more interested in what Wendy was saying to Tom. He strained his ears to hear, but he couldn't make out a word. "Did she call Tom something weird just now?" he asked. "Scruffy?"

"She has a pet name for everybody she likes," Sarah explained. "She names people after what she considers their most prominent body parts. She's just teasing him about his lame half-assed beard and the fact that he doesn't own an iron."

"Oh, yeah? What's her name for *you*?"

"Tushy." Sarah waved her hand behind her tight little ass in her jogging pants.

That sounded too much like Wendy for Sarah to be making this up. He tested her. "What's Wendy's name for me?" He wanted to know more about this pet name habit. He also wondered if she liked him enough to have named him.

"Cheekbones," Sarah said instantly, without thinking.

Daniel eyed her doubtfully. He wasn't sure whether it was a good thing or a bad thing that Wendy had named him Cheekbones. He would have preferred Biceps.

"Listen," Sarah said, "I'm not going to tell you or Wendy what to do, but . . . she let you know she's in trouble with the firm, right?"

He nodded. He was feeling more and more guilty about taking her Darkness Fallz account.

"Her job was already in jeopardy," Sarah said, "and now she's expending extra resources by calling Tom and me out here to help her. She needs a win on this case. She does *not* need to start a relationship with you. Our bosses hate the Blackstone Firm."

Daniel knew Sarah had Wendy's best interests at heart. And though he regularly lied on the job for the sake of his clients, it pained him to think about lying to Sarah.

"I hear you," he said.

But he wasn't making any promises.

13

〜

Wendy was starving. She figured a full stomach would do Daniel a world of good. And the tension in her room was getting so thick that they wouldn't be able to move soon. She convinced them all to go with her down to the food court in the mall attached to the casino in search of brunch.

As they slid their trays onto a table together, they discussed a plan of action, with Sarah helping Daniel and Tom assisting Wendy with the day's chores. After they'd eaten, Tom stood to get them all coffee. He was well versed in getting Wendy and Sarah coffee. This had been their version of hazing him when he joined the firm. Daniel said he couldn't stay because he needed to leave to check on Colton, whom he hadn't babysat all morning.

As he rose, Wendy couldn't let him go without some moral support. Impulsively she hugged him around

the waist. He put his arms around her, too, and gave
her a quick squeeze. Electricity shot through her at his
touch. Surprised, she tried not to miss a beat as she
said, "Call me if you need me. Or fall down."

He waved vaguely and headed for the corridor back
to the hotel. She watched him until he disappeared
around the corner. He was walking normally now, a
fast gait that meant he was all business.

Finally she turned around and realized Sarah was
watching her. Wendy plopped down across from her
at the table.

"Wow," Sarah said. "After talking to him about
work for just a few minutes, I'm thinking, Mr. Blackstone, if only I could shadow you for a month."

"He's good," Wendy acknowledged, trying to tamp
down the hint of pride she heard in her own voice.
"The thing is, he doesn't give a shit about this job.
I would kill to have his talent. It's totally wasted on
him."

"I got that impression, too." Sarah arched one eyebrow. "So, tell me what's going on between you two.
If I hadn't seen his head in your lap, I still would have
been able to tell you're together by the way you were
acting."

Wendy eyed her suspiciously. "How was I acting?"

"Kind of, ah . . ." Sarah looked into space, searching
for the words. "Like a lady."

Wendy snorted.

"Like you were very concerned that he heard you,

and you heard him, and you understood each other. Normally you wouldn't bother. If a guy didn't agree with you, at the slightest provocation you would quote a feminist philosopher."

"Or just tell the guy to fuck off," Wendy added.

"Or both," Sarah said.

"There has been all kinds of that," Wendy said. "I've been giving him lots of attitude. You just haven't seen it."

"Oh *really*," Sarah said. "Did you bend him over your knee and smack that tight ass?"

Past Sarah's shoulder, Wendy saw Tom stop short a few feet from them with a cardboard holder and three coffees.

Seeing Wendy's face, Sarah's eyes widened. "What is it?" Sarah whirled to glance behind her. "Oh, Tom! Thank God. The way Wendy looked, I thought you were Daniel, eavesdropping on us."

Tom sauntered over to the table and sat down, eyeing Sarah. "You think it's good business policy for Wendy to slap Daniel Blackstone on the ass?"

"I think she already has," Sarah said.

Wendy kicked Sarah under the table.

"Metaphorically," Sarah said without missing a beat. "I was just making fun of the way Wendy talks about men when you're not around. Wait, you didn't need to know that, either." She looked to Wendy for help.

"We both apologize," Wendy said, trying her best

to sound like Audrey Hepburn. "We are very sorry you walked in on our sexist language. Sometimes in our private discussions, we are not very professional."

"Professional?" Tom's brows shot up. "You two? I think we left that place about five minutes after I started work." He put his chin in his hand, settling in to find out more.

Wendy gave them the brief version of everything that had happened in the past three days. She mentioned but downplayed Daniel's suspicion that Rick was her attacker. Last night she'd been so sure he was right, after brushing past the Colton-like character in the club. But in the bright light of day, she wasn't so sure anymore—though she was still wary of passersby and kept one hand over the top of her paper cup of coffee.

Since they were so curious, bordering on disbelieving, she unfurled her bun and showed them the three places where her hair had been lopped off, and the gash stitched together in the back of her head. She explained that the attacks were why she'd stayed the last two nights in Daniel's room. As she pinned her hair up again, Sarah and Tom grilled her about why the police hadn't done anything, and then about what else had been going on between her and Daniel.

"How much do you know about this guy?" Tom demanded.

Wendy opened her mouth to explain that she'd known Daniel by reputation her entire adult life—and then stopped. Tom had turned the tables on her somehow, making her feel like he was her older brother rather than her younger one, and she needed to defend her boyfriend to him. "Daniel's not my boyfriend," she said testily. "I don't *need* to know anything about him."

"It sounds like you've been tumbling all over each other like puppies," Tom insisted.

"No, that would be you and your girlfriend, Miss New Jersey," Wendy countered.

"Whoa whoa whoa," Sarah said, putting a hand between them to interrupt their glares at each other. "Seriously, Wendy, we need to talk about what tack Tom and I are supposed to be taking when it comes to Colton, who's officially a client for a rival PR firm."

Wendy stared at her without speaking.

"What?" Sarah asked.

"Are you wearing a bra?"

Sarah hung her head. "No."

Tom looked at the ceiling.

"We need to take care of this," Wendy said, sweeping her hand in a way that indicated all of Sarah. "Come with me. Walk and talk." She raked her chair back from the table and led them out of the food court, into the mall. In a high-end shoe store, she chose an ankle boot with a three-inch heel and approached the counter. "We'd like to try this in a seven, please." Then she sat across from Sarah and Tom where they'd settled on the store's low seats. "I thought I'd made it clear what tack you should take," she told them. "Daniel and I are working together to make it look like Lorelei and Colton are reuniting. I need you guys to help us any way you can, and that includes helping Daniel."

"But what if I just *happen* to skew Lorelei's PR in a way that makes her look good and Colton look bad?" Tom asked.

"And there are so many ways I could sabotage Colton's PR without Daniel knowing," Sarah added.

"No," Wendy said. "I don't want to screw Daniel over."

"Why not?" Tom asked suspiciously.

"He's with the Blackstone Firm, in case you hadn't noticed," Sarah said. "Screwing them over is practically part of Stargazer's mission statement."

"Daniel and I have been working together some since we've been here," Wendy reminded them. "He's had the opportunity to screw me over, and he hasn't. I've had the opportunity to screw him over, and I haven't."

"But now *we're* here," Tom pointed out.

"And you need to screw him over if you can," Sarah told Wendy. "Katelyn knows you called us to help you. With extra resources added to your tab, you'd better come through with something spectacular."

"That doesn't have to include sabotaging Daniel," Wendy protested. "It could simply be doing my job and getting Lorelei out of trouble."

"And getting her album nominated for a Grammy," Tom said, "because at this point, I don't think just doing your job is going to cut it."

"Nah." Wendy waved away his concerns with a confidence she didn't feel. "Lorelei will record a beautiful mini-concert in an hour, and she'll do great at the awards show tomorrow night. Everything will turn around for her. You'll see."

The salesman came out with the shoes then. He offered them to Wendy, but Wendy pointed to Sarah. After he left, Sarah held the box as if she wasn't sure what to do with it. "These are for me? What's wrong with what I have on? I just bought these." She stuck out one sad Mary Jane with a hiking tread.

"What's wrong with them," Wendy said, "is that you're in Vegas, where everybody goes out of their way to look good. You're part of my posse. You're a reflection on me. You can't dress like you teach kindergartners at a Montessori school. We're getting a scarf and chunky earrings, too, to make what you're wearing into something presentable. Or just cover it up. And then you are marching right back to your room to put on a bra."

With a grimace, Sarah tried the boots on. "They fit, but Wendy. I'm running a marathon in two weeks. I'm not willing to break my ankle in heels just because you're embarrassed to be seen with me."

"Precisely because you run marathons, you could punch holes in steel plate with your ankles." Remembering Tom, Wendy turned to him. "You're very tolerant of us while we conduct this meeting in a women's shoe store. Thank you."

"No problem." He grinned.

"Are you putting up with it, or are you kind of enjoying it?"

"I'm kind of enjoying it. Taking notes like David Attenborough."

"You'll make somebody an excellent husband."

Tom put up his hands. "Hold on there, cowgirl."

"Not for *me*, Scruffy! You're just a baby." Running her eye up and down him, she appraised his usual attire. "You just need to iron."

"I don't iron."

"Send your clothes out to be pressed, then, and charge it to my room. Jesus." She turned her sights on Sarah again. "Do you have something to wear to Lorelei's birthday party tonight?"

Sarah gestured to what she was wearing. "This?"

Wendy took a deep breath and prayed to God for forbearance. Then she said, "I'll give you a hint. Sequins."

"Then, no." Sarah stuck out her bottom lip.

Wendy shook her head in disgust. "When I get a minute this afternoon, I'll buy you a dress and have it delivered to your room."

"I feel like your mistress." Sarah grinned.

"Speaking of inappropriate relationships," Tom spoke up, "seriously, Wendy, what are you going to do about Daniel Blackstone?"

Wendy glanced around the shoe store to make sure they wouldn't be overheard, then scowled at him. "Why do I have to *do* anything about Daniel Blackstone?"

"Because his head was in your lap!" Sarah exclaimed, exasperated.

"You love saying that," Wendy grumbled.

"I'm just dishing it back out, girlfriend," Sarah said. "I can't believe this day has finally come. You and Daniel have both met your match. Only, you're not really a match for him. Not long-term. If this is a fling that will be over when you go back to New York, that's one thing. If you think you can keep meeting in New York without anybody finding out, I don't know. That's really iffy. And Stargazer can*not* find out about this, Wendy."

Wendy's stomach twisted. "It's not against company policy to have a relationship with the Blackstone Firm," she protested.

"It might as well be," Tom said. "That's the first thing I learned in this job."

"And they already don't like you, Wendy," Sarah said. "In case you forgot, they *fired* you on Monday, but you clung to Archie's leg and he couldn't shake you off."

"Plus, I've been doing a really good job of keeping Zane Taylor clean," Tom volunteered. "Maybe too good. I've told the bosses that you laid the groundwork, but they don't listen when they don't want to hear it. And now this photo of Lorelei is making the rounds."

"You can't give them another excuse," Sarah insisted. "You've got to get Lorelei out of this scrape, *and* you've got to dump Daniel."

Wendy grimaced. "What if I didn't dump him? Isn't there another way out of this?"

"He can't leave the Blackstone Firm," Tom said. "It

practically belongs to him. You could leave Stargazer and—"

"No!"

"—go to work for—"

"No!"

"It's not that bad, Wendy," Sarah broke in. "There are plenty of PR firms that—"

"No!"

"Hey!" Sarah put her hand on Wendy's thigh. "We know you're scared."

"I'm not." Wendy rose and pointed to the counter, indicating that Sarah should pay for her shoes so they could move on to the next item of clothing. "There's nothing to be scared of. The only reason I would lose my job is if Daniel and I really fell for each other. I'm not going to let that happen."

Midafternoon, Daniel found Wendy in their room. She'd draped her suit jacket over the back of the desk chair, so he got a better look at her breasts than he had that morning. The sight heated his blood. He made a valiant effort to stare at her face instead while he waited for her to acknowledge him.

She'd set up her laptop on the desk rather than balancing it on her thighs on the bed, which told him that things had gotten serious. She even held up one finger so he would hold his thoughts while she finished an e-mail. "There!" She tapped the trackpad with a flourish and spun in the desk chair to face him. "How are you feeling?" she asked, beaming at him.

"Better, after eating," he said. "How do *you* feel? I've stopped asking you, but you're the one with stitches."

"A hundred percent. Lorelei's TV appearance went *so well*. Did you see it?"

He sat on the bed, very close to her chair, and tried not to stare at the tempting hem of her skirt as she crossed her toned legs in front of him. Wendy looked very sexy in skirts. "Colton and I both watched it, and then I watched it again online. You and your crew did a super job setting that up and getting the video out there."

"It turned out great," Wendy agreed. "I could have kissed that girl right there in the studio, but PR professionals do not inadvertently start lesbian rumors about their clients."

Daniel laughed. "I can tell Lorelei's public image is turning around because of that video, and people are getting excited about the fact that she and Colton might be back together. I only wish there was something else we could do."

"Something *else*?" Wendy exclaimed. "I don't know how you work at the Blackstone Firm, but over at Stargazer we are tired. Maybe we're underachieving."

Daniel shook his head. "It's just that Lorelei and Colton's bad PR has been *incredibly* bad. In order to counteract that, the good PR has to be over the top. Their apparent reunion and your video are steps in the right direction, but I'm not sure we're there yet. I'm still thinking. Maybe I'll come up with something."

Wendy was looking at him like he was insane, so he shrugged and changed the subject. "Thank you for bringing Sarah out here to help. I know it was really for Lorelei, and only incidentally for Colton or for me, but I appreciate it all the same. Sarah is good at what she does."

"She thinks the same thing about you," Wendy said. "She told me you were like a master class in this business."

"Well," he said quietly. "It's second nature now. I grew up with it. Couldn't get away from it. I . . ."

She raised her eyebrows, probably wondering why he'd stopped talking. And why he was talking about himself voluntarily. Good call.

He started over. "I know it was just a big mistake to be asleep on your lap when your colleagues came into the room. I feel awful about it. Sarah gave me a talking-to."

"Yeah," Wendy said regretfully, "Sarah does that."

"I, um . . ." He was *never* tongue-tied, but Wendy had this effect on him. She watched him with concern in her blue eyes as his speech ground to a halt. He doubted he would have gotten himself in this fix with her if she'd only been kind. Or only brilliant at her job. Or only hilarious, making him laugh like he hadn't laughed since high school.

Or only sexy. He found his gaze drifting from her eyes down to her perfectly polished lips, and farther down to her breasts again. Two nights alone with her in this hotel room and he hadn't seen her bare breasts, hadn't even touched them. That was how smooth he was around her.

He couldn't be tongue-tied now, though. He had to tell her. Reaching across the space between them and taking her hands in his, he said, "I haven't made any secret of how I feel about you. I think some of it has been welcome and some of it hasn't, which I really regret. But I never, ever intended to get you in trouble at work. If that's going to happen, but we're still uneasy about this guy who likes your hair so much, maybe you could stay in Sarah's room instead of mine."

"Oh," Wendy said to their clasped hands.

"I want to be honest about this," Daniel said. "I've enjoyed living with you. I hope you'll stay." Of course, if he'd really been honest, he would have said a whole lot more.

Wendy nodded. "Then I'll be honest with you. We can't have any kind of long-term relationship. Not while you're with the Blackstone Firm and I'm with Stargazer."

His heart sank. He'd wanted to clear the air with her—to a point. But now that she'd stated her true feelings, ambiguity didn't sound so bad.

"Sarah and Tom won't rat me out," Wendy went on. "Stargazer has no way of knowing you and I are together out here. So as long as we're in Vegas, as far as I'm concerned, we can do anything we want."

They shared a long, serious look. Daniel's heart pulsed painfully in his chest. Sometimes clarity was very, very good.

Wendy sat back in her chair and smiled craftily at him. "Guess what? While we've been chatting, I've come up with that over-the-top idea you wanted, the one that will rescue Lorelei and Colton once and for all." Her words were businesslike, but her come-hither smile told him they were done with work for now.

He whispered, "Do tell."

14

It's going to sound crazy," Wendy said, "but hear me out."

"Mmmmm-kay," Daniel said in such a knowing tone that she nearly jumped out of her skin in anticipation. Though he gave her the impression of consciousness of his own body and looks, he was unself-consciously sexy, legs crossed casually on the edge of the bed in his dark suit pants, crisp white shirt open at the throat, dark hair perfect, dark eyes on her.

"Lorelei is great at taking scandalous photos," Wendy said. "She's known for it. It's never brought her anything but trouble, but if we brainstormed, maybe we could turn that around. The thing about Lorelei and her exhibitionism is . . . she's got a killer body."

Daniel nodded. "If you have a thing for bony twenty-one-year-olds."

Wendy laughed. "Most people do. And if she were

to post the right pictures of her elbow or her carefully pedicured big toe or worse, that might actually make for good PR. But that's not what she does. She takes the grossest, most unflattering shot possible and posts that, making herself look like a drunken slob."

"Which she is," Daniel pointed out. "It's just that she's a beautiful drunken slob, and her photos don't do her justice."

"Exactly," Wendy said. "See, you're so difficult to work with—"

"Me!" he exclaimed.

"—but we really are on the same page. Because here's what I was thinking. Maybe we could take some test shots to see what looks best on camera."

A smile crept across Daniel's face as he caught her meaning. "And we don't want to disturb her," he said. "She's probably doing something really important, like staring into space, or embroiling herself in an online battle with her high school choir director. We can take care of this ourselves."

He put his hands on Wendy's knees and rolled her office chair to the edge of the bed, right in front of him.

The sudden manhandling was so out of character for him, and so titillating for her, that she sat there dazed for a moment, staring at him without speaking, enjoying the tingles that still raced through her blood.

He handed her his phone. "Try your cleavage first, and we'll go from there."

Heart beating wildly, she examined his phone to

figure out where the camera buttons were, then aimed the lens down her blouse and clicked.

He took the phone back from her before she could even view the picture herself. Suddenly embarrassed, she tried to snatch it away from him. He held it above his head and gently slapped at her hands until she withdrew them. He peered at the screen, then at her. He tilted his head, considering her. She felt herself blushing, thinking of him examining her cleavage, waiting for his verdict.

"A little higher, I think, and centered better. And we need to show a little more." He placed the phone on the bed and reached both hands toward her neckline. She watched him coming, instinctively throwing her shoulders back to give him better access to her breasts.

His hands stopped inches from her blouse. He was watching her. He asked softly, "May I?"

"Of course," she said casually. "Anything for Lorelei's PR."

He bit his lip to keep from laughing. She suppressed a shudder as his fingers slipped past the neckline of her blouse to explore the lace edge of her bra. "I don't know," he whispered. "We're probably going to have to adjust all this." His fingers trailed down to unfasten the first button of her shirt.

She tried to enjoy the warm waves of excitement that washed over her as his hands moved in slow motion. But relaxing was impossible with this tight thread of anticipation running through her and making her skin burn. He gently tugged the sides of her shirt apart and smoothed them back, deliberately pressing her breasts and stroking her nipples beneath the silk. He cupped her breasts in his palms as he tugged her bra lower to expose more of her cleavage. It was all she could do to hold in a groan of pleasure as he touched her through the lace.

"There," he said. Holding her gaze, he felt around for the phone. He glanced at it, adjusted the settings, and then reached over to point it down over her chest. The camera flashed, warming her bare skin, and the warmth seemed to remain and pool in the cups of her bra.

This time he offered her the phone. They put their heads close together to look at the photo.

"Wow," Wendy said. "That's an improvement." It was amazing how buxom she looked with her breasts and lacy bra out of context. She could hear Daniel breathing beside her, smell his cologne.

He looked over at her, dark eyes questioning, asking her permission to go on.

She winked at him.

"Let's try something different," he said. "Switch places with me."

She let him have her chair, and she shifted to the edge of the bed.

"Spread your legs a little," he suggested.

She laughed and felt her cheeks turn flaming red, but she obeyed him, inching her knees farther apart. He slid the phone under her skirt and up her thigh.

"Hold still," he said.

This time she didn't laugh, just watched him. He looked back at her, half smiling, eyes black.

She blinked as the phone flashed. She wasn't sure where the light in her eyes was coming from: out from under her skirt, up her blouse and out her neckline, or all in her own mind.

Slowly he slid the phone out from between her legs. His grin gave away that he might be enjoying himself a little.

"Is it a good picture?" she asked. "Let me see."

He turned the screen around and showed it to her. There were her panties all right, and the lining of her skirt, and her thighs looking unnaturally white in the bright flash.

"Take a few more," she suggested. "I'm not smiling in this one."

He burst into laughter, and she was so surprised that she forgot to laugh herself. "This job," he grumbled, still chuckling. Without ceremony, he reached forward, grabbed her hips, and dragged her to the very edge of the bed. He put one hand on each of her knees and spread her legs wide.

"Now," he said, his voice more gentle than she'd ever heard it. He slipped his phone underneath the edge of her skirt. She strained to keep from jumping as she felt his whole hand on the inside of her thigh, very close to her panties. "A little farther apart. We want a good view this time." Obediently she opened her legs further. She heard the phone click, saw the flash, and felt the heat, whether it was her imagination or not.

"Hold still," he said. He took several more photos and then drew the phone out to look at it.

"Well?" she asked gamely.

"It seems awfully innocent and tame," he said. "I think we need something else."

"Like what?"

"A prop."

She bit her lip and repeated, "Like what?"

He held up his hand and splayed his fingers.

She widened her eyes at him. He grinned at her.

"Let's try it and see how it looks," she said.

He moved his hand up her thigh again. She sucked in a sharp breath as he rested his fingers on her panties. She was sure he could feel how wet she was through the silk. His palm rested possessively on her mound. An electric zap of pleasure moved across her chest and down her arms.

She heard the camera snap.

He peered at the screen. "It's hard for me to get a good angle with one hand." Then he stood and turned toward the desk. He must have decided enough was enough, and now it was time to get back to work.

Recess was over.

Supremely disappointed, but determined not to show it, she kept a smile pasted on her face and inched her knees back together.

He turned to face the bed again, holding out her phone, which he'd grabbed from the desk. "Why don't you take some with *your* phone? That will free me up to touch you."

She'd never felt such an intense mixture of relief and excitement. Recess wasn't over after all.

Ever so slowly he came down from his full height and kneeled on the carpet in front of her, watching her all the while. "Now then," he said, grasping both her wrists. "Put the phone here and wait until I tell you." He positioned the phone at the opening of her skirt.

She braced for his touch, and then it came. She shivered at the rush of sparks as he reached once more up her thighs to her panties. This time his fingers slipped past the lacy edge.

She held her breath, anticipating what he would do next, uneasy with the knowledge that she'd completely lost control of this situation, yet dizzy with the thrill of it. Her afternoon honed to this point: feeling his fingers where they shouldn't be and wondering how far they would go.

His fingertips stopped at the edge of her, stroking her clit and making her squirm. "That would probably make a good shot," he growled. "Give it a try."

She took the picture, sighing at the sudden warmth of the flash.

"Let's see," he said, sliding his hand out of her skirt and reaching for her phone. He examined the picture critically. "The prop is good, but the shot is too dark. See for yourself." He handed it to her.

She peered at the photo. His big hand disappeared beneath her pale pink panties, all lit brilliantly by the flash and clear as day. She rushed wet again at the sight.

"Let's try taking your skirt off," he suggested. "To improve the lighting."

She stood. There wasn't much room with him kneeling in front of her, so the fabric of her skirt brushed his chin as he gazed up at her. He didn't blink.

She reached behind her with both hands and unclasped the waistband of her skirt, then unzipped it down the back and let the material drop. It grazed his nose and fell to the floor. Now his head was level with her panties.

"Do you think you'll be able to see me better now?" she asked.

"One way to find out. Why don't you sit back down?"

She sat on the bed and waited for him to hand her the phone, but he slid it onto the desk.

So recess *was* over this time. Now they were getting down to business.

He shoved his fingers past her panties. His hand didn't pause there. His fingers reached inside her, shallowly at first, testing. He must have felt immediately how wet she was for him, because he pushed deeper. His eyes never left hers. His lips parted. "You know, the bottom of your blouse is in the way of a good picture."

"Can you help me?"

Nodding, he shifted forward, his fingers moving even farther inside her so that she groaned. With his other hand he reached for the next button of her blouse and unfastened it, then moved down to the next. Still caressing her inside with one hand, he moved the halves of her blouse aside, revealing her lacy bra. She panted, her breasts rising and falling rapidly.

"Better?" she asked breathlessly.

"I think we need to try a new prop."

He must feel the way she tightened around his fingers. She was excited and a little frightened. "Like what?" she breathed.

"My mouth." Slowly he pulled his fingers out of her and rubbed his thumb back and forth across her slick clit. "Right here. We're going to have to take your panties off, though, because they're in the way." He used both hands to slide her panties down. She half stood to let him ease them off her hips, then picked up her feet. He pulled her underwear down and off her toes and kneeled there with the silk crumpled in one hand, watching her.

"Lie down," he said firmly.

She eased down and let the softness of the duvet surround her. She loved being exposed for him, and the electric anticipation as she waited, staring at the white ceiling, listening to the soft drone of the air conditioner, wondering when he would touch her. The silence and stillness were so complete for long seconds that he must be looking her over. At the thought, a new wave of pleasure nearly made her cry out.

There. He was touching her at two small points, his long fingers teasing her open. Those fingers pushed into her again, farther than before. She simultaneously squirmed with discomfort at how far he had invaded her and lifted her hips so he could reach farther inside.

There. Now his mouth was on her, a warm circle that covered her clit and lapped at her.

"Ah." She felt like saying a lot more, but she just dug her back and elbows into the soft bed and tilted her pelvis up to him.

He began to fuck her with his tongue. She cried out and gripped the duvet in both fists as she felt herself climbing toward orgasm. His tongue was deep inside her. His thumb massaged her clit. Her body jerked upward against him, and she came. A warm shock ran through her, a sensation too good to withstand. His mouth and his hands stayed with her as she gasped and bucked under him for long minutes of bliss. Slowly the waves faded, replaced by an awareness of cool air touching her wetness.

Without warning he scooped her up—his hand covered her bare ass, which was all she had time to note—and set her down at the head of the bed with her back against the pillows. He kicked off his shoes and stretched out on the other side, facing her.

She reached toward his crotch. He didn't stop her. Beneath the expensive cloth of his pants, his dick was thick and hard. "Your turn," she said.

Across the room, his phone rang. They gazed at each other for a few moments, listening to it. She'd heard his normal ringtone before. She knew this was a special ring he'd programmed for an unusually problematic client. She did the same thing on her own phone. She asked, "Who is it?"

"Victor Moore," he said flatly.

"Better get it. His storybook marriage to Olivia Query may be in trouble." As soon as the sarcastic words had left her mouth, Wendy was sorry. She wanted to give Daniel a blow job, not drive him away.

He did roll off the bed then, but he didn't seem offended. He reached for his phone on the desk. "Hello, Victor," he said. "No, this isn't a bad time at all." Looking at Wendy, Daniel shot himself in the head with his finger.

She covered her mouth with her hand so she wouldn't giggle out loud. All of a sudden she was the floozy mistress in the middle of Daniel's workday, and he was her extracurricular activity.

She knew their session had to come to an end now so they could follow their clients to rehearsal. But she enjoyed a few more minutes of Daniel's dark eyes roving up and down her body while he listened to Victor, his white shirt rumpled, his collar askew, his dark hair as wild as she'd ever seen it.

"It's not something we can discuss over the phone?" He ran his hand back through his hair, mussing it further. "No, I'm in Vegas with another client this week—"

Wendy pointed to herself and mouthed, "Me?"

Daniel grinned at her. Ah, how she loved those cheekbones.

"—but I'll come to L.A. as soon as I can. Yes. Call my office if they can help you with anything in the meantime." He wrapped up the call and set the phone down. "He's either dying or he needs advice on choosing a brand of dishwashing detergent," he told Wendy. "Good actor, though." He glanced at his watch.

"Don't tell me," Wendy said. "Rain check?"

He nodded. "I'm so sorry."

"How sorry *are* you?"

With a devilish grin, he closed the space between them, crawled onto the bed, roughly moved the cup of her bra aside, and took her nipple into his mouth. Releasing her, he murmured, "Pretty . . ." He circled her breast with his tongue. ". . . damn . . ." He centered on her nipple again and suckled her until she cried out with pleasure. ". . . sorry," he sighed, pulling her bra cup back into place.

Half standing, he slid both their phones from the desk and offered his to her. "Trade?"

They spent a few minutes side by side on the bed, thumbing through each other's phones, deleting the dirty pictures.

"Oh man," he murmured, "it's a real shame to trash this one." He showed it to her.

She looked, blushed, and went back to deleting the photos on his phone. She'd reached the end of her porn shots, apparently, because the next photo was of Daniel scowling next to a giddy-looking young brunette in expensive sunglasses. Only their heads were in the shot, close-up, as if the girl had held the phone at arm's length and taken the picture herself. Wendy showed it to him. "Is this your sister?"

He glanced at it and smiled. "Yeah." He went back to perusing her phone.

"Sorry. I didn't mean to browse your photos. I didn't realize I was done deleting."

"You can look," he said.

So, curious, she swiped the screen. The next photo back in time was a scene she recognized: the view of the street from a front room of the Beverly Hilton. The next view was familiar, too: Chicago. And the next: San Francisco. She said, "You take a lot of pictures from your hotel rooms."

"Wishful thinking, I guess. I always want to see the sights in cities where I'm working. I never have time. I take a picture of what I can't have." He held out her phone. She accepted it and gave him his. He took it from her and snapped her picture.

She blinked against the afterimage of the unexpected flash. "Delete that. I'm dishabille."

He laughed heartily. "You're more than dishabille. That's not clear in the picture, though." He held the phone up for her to see.

True, her hair spilled over her shoulders and down her chest, hiding her bare skin. But she still didn't recognize herself. The girl in the picture looked like a dazed blonde who'd just been thoroughly fucked.

He pocketed his phone. "I have a confession to make. Now I really do have that over-the-top idea to save Lorelei and Colton's careers, and yours."

"Which you got while going down on me?"

"No, while talking to Victor."

Suddenly very, very tired, Wendy rubbed her eyes. This was smearing her carefully applied makeup, she realized too late. Being human did not mix with this job. "What's your idea?"

"Colton and Lorelei will get married." Daniel glanced at his watch again.

Wendy asked, "To each other?"

"Of course, to each other. We're here in Vegas, so we can have it taken care of tonight, and it will be in the news tomorrow. We're rehabilitating their public images, but that takes time. We need people to tune in to the awards show *tomorrow*. Do you see how getting them married would help? It will be perfect."

"You and I have different definitions of *perfect*."

Her words came out angrier than she intended. As Daniel watched her somberly, she realized she was letting her emotions get in the way of what ought to be a straightforward PR fix.

"I do see how it would help, actually," she admitted. "When they're not serious and he's taking pictures of her ass, she seems like a ho. But if they're married, or even if the rumor circulates, it seems like they're intimate and playful, and the millions of people following their every move are somehow invading their privacy."

"Exactly."

"And they'll tune in to the show because they want *more*."

Daniel pointed at her. "See?"

"Or . . ." She couldn't believe she was actually thinking through this possibility, but she was. "That's the best-case scenario. More likely, people will think Lorelei and Colton got plastered and decided to get married the same night they got matching portraits of George Washington tattooed on their ass cheeks."

"Lorelei has run out of room for art on her ass cheeks," Daniel pointed out.

"No," Wendy said firmly, "I don't want to marry Lorelei off to that fountain pisser just to solve a public relations problem. That is *your* modus operandi, not mine."

"Just present the idea to her," Daniel said. "What if she agrees?"

"She won't agree. She has a better head on her shoulders than that." Wendy realized as she uttered these words that they weren't true.

"Can you think of an alternative?" Daniel challenged her.

"Fake a wedding," Wendy said.

"That's not going to work," Daniel said. "We'll have a leak. A lower-level employee at a Las Vegas wedding chapel will sacrifice a job just to nab a few thousand dollars for spilling the real story to a tabloid. But I'll tell you what *will* work. We'll put Lorelei and Colton at a real wedding ceremony tonight. Afterward, they and the chapel employees can swear up and down to the tabloids that it wasn't Lorelei and Colton who got married, but another couple. Lorelei and Colton will be telling the truth, so they'll sound sincere. But the press won't believe them, and we'll get our positive PR anyway."

"Now *that's* perfect," Wendy declared. She didn't think they could pull it off, but in theory, it was perfect. "How are we supposed to find a couple getting married? Just hang around the chapel and wait for someone to drive up? People like that *definitely* won't stay quiet for the tabloids, because they're happy about their own wedding."

Daniel was somber. He rolled away from her, rounded to her side of the bed, and went down on one knee on the carpet.

"No," she said automatically.

He reached for her hand. She held it behind her back. He said, "Give it."

"No," she said, but he was stronger than her, and she didn't want to struggle. He was fully clothed and she was wearing nothing but an unbuttoned shirt and a bra. She felt suddenly—and belatedly—self-conscious.

He pulled her arm from behind her back. "Wendy, will you marry me?"

"Nuh-uh."

He tilted his head, wearing a bemused expression. "You're taking this way too seriously. We'll stay married on paper for a few weeks, until the awards show is done, Lorelei starts her concert tour, Colton gets his movie role, and this all blows over. Then, way before Stargazer has any reason to be suspicious, we'll get a divorce."

She pulled away from him and threw up her

hands—carefully, so the movement didn't dislodge her hair from covering her. "I don't want to get divorced."

He still kneeled on the floor in his beautifully tailored suit pants, frowning up at her, imploring her with his dark gaze. Then his eyes fell, and he turned away to look out at the bright Strip, mirrored windows of the hotels across the street glinting in the daylight. He was calculating a new way to start a marriage rumor about Lorelei and Colton. Or maybe—just maybe—Wendy had hurt his feelings.

"Even if we agree it means nothing spiritually," she said more gently, "it still means something legally. You could take me for half of what I'm worth."

He turned back to her, eyes glinting, knowing she was back in the discussion. "You could take me for half of what I'm worth, too, and I'm worth a lot more than you. I'm trusting you not to do that, just like I've trusted you before."

"I seem to recall that when you said you trusted me before, you followed that up with, 'I can ruin you.' When you tell me you can ruin me and you tell me how much money you have, you might as well go ahead and threaten to have me killed."

"I promise I won't have you killed. Not for this."

She considered him on the floor in front of her. He was willing to attach himself to a woman—she assumed for the first time ever, though they should probably have that discussion—just for the sake of his job. Obviously his life didn't hold anything else of value. He'd told her as much.

She was in the same boat. She had no personal life to speak of. She had plenty of friends, with Sarah at the top of the list, but all of them had significant others. She was the go-to person when the significant other was unavailable. She was everyone's backup plan. This wasn't much to forfeit, on paper, for a couple of weeks.

Because what she'd be saving was her job. A wedding rumor would truly put Lorelei over the top in terms of positive public interest. As long as she played a ferocious set of songs at the awards show, tickets for her concert tour would start to fly. Her tour would be a success. Her album sales would follow. Wendy would get her raise and her promotion. By the time anyone caught a whiff that the wedding rumor had been wrong, just as Lorelei had been insisting all along, they would be in the clear.

All Wendy had to do was suffer through a short ceremony and sign a piece of paper binding her, however temporarily, to the man waiting in front of her. A handsome, brilliant, dangerously sexy man who was exactly as lost as she was, and who had exactly as little to lose by doing this.

She said, "Yes."

15

*G*reat," Daniel said on an exhalation, which sounded like relief. He nudged Wendy's laptop aside and opened his own on the desk. "Let me see what I can set up before I go."

Now that his back was turned and the clicks of his keyboard filled the silence, Wendy slid off the bed. She buttoned her blouse, which seemed awfully wrinkled, but she had no time to re-iron. Daniel wasn't the only one with a busy afternoon. She found her skirt and shimmied into it, then searched the floor for her panties. Their whereabouts were not immediately apparent. She felt kind of stupid about this. A lady should always know where her underwear was.

She looked up at Daniel. He was rising from the chair to pull her panties out of his pocket. He held them out to her.

She took the wad of silk. "You had my panties in your pocket," she complained, half accusing, half teasing.

"Sorry."

"Were you going to give them back?"

He gave her a brilliant smile. "Maybe."

She couldn't help grinning back at him. For that brief moment, the complications and jealousies between them fell away, as they did every so often, as if their relationship were meant to be.

Then he turned back to his laptop, and she wiggled into her panties.

"This is a problem," he called. "All the wedding chapels close at midnight or so. I had a four a.m., end-of-the-night wedding in mind."

"That would be good, but this is better," Wendy said to the mirror over the dresser as she ran a brush through her hair and repinned the bun hiding her missing locks. "Lorelei is supposed to cut her birthday cake at midnight. We'll schedule the wedding for eleven thirty. Around eleven we'll spring the whole thing on her and Colton. We'll ask them to be our witnesses, and we'll all take Colton's limo to the chapel. The paparazzi will see them leaving the casino and go wild. Some of them will follow the limo straight to the chapel."

Daniel spun in his chair to beam at her. "Right!"

"We'll get lots more attention that way than if we do it in the wee hours," Wendy went on. "Some photographers will have given up and gone to bed by four, but this will be prime time. Then we'll skate back into the casino just in time for Lorelei's cake cutting. If we're fashionably late, so much the better."

"Colton and Lorelei will act innocent," Daniel said, "because they *will* be. For once. But the tabloids will assume they got married on her big day of celebration, right before their TV reunion, and they're just being coy about it. Wow." He turned back to the laptop and resumed typing. "We may be too good at this."

"That's what I've been saying."

He ignored that comment. "There's no blood test or waiting period, but we do both have to apply for a marriage license. Can you meet me at the county clerk's office at five?"

"It's going to be tight." She retrieved her phone from the bed and thumbed through her schedule. "I have to get changed for the party fairly early so I can supervise. There is to be absolutely no penis cake."

"Good thinking," he said without turning around. "Photos of penis cake have sabotaged many a starlet's career."

"I've got so much to do before then. I can delegate more of this to Tom, though."

"Four thirty?" Daniel asked.

"So noted. Listen . . ." Wendy secured her phone in her computer bag, thinking hard all the while. "I'll have to get rid of Tom and Sarah. Send them back to New York tonight on the red-eye."

Daniel looked over his shoulder at her. "Why?"

"If they find out what we're doing, they won't let me."

His expression turned somber. "Okay." He glanced at his screen. "Here's an eleven thirty opening for a wedding ceremony tonight. I can reserve it online. Do you want a drive-through wedding?"

"No," she said, crossing behind him to look over his shoulder at the web page littered with tacky hearts. "If it's outdoors, the paparazzi will see it's not Lorelei and Colton getting married. It's . . ." *Us,* she should say. *Us.* She couldn't bring herself to say it.

He'd already moved on. "Photos?"

"Absolutely not. If there are no photos, they can't leak."

"Right. Do you want the ceremony to be officiated by Elvis?"

"Yes, duh." She reached around him to fold her own laptop. "I've got to run."

"See you at the clerk's office at four thirty," he reminded her.

She gave him a short nod. She knew how bad an idea this was. She'd argued herself into acquiescing, but in her heart, she knew.

"Wendy." Daniel stood and wrapped her in his arms.

She tried to relax and enjoy the hug. The tingles were back, for one thing. Her heart raced any time he touched her. And hugging seemed rare and strange for him. She felt lucky for the privilege. But this was all wrong. And she still held her laptop sandwiched between them.

He kissed her forehead, ran his hands up to her shoulders, and held her there while he looked her in the eye. "It will be fine, I promise. I won't let this go bad."

It already had, but she couldn't think about that. She stuffed her computer in her bag on her way out the door, headed to her next appointment.

"We deleted all the pictures when we were done," Wendy told Sarah.

"That doesn't mean it didn't happen," Sarah said.

"I guess not," Wendy said. "But I'm not the type of girl to encounter a sexy man in a hotel room and say, 'This is inappropriate and we should probably stop.'"

"No, you're not," Sarah agreed.

Lorelei's party would start any minute in the posh rooftop club of the casino. Wendy had spent the last hour checking and rechecking every detail from the caterer to the carefully screened photographers who would be allowed to take pictures of the cake-cutting at midnight. Sarah had joined her for the last fifteen minutes of frantic supervision. Now they both sat in cushioned chairs in the outdoor section of the club overlooking the Strip.

While they'd been sitting, Wendy had told Sarah casually that she should grab the red-eye back to New York. In fact, Wendy had already arranged with Star-gazer to book the midnight flight for Sarah and Tom. Their work here was largely done. If they made it into the office tomorrow, the bosses would think Wendy's problems with Lorelei weren't so serious. Sarah had watched her gravely while Wendy explained this half-truth. She felt like death for misleading Sarah, and worse because Sarah would guess what was really going on and refuse to let Wendy go through with it.

Panicked, Wendy had launched into a description of what she and Daniel had been up to in the hotel room. If she admitted that they'd taken their relationship to the next level, maybe it would seem to Sarah that she wasn't hiding anything else. So far it seemed to be working.

"In the beginning," Wendy went on, "it was all completely innocent. Well, as innocent as dirty pictures can be. The next minute he was going down on me."

Sarah arched one eyebrow. "What if he'd been a pervert who uploaded your porn shots to the Internet?"

"If my face had been in them I would have been concerned, but it wasn't. They were just crotch shots. You can upload my cooch to the Internet all day and I won't mind, as long as my name isn't attached. That is precisely why I've never had *Wendy* tattooed across my labia."

Sarah snapped her fingers. "Damn it! I wish you'd said something before I got my labia tattoo last week."

"Do your labia say *Sarah*? You can always get it changed, like dumbass stars when they break up with the girlfriends named in their tattoos. That way, when you took crotch shots in the future, nobody would recognize you. What could you get it changed to? Saaaa . . ." She sounded it out.

"Saaaa . . ." Sarah joined in. The pitch of her voice changed like a passing ambulance as she looked around the candlelit patio to make sure none of the waiters listened in on their discussion of their labia tattoos.

Wendy said, "Saaaaaaalad. Taste a sample of my sexy salad."

"Sex salad," Sarah said. "My salad bar of sex."

"Take what you want and leave the rest," Wendy said.

Sarah said, "All you can eat."

They both shrieked with laughter and immediately shushed each other, trying to look innocent while several waiters inside pressed their faces against the glass wall of the club to peer at them.

Sarah choked out, "What are you going to tell your kids when they ask how you got together with Daniel? That is the most unwholesome damn thing I ever heard. You'll have to make up some shit about going to Paris."

Wendy grinned right through Sarah's offhand comment about children. The longer Wendy's fake relationship with Daniel went on, and the more pretend-serious it became, the more it hurt to joke about the trappings of a serious relationship that would never be. "Oh, we went to Paris, all right." She winked.

"Yes! Daniel had salad in Paris."

"Paris is famous for its salads, you know."

Sarah looked perplexed. "I thought that was Bangkok."

They both glanced toward the glass wall again as music began throbbing from the sound system. Straining her eyes to see through the shadows, Wendy realized that security was letting in the guests. "That's my cue," she told Sarah.

As Wendy rose, she braced for the suspicious comment she'd been expecting from Sarah. But Sarah kept her lips zipped, and Wendy couldn't worry about it. She had too much else to do.

And she was proud of herself for the job she'd done that day. Between the endless press releases, the media calls, Lorelei's TV appearance, and this party, Wendy had also managed to enjoy oral sex with Daniel, meet him for a marriage license, run a few more errands, and purchase a party outfit for Sarah. With her hair swept up and her makeup done correctly, Sarah was as beautiful as any plastic starlet who'd scored an invitation to this party. Her tiny dress hugged her athletic body, and her gold sandals were exactly right. This makeover was the crowning achievement of Wendy's day. She honestly believed her bosses were fools if they fired her. That knowledge would be cold comfort if she did get axed, but it was something.

She made her way into the club, which was quickly growing crowded. After that, her sense that she had a handle on her life and command of her job faded into a blur of sequins, laughter, and vague dread. Lorelei and Colton arrived together as planned, with Daniel close behind. Lorelei was photographed by a legitimate entertainment mag while having an animated conversation with a rock legend who'd been close friends with her mom and had nevertheless survived. This was a publicity coup, but Wendy found herself standing in a corner, smiling vaguely at the scene as it unfolded in front of her, and in her head yelling at herself to wake up. She wasn't drinking, but she felt besotted with worry about what she was about to do with Daniel.

She did return to reality for a moment when Sarah and Tom hugged her good-bye before snagging their bags from their rooms and hurrying for their flight. Sarah had drunk more than usual during her short stay at the party. She leaned into Tom as they left. In the last glimpse Wendy caught of them as they exited the club, Tom was laughing and putting his arm around Sarah.

Poor Sarah. This was what her marriage should have looked like. Wendy couldn't picture Sarah with Tom. The two of them seemed to have the same type of sibling relationship that Wendy enjoyed with Tom. But Sarah deserved to dress up. She deserved to go out. She deserved to have the arm of an adoring man around her, happy that she was having fun, rather than a husband who never wanted to do anything with her and, on the rare occasion when he gave in, acted like the night was all about him. Wendy sighed across the room and into the empty doorway where Sarah and Tom had been.

The chill that wrapped around her bare shoulders wasn't caused by Sarah's plight, though, or the club's air conditioning system. It was about Wendy herself. *She* deserved to dress up and go out and be valued like this, too. At some point, though, she'd forgotten. She'd given up. So she might as well get married to a professional acquaintance for business purposes.

One she'd completely fallen for, she thought with dismay as she spotted Daniel in the shadows, coming toward her. Her heart sped into overdrive. Her brain woke up, hoping for the chance to joke with him, like a kid in grade school about to be let outside onto the playground. She tried to back herself down. He didn't consider her the highlight of his evening. He needed to find her and discuss a PR matter with her so he could check it off his list.

But when he stopped very close to her, he didn't sound businesslike at all. He eyed her up and down and murmured, "Is that what you're going to wear?"

"I know," she said, feeling herself blush. "Tacky for a wedding. But changing clothes or wearing something that didn't look right for this party would draw attention we don't want."

"It's not tacky," he said. "It's completely appropriate for you to get married in a red sequined minidress."

"Thanks, I think."

"You look stunningly beautiful," he whispered. "You always do." He reached out to touch a tendril of her hair. "When we were talking about the wedding this afternoon, we forgot something. Rings."

"I didn't forget," she said triumphantly, opening her purse. Looking past him to make sure his body hid her hands from a nosy crowd, she pulled out the cheap, pre-engraved gold ring. She'd bought it on a whim from a cart in the middle of the mall food court as an ironic protest.

Handing it to him, she said, "It has a message on the inside. I wanted to get you one that said, 'Happily ever after for at least a few weeks,' but they were all out."

He held it between them and peered at the tiny letters in the dim light. "'Happiness,'" he read. "Thank you, Wendy." He cracked his gorgeous smile.

But just as quickly, an awkward silence settled over them. Wendy dropped his ring back in her purse.

"Oh, I got you one, too." He reached into the inside pocket of his suit jacket and held the ring out to her.

Her lips parted, but she was so surprised that she couldn't even gasp at the enormous diamond on a delicate band. She had hardly any breath to choke out, "Is that real?"

"Of course it's real!" If he'd had facial expressions, she would have thought he was almost offended.

"Did you expense it?" she squeaked.

"No!" He hid it in his pocket, then took both her hands in his. "Everything we do from here on out is real."

She stared at the lapel of his coat, where the ring had disappeared. She should have bought him a real ring instead of a toy. Or should she? They stood in a rushing river with their former lives as corporate enemies on one bank and a future as lovers on the other. Every time she made a decision to head one way, he turned in the opposite direction.

"Wendy," he said. "Are you still with me?"

She nodded.

He watched her for a moment more, looking for something in her eyes. Whether he found it or not, she had no idea, but he let her hands go. "Now we need to tell Lorelei and Colton that we're getting married and we want them to be witnesses. Remind Lorelei we work for rival companies and we have to keep it secret. That way, she won't squeal in the middle of the party."

"I know," Wendy said. "We went over this before."

"Just making sure." He put his hand on her shoulder. "You don't look well."

Right. She needed to get over her sentimental squeamishness. She still had a job to do.

She stood on her tiptoes and kissed him on the lips. "See you at the limo."

"Would you like to say a few words?" Elvis asked Wendy.

She glanced at him, then over his shoulders at the massive display of plastic calla lilies on the dais where they stood. Daniel waited in front of her.

Lorelei and Colton watched from the red carpet that stretched down the aisle of the tiny chapel, standing at a noticeable distance from each other. She thought she'd seen them having an argument at the party. She'd been afraid Lorelei or Colton would storm out of the club, and she'd hurried over to placate them. But they'd insisted everything was fine.

The aisle stretched past four rows of empty pews to the chapel doors. There were no windows for photographers to take pictures through, thank God, or all this would have been for nothing. There were windows above the doors, though. Both bodyguards and Colton's driver waited outside, guarding their privacy from the paparazzi. Their cigarette smoke curled behind the glass.

No, Wendy thought. She didn't want to say a few words at her own wedding. She just wanted to get this over with.

But Daniel looked haggard at the end of his fourth long night in a row, with the purple bruise not quite faded under one eye, and oh so handsome. She probably shouldn't, but she did have something to say to him.

"Daniel," she began.

His eyes widened at her, warning her not to make a joke and give them away.

She wanted to tell him to chillax. Instead, she said, "This year, I've traveled to Los Angeles, Seattle, Paris, and Rome to assist the rich and famous with their problems. This month I've resurrected the career of Satan and his band, and I've tried and failed to stop a rock princess from having her bare buttocks posted online."

Wendy was interrupted by a farting noise. She, Daniel, and Elvis all looked toward the red carpet. Lorelei's tongue was sticking out. She was blowing Wendy a gentle raspberry.

Wendy turned back to Daniel. "And yet I can unequivocally say that the most interesting time of my whole life has been the time I've spent with you."

She expected his face to remain unchanged, even if his emotion actually went from patient to exasperated. To her astonishment, she detected a movement in his jaw, as if she'd elicited an actual emotion so strong that it made his face move—almost into a facial expression. She still couldn't tell which one.

As she was contemplating this, Elvis turned to Daniel. She thought Elvis would have to remind Daniel that he was being asked to say a few words at his own wedding. She hoped not, because if Daniel seemed too bored, Lorelei and Colton might suspect the whole wedding was a publicity ploy.

To her surprise, Daniel said, "Wendy," looking straight at her. "When you make me laugh, I feel like I'm finally alive again."

His expression could have been anything. Anger? Fear? Love? This last thought made tears form at the corners of her eyes. To keep herself from crying, she stuck out her bottom lip in fake sympathy for him.

He laughed. There in the middle of their cheeseball wedding, he genuinely laughed with the corners of his dark eyes crinkling. He stepped forward and took her hand.

Elvis moved forward through the ceremony. Wendy watched Daniel grinning at her. Her hand tingled where her palm met his. The tingle spread warmly up her arm and across her chest.

"Do you have any vows?" Elvis asked next.

Daniel cut his eyes toward Elvis, then back toward Wendy, and his lips parted. He was about to make up an excuse. Or, worse, a vow he didn't mean.

Wendy cut him off. "Better not," she said. "After all, it's Vegas."

This time everyone laughed, but Daniel's eyes looked worried. He squeezed her hand as if to give them both the strength to get through the rest of this.

Elvis said, "Then, by the power vested in me by the state of Nevada, I now pronounce you husband and wife."

Wendy went cold. She actually felt all the blood draining out of her brain, and she thought she might faint. She was calculating how *that* rumor would spread through the tabloids, and whether it would get warped into good publicity or bad publicity for Lorelei, when Daniel stepped forward and reached one stable hand around the small of her back.

"You may—" Elvis said.

Daniel pushed his other hand into her hair.

"—kiss the—"

Daniel eased her backward. His dark eyes met her eyes for a moment before his lips found hers.

He kissed her deeply, but she felt more than the kiss. She felt her whole body melting into his.

It was going to be really bad when they got divorced.

Lorelei and Colton burst into applause and wolf whistles. High-class. But it made Wendy happy, and when Daniel finally broke the kiss and stood her up straight, he was laughing again.

Mission accomplished.

In the wee hours of the morning, when most of the party guests had stumbled down to the casino to lose some money before finally making it back to their hotel rooms, and the pounding music had shut down, Lorelei swayed her way across the club to bring Wendy a flute of champagne. "To you," she said, tapping Wendy's glass with her own.

Wendy took a long sip. She needed it.

But then she said, "No, to *you*. I didn't expect the press to ask you about my wedding. I didn't prep you, but you handled it exactly right. You denied you got married, but you never said you'd been to your PR rep's wedding, so you didn't throw me to the wolves. I'm proud of you!"

"You told me not to admit I was friends with anybody who wasn't famous," Lorelei said.

"I did tell you that, but I didn't expect you to remember it when you were under pressure." Wendy leaned back against the wall, satisfied. "My little chickadee has flown away. You don't need me anymore."

Lorelei gasped. "No! You're quitting?"

"Of course not! I couldn't quit anyway. Your contract is with Stargazer. I could quit the company, but I couldn't quit you. They'd just send someone else. I'm saying your crisis is over."

"Well, I might let you go back home now. But I still want you to handle stuff for me when it comes up." Lorelei pointed her flute at Wendy. "And when there's an event like this, I want you to come party with me."

"Even if I'm the downer?"

"Especially if you're the downer. I had a lot of fun with you this week. I know you said I'm not supposed to be friends with bodyguards and hairdressers and people like that, but I feel like you and I are friends, and not just because I'm paying you."

"I feel like that, too," Wendy said honestly. "I've felt like that ever since the first morning when I heard you sing. I knew you were special. And I already thought you had killer taste in shoes. Come here, pretty girl."

They hugged each other, careful not to spill their champagne. Wendy rubbed Lorelei's bare arm and was surprised to feel chill bumps. She was a real person, of course—Wendy's job was all about helping the stars when they turned up human—but it still came as a little shock when Lorelei looked so flawless.

Wendy let her go. "Let's talk about tomorrow, because we'll both be so busy that we might lose track of each other. Daniel and I have arranged for you and your whole posse to ride back to Los Angeles with

Colton in his limo. You'll hop in and be off the instant the show is over."

"Really?" Lorelei complained. "What a bummer!"

Wendy shook her head firmly. "Sorry. Right now, during the week with the city kind of dead, it's reasonably safe for you to go out. After the show on Friday night, when so many extra people have been pumped into town for the awards show and the weekend, and when they've seen your awesome act onstage, you won't be able to go anywhere. You had a great party tonight. Know beforehand that you'll spend tomorrow night in the limo, sipping more champagne. When you get to L.A., they'll drop you at home, and you'll sleep until Tuesday."

"The paparazzi will be camped outside my house when I get there," Lorelei griped. "They'll see me getting out of Colton's limo, and they'll think we really did get married. You know, some tabloids don't like him and think he's overconfident. They call him Colton Fart."

"That," Wendy said, "is my husband's problem."

"I don't know," Lorelei said. "Until they figure out we really didn't get married, do you think they'll call *me* Lorelei Fart?"

"Maybe," Wendy acknowledged, "but it's cute. Colton Fart is not cute. Colton sounds as big as mountains, and his fart would be powerful. Lorelei Fart sounds like a baby passing gas, or a little fairy."

Lorelei laughed. "Why do I ask you stuff?"

Wendy yawned. "I don't know."

"Okay, I'll ride with Colton back to L.A.," Lorelei said, tilting a little on her high heels. Wendy could tell she would need to have this whole conversation again with the wardrobe mistress.

"Now you're going to bed, right?" Wendy checked. She didn't have to add that she wanted Lorelei to go to bed alone, without Colton. He'd left a few minutes before with his bodyguard and driver. Wendy thought again that something had gone wrong between him and Lorelei. But after all, this was what Wendy had wanted for Lorelei: to pretend to fall in love, not actually do it. Actually doing it was Wendy's mistake alone.

"Promise me you won't get up until you need to go to the theater tomorrow for the show," Wendy said. "I'll come wake you."

"Okay," Lorelei said. "What are *you* doing now? You're going to bed, too, finally, right? With Daniel." She gave Wendy an exaggerated wink.

"Ha," Wendy said, unable to call up enough mirth. "Not like you mean. Daniel told me he has to get up in three hours for a breakfast appointment. I am like, screw that. I'm sleeping for *four* hours before I go back to work."

It was just as well. She wasn't sure whether they were supposed to have a wedding night or not. The inevitable awkward scene was more than she could handle, dead as she felt.

Still, she found herself touching the strangely heavy ring on her finger and searching the shadows of the club for Daniel. He'd sent Colton to bed with other members of his entourage so he could wait for her . . . and there he was at the long, dark bar, sipping from a tumbler and watching her over the rim.

"But after the awards show tomorrow night"— Lorelei grinned—"you and Daniel are going to bed."

16

$\sim$

Rumors are running rampant that last night, embattled exes Colton Farr and Lorelei Vogel took a break from her twenty-first-and-a-half birthday party at posh club Wet Dream to get hitched at a Las Vegas chapel. Farr acknowledges he and Vogel are back together but has vehemently denied they are married.

We caught up with Vogel after she returned to her party. She elaborated when we asked whether the wedding was genuine or a stunt. "Two dear friends of ours did get married," she told us. "The wedding wasn't staged for publicity. If you'd been there, you would have known this was true. It was only a Vegas quickie marriage, but it was the most romantic wedding I've ever been to. I have never seen two people more in love."

Fond words about that mystery couple—or perhaps coy words about herself and Farr?

Farr will emcee the Hot Choice Awards televised
live tonight at 8 p.m. (EDT), and Vogel's newly formed
band will be the featured musical guest.

Daniel didn't have time for his morning routine of
room service breakfast and online perusal of what he
was missing in politics. But as he carefully unlocked
the door so he wouldn't wake Wendy and stepped
into the hall, the national newspaper was waiting. He
quietly closed the door behind him and turned to the
entertainment section. The little article about Colton
and Lorelei was one of the front-page blurbs.

Daniel wanted to burst back into the room, shake
Wendy awake, and give her a huge hug with the news.
She would likely kill him, though, if she felt like he'd
felt when his alarm went off.

He plastered the paper against the wall and pulled
his pen from his coat. Outlining the blurb with a
heart, he scribbled in the margin, "Job saved! Great
work!" He snuck back into the room and set the paper
next to her laptop, where she would see it first thing.
With a final long look back at her, just the golden mess
of her hair visible above the covers, he shut the door.

He was already in the elevator when he began to
have second thoughts. A *heart*? He'd encircled the
blurb with a *heart*? He hadn't done something that
dorky since his punk band dedicated a song to a girl
he liked who promptly walked out of the club in re-

sponse. And *Job saved! Great work!* was something he would say to one of his employees, not his wife.

He entertained the thought of going back to the room and retrieving the paper before she could see it, like a total loser. Glancing at his watch, he saw that would make him late for breakfast with a second movie producer interested in having Colton audition. He tried to get his head back into work and let Wendy go.

Only he couldn't. All through his meal with the producer, he thought about the way her hair had spun golden across the pillows. When their meeting ended, he found she'd texted him in response to the newspaper article—*Yay!!!!*—and he stared at one word and four exclamation points for a long time, trying and failing to come up with something clever to text back. For the next few hours, as he met with reporters gathered at the theater to cover the awards show, he remembered his night with her, how he'd spent his scant three hours of sleep spooning her with his hands underneath her T-shirt, on her breasts, and she had folded her hands possessively over his. Finally, when he got a free moment an hour before the awards show began, he called her.

"Hey, lovah," she answered.

"Where are you?"

"In Lorelei's dressing room, getting our hair done. Where are *you*?"

"In Colton's dressing room, making sure he doesn't produce a flask." He grinned at Wendy's musical laughter.

Colton scowled across the room at him, and not because he'd heard Daniel's low words. More likely, he was confused that Daniel was laughing. Daniel was confused, too. Confused and happy. He stepped into the bustling corridor.

"When's your flight to L.A.?" Wendy asked.

"Tomorrow afternoon. How about your flight to New York?" He didn't cross his fingers, but he wanted to.

"Same time," she said. "So, what's on your schedule after this show?"

The loaded tone of her voice made his groin tighten. He said, "A honeymoon."

"I can't wait," she whispered.

After they hung up, he called for reservations at the nicest restaurant he could think of. It was a huge struggle, possibly the single hardest thing he'd done on this trip, to wipe the smile off his face before he reentered Colton's dressing room.

Hours later, as the awards show drew to a close, he stood at the back of the packed theater, watching Colton announce the last number from Lorelei and her band. As soon as the most anticipated award was announced and the credits rolled, Colton and Lorelei would be hustled by security into the waiting limo and hurried out of town. With only five minutes of air time left for the stars to screw up, Daniel started to relax. His job here was done.

A movement in the corner of his eye caught his attention. Wendy had the same idea he'd had. On the other side of the theater, she came in through another back door and leaned against the wall, watching Lorelei's band start playing in a cloud of dry-ice fog. Then Wendy saw Daniel and smiled. They walked toward each other and met in the middle.

For the rest of the song, they stood next to each other. He didn't want her to catch him staring at her, but he took surreptitious glances. She wore a stylish gray suit with a deep blue blouse that made her eyes stand out, as blue as the Vegas sky. She'd caught her hair back in a long, loose ponytail.

Gorgeous as she was, though, the prettiest thing about her was her smile. Seeming to forget he stood beside her, she gazed at Lorelei onstage like a proud sister. He was glad this job had finally worked out for her. She deserved this moment.

The song ended. The applause was thunderous. Lorelei bowed for the standing ovation long after the on-air lights had blinked off and the show had cut to the last commercial. When the crowd finally died down to the point that they could hear each other, Daniel leaned over and said in Wendy's ear, "Wow."

Wendy beamed. "Isn't she great?"

"She is," Daniel said. "Her concert tour is definitely saved."

"And Colton has been riveting and charming!" Wendy sounded exactly as astonished by this as Daniel felt.

He laughed. "You told me a couple of days ago that everyone famous has some talent. I'm beginning to see your point. Colton has been totally unlike himself to-night. He's a terrific actor."

"See?" Wendy's smile faded as she asked, "Have you noticed he and Lorelei aren't as into each other as they were when we caught them macking on the couch? I think they had a fight."

"He hasn't mentioned it to me," Daniel said, "but yeah, I think they've cooled off. I hope it won't be a problem. I've been thinking a lot about something else you said, that we need to make sure our solutions for the stars are what's good for them long-term. I've tried to impress on him that even if he and Lorelei break up for good, he can't attack her again, publicly or otherwise. That's not how adults operate, even famous ones."

"Unless he gets a reality show."

Daniel almost didn't say it because he didn't want to jinx it. But he was becoming accustomed to sharing everything with Wendy, and he couldn't keep this in. "Talks are going well. I think we'll get him a movie. A big one."

Wendy nodded and grinned. "After his performance tonight, I'd say it's a sure thing." She held out her arms.

Daniel walked into her hug. His whole body woke up when she whispered in his ear, "Congratulations." As the on-air lights blinked and the audience obediently applauded for Colton's last stage entrance and the last award, Daniel and Wendy gave each other one last squeeze and backed away. He noticed she still wore the diamond ring.

.

"You really know how to take a girl to dinner," Wendy said.

They sat at a terrace table for two, with tourists strolling the Strip below them, palm trees and strings of lights above them, and a gentle breeze fingering Daniel's hair. She hadn't seen service like this since a stop at Commander's Palace on a mission to New Orleans last year. The food was delicious, plentiful, and not too eccentric, just the way this West Virginia girl liked it. And after her half of a bottle of wine, she'd lost most of her worries over where the night was leading them.

Maybe the wine was tricking her, but she thought he was enjoying himself as much as she was, even though he hadn't said so. She teased him, "You're being awfully quiet, even for a quiet person. What's wrong? Having second thoughts?"

"Actually, yes."

She kept smiling. There was no reason to be angry with him about this. He'd said from the outset that this wedding, though real, wasn't serious. If she'd fallen for him in the meantime and was beginning to be sorry the marriage meant nothing, that was her own fault.

He said, "I wanted us to get married because it solved a problem. That's what I do."

"Right," she said sharply, wishing her tone would cut him off.

No such luck. "You told me you didn't want to do it, and I bullied you into it."

"Oh." This wasn't what she'd expected him to say. "Well," she began again in a softer tone, "you made a logical argument and I agreed with you. I wouldn't say you bullied me."

"I know women take weddings very seriously," he said. "There are so many reality shows about weddings and cakes and dresses. People have subscriptions to whole magazines about this, and they keep the subscriptions even when they're not getting married. Women pick out their wedding dresses when they're eight years old."

"You sound awfully familiar with this scenario, Mr. Blackstone. Do you have a collection of veils that you want to tell me about?"

He winked at her. Then shushed her because she was laughing too loudly.

"No," he said, "but I've dated this scenario repeatedly, and my sister is the same way. I knew all that, Wendy, but I made you feel, if that was your personal position, that you should give it up for the sake of business. That's what I'm sorry for. I was watching your face during the ceremony. There was one point when I was sure you were going to faint."

"And that would have been terrible PR," Wendy joked. "Difficult to cover up. These pesky ambulances that keep following us around."

"You're not listening to me."

"I am," she said with equal gravity. "I hear you. But I'm not that girl. I've met this girl you're describing. There are a lot of her out there. That girl is in love with weddings, or with the idea of getting married. I was never like that. In West Virginia, people didn't understand me. When I first got to New York, though, I thought I would get married someday. I would meet some fast-talking funny guy who loved art and good parties and traveling. He was part of my new future.

"But even then, I concentrated more on the fact that we would be soul mates and we would bop around New York together. The idea of what dress I would wear to my wedding never entered my mind, I promise you. And gradually, even the idea of this guy faded, because he didn't exist. I dated, but nothing ever lasted. I discovered, to my utter astonishment, that I am hard to get along with."

She choked a little on her last few words and was embarrassed into silence. He watched her solemnly, his face unreadable as ever. The neon lights of the Strip danced behind him.

She found her voice again. "Even when I thought it would happen, I didn't care so much about the wedding itself. I cared about the vow. Some people wouldn't want to swear to love someone for the rest of their lives if they didn't really mean it because God would be watching them. Some people wouldn't want the government to sign off on that officially if they didn't mean it. But to me, the person I feel like I'm letting down is myself. I mean, both our jobs are set up around spinning the facts. Coming as close as we can to lying without going over. Going ahead and lying if that's what we need to do to get the job done. But at the end of the day, I guess I don't want to lie about *that*. I don't want to lie to myself, about myself."

He took a sip of wine. The cheap gold band she'd given him glowed on his finger in the soft light. She marveled all over again at how he could look so masculine and elegant simultaneously. But what she saw was what she got: a professional, an elitist, with his priorities in all the wrong places, but at heart a genuinely kind man.

She prompted him, "You're *still* awfully quiet for a quiet guy."

He smiled grimly. "You've made me feel worse."

"Don't. I could have said no." She reached forward and covered his hand with hers. "Anyway, to me, the real beauty of a wedding isn't the dress or the flowers or the chapel or Elvis. It's finding the right person to be with, and—"

He broke in, "I already have."

She flushed with warmth. "I was about to say the same thing."

He looked at their hands on the table for a moment, then looked up at her. He held her gaze for so long that her skin tingled with anticipation. She knew exactly what he meant by that look, and what he wanted.

However, because he was Daniel, he asked politely, "Would you like dessert?"

"Yes, I would," she said with gusto. "If you know what I mean."

He gaped at her in outrage but couldn't hold the expression when he was overtaken by a laughing fit. He held up one finger and the check suddenly appeared in front of him. As he took out his wallet, he said under his breath, "This night is going to be even better than I thought."

He shut the door of their room behind them. The lamps were off. The only light was the neon in the panoramic view of the casinos across the street. She watched his body move in that soft glow as he turned the dead bolt. They were locked in together.

He turned and stopped, seeming surprised that she was watching him. The vague light softened his features but highlighted his cheekbones and the perfect arch of his brow, like a stylized sculpture of a man rather than the real thing. His eyes were so dark that in the shadows, she could only tell he was looking at her by the reflection of the window, a light in his eye that disappeared momentarily when he blinked.

The silence stretched into awkwardness. She wanted to tell him that *he* might be racking his brain for something to say in the uncomfortable silence, but *she* was not. She was content to pause in this rare, magical space between one stage of their relationship and the next, taking in how handsome he was, and how lucky she was that he had ever kissed her.

His lips parted. He took a slow breath to speak. She was afraid he would say he'd changed his mind. They'd gotten married for work, and now they should go their separate ways.

To prevent those words from crossing his lips, she spoke up so suddenly that he blinked again. "My friends will die when I tell them we waited until we got married to have sex."

He threw back his head and laughed. Then tried to stop himself from laughing and couldn't, holding his side and choking a little.

She loved to watch him laugh. It happened so rarely, and this was the longest she'd seen his laughter go on. To prolong it a bit more, she added, "I don't know about you, but saving myself for marriage is somewhat out of character for me."

Still laughing, he placed one hand on the wall behind her and leaned in, so close that she caught a whiff of his cologne. She suppressed a shudder at the chill that raced through her.

He said, "I'm glad you wanted to be pure for me."

Now Wendy cracked up. Through her giggles, she said, "Sorry. I haven't been pure since I was fifteen. And if my virginal status in the marriage bed is important to you, we should never discuss my sophomore year in college. Also, 2009."

"It's the thought that counts," he said in a sexy rumble. Still bracing himself on the wall above her with one hand, he used the other hand to stroke a lock of hair that framed her face. "But that's okay. I like my women experienced."

Her snort of laughter was cut short as he kissed her.

He held her in place while he explored her mouth, his tongue delving deep, his teeth nipping at her lips. His hand slid seductively down her neck, pressed her breast underneath her silk blouse, and sneaked past the waistband of her trousers to stroke her through her panties. This time she didn't mind that he could feel how wet she was.

He removed his hands from her and stood up straight.

She opened her eyes, blinking at him in the darkness. She'd made a joke out of sex before, but she was past that stage now, and if he tried to get out of it, she was going to be angry. "Why'd you stop?" she whispered.

"We're married now," he growled, "and I'm a gentleman. I'm not going to spend our wedding night fucking you against the wall."

"Really?" she asked, letting him hear her disappointment. "Are you *ever* going to fuck me against the wall? Because that gentleman thing is overrated in my opinion."

"Later in our marriage," he promised her. "When we're older, and we plan a rare escape, trying to recapture the youthful exuberance we used to have in our relationship."

"Oh." That sucked. This whole joke sucked.

"Like, tomorrow." He led her over to the bed. The stripes of moonlight and colored light rippled over his features as he moved. He stopped her at the foot of the bed and gently pushed her suit jacket off her shoulders. "Turn around and let me unzip you," he said.

She faced the dresser with the mirror above it. Her ponytail was intact so far, her figure looking pretty good in suit pants she'd had made on a trip to Hong Kong. The dark figure of Daniel stood over her, watching her in the mirror, then focusing on the catch at the back of her neck. She felt it unfasten and the zipper move down her back, and she shuddered.

Still watching her, he unclasped her bra, then moved his hands beneath her clothes, brushing along her skin. In the mirror she could see his hands skimming her body, moving around to her front, just as she felt her breasts tingling with his touch. His fingers thumbed her nipples until a gasp escaped her lips.

And then his mouth was on her neck, making all her senses go wild. She couldn't get enough air as she lowered her chin to give him better access to the back of her neck. Just as she thought she couldn't stand any more, he moved her blouse and bra together off her arms and down her body, letting the garments pool on the floor. He nudged her pants down her hips. She stood in front of the mirror in nothing but her panties and high heels.

"You are beautiful," he whispered. "I can hardly believe you're mine." He slipped one hand from her breast down her side, along her hip, to cover her panties with his warmth. His fingers explored downward.

Suddenly his hand stopped, and his eyes widened at her in the mirror. He growled, "Are these crotchless panties?"

"Maybe."

"Did you bring these with you to Vegas from New York, like you knew you would need them?"

She'd bought them in another mad dash through the mall that afternoon. She *should* have brought some from home, because just when she didn't bring them, she needed them. They were like the bunny ears and clip-on tail in that regard. But Daniel seemed outraged, and she found this funny. So she only pointed out, "You brought latex gloves."

He continued to stare at her.

"I thought I might get married while I was here," she said, "and then I would need them."

"We will talk about this later."

"Really? Will you punish me?"

"Definitely."

"Will you spank me?"

"I think the punishment should fit the crime, don't you?" He pushed his fingers inside her.

She arched her back, allowing his fingers to shove deeper. Her ass rubbed against the front of his pants, and she found out how hard he was for her. She felt coiled and tight, ready to spring.

Finally she turned to face him and started to unbutton his shirt from the top. He unbuttoned from the bottom and they met in the middle, his fingers still slick from being inside her. She moved the sides of his shirt away and slid the sleeves down his arms and off him, letting the carefully tailored garment crumple to the floor and wondering whether this was bothering him right now. It didn't seem to bother him. Before she'd even had time to run her hands across his solid muscles, so beautiful in the moonlight, he'd bent his head to suckle her breast.

It was hard for her to concentrate while she endured such pleasure, but she managed to reach forward and fumble with his belt buckle, then the catch of his suit pants and his zipper. She tried to push everything down together. He raised his head and took over for her, kicking off his shoes and disrobing completely. He sat down on the bed, gorgeous in the moonlight like a marble statue, the planes of his muscles shining in contrast with the dark shadows between them.

She didn't want to ruin the mood by bringing this up, but she had to. "I'm on the pill, but do you have a—"

As she said this, he was already reaching for his pants. He pulled out his wallet and unfolded it to find a condom. He looked into her eyes and paused a moment, as if he understood what she was thinking. It was so strange that she was on the pill, protected from pregnancy, yet they were still using a condom like they hardly knew each other, like this was sex with a near stranger. Which it was.

Except that they were married.

The moment passed. He sheathed himself. Before she could step away or think of a joke, he was pulling her by the wrists toward him, then by the buttocks, pressing her center down on his erect cock. He brought her down on him so far that it took her breath away. He urged her to impale herself on him over and over, until she was boneless with want.

He lifted her off him and stood up. Then he turned her around and pressed her down until her head was on the bed, her ponytail spilling across the covers. Her ass was thrust in the air, higher than it should have been courtesy of her high heels, waiting for him. He ran his fingers up and down her crease, moving her slickness around, and then once more inserted himself through the hole in her panties, finding her center and then shoving himself all the way inside her at once, making her cry out.

"Touch yourself," he whispered.

Obediently she lowered one shoulder to the bed to brace herself while she reached back with the other hand to finger her clit. Her whole sex immediately clenched around him. He cursed and grasped her by both hips, his fingers digging into her flesh as he thrust himself into her harder and faster.

She lost herself, spiraling out of control under her hand as she came. His dick pounded inside her until, with a final groan, he found his own release.

Panting into her shoulder, he stroked her a few more times before easing down onto the bed, cradling her body against his.

She took a few deep, satisfied breaths. Finally she said, "Well, that'll leave a mark."

He eased a possessive hand over her bruised hip.

They lay together for a few quiet minutes. Wendy got lost in them. She closed her eyes and let herself enjoy the sensations: the warmth of his body all along hers, the tingles that still ran up and down her arms, the shakiness she felt deep inside.

He murmured, "You're uncharacteristically quiet, even for a quiet person."

She snorted. "I just got my brains fucked out. Give me a minute."

He rolled away from her, off the bed. She bounced a little at the sudden shift of his weight. "I'll give you five." He smacked her ass.

"Oh, it's going to be like that, is it?" Her mouth was still full of sass, but her body didn't have the energy to back it up. She watched, motionless, as he walked toward the bathroom, exquisitely naked.

He turned suddenly. "Do you need your hair washed?"

"You enjoyed that?"

"Yes," he said immediately.

"I washed it this morning. I managed with just two hands. Apparently I only need help when I'm hurt and pitiful."

He made it back to the bed in two long strides. His muscular arms held him hovering above her as he growled, "You have never been pitiful in your life."

He kissed her. Both hands cradled her head and

held her steady while his tongue swept inside her mouth, possessing her totally. With a final peck on the lips, he lifted himself from her and closed himself in the bathroom.

She hugged herself on the bed, her body awash in the afterglow, her mind for once a decadent blank.

When he stepped back into the bedroom in a cloud of steam, she was still huddled on the bed in exactly the same position as when he'd left her. As he'd figured, he was hard for her again already. If she'd fallen asleep, he was going to explode.

But as he moved closer, she turned her head to look up at him. "I guess you've come for that favor I offered you yesterday."

He sat down beside her on the edge of the bed. "Yes."

She slid onto the floor and walked on her knees until she was directly in front of him. He reached to the back of her head and carefully pulled out the band holding her ponytail. Her curls spilled past her shoulders, covering her breasts. Only her nipples peeked out.

"You are beautiful," he told her reverently. "You have always been beautiful. I've wanted you since college."

She looked up at him through long lashes. "What are you really saying? You thought about me while you masturbated?"

He laughed shortly. "That might have happened, but for the record, we are neither confirming nor denying."

He took in a sharp breath as she reached for him. Exhaled again in a huff as she wrapped her hand around his dick.

"Did it feel like this?" she asked, watching him.

He shook his head. "No, this is better."

He ached with pleasure as she massaged him slowly, her hands moving up and down his erect shaft. Finally she scooted forward until her lips nearly touched the tip of him. Looking up at him, she asked, "Is this what you wanted when you masturbated? Is this what you pictured when you came?"

"Yes," he said, one syllable that transformed into a gasp as she put out her tongue to taste him.

"You know," she said casually, as if he couldn't feel her warm breath on his cock, "Sarah and Tom told me yesterday that I do anything you tell me without complaining. They seem to think you have some kind of power over me."

"Let's see." He placed one hand under her chin and gently guided her forward.

He loved how she looked as she sucked him, her thick hair brushed back over her shoulders so he could see her face. One long tendril, dark with dampness, snaked down her forehead and stuck to her cheek.

On a sigh at a particularly intense stroke of her tongue, he commented, "Don't worry. This won't take long."

She managed to remove her lips from him before she bent her head in a fit of coughing and laughing. When she'd collected herself, she looked up at him and grinned. "Don't make me laugh when your dick is in my mouth."

"Sorry."

"Injuries." She opened her mouth wide and took him inside her.

As she kneeled at his feet and sucked his cock greedily, he flashed back to two nights before, when he'd watched her pole dance for him, all tease and no strip. This woman had been bullied, but she still found the strength to give him freely what another man had coerced from her. Daniel took it gratefully. She stroked and circled his member with her tongue, and he groaned with pleasure.

When he wove his fingers into her hair so that she couldn't have backed away if she tried, she opened wider for him and sucked him more eagerly. She was only playacting at being his submissive lover, he knew, but she seemed to be enjoying every second. He felt the same way.

Of course, they weren't *really* playacting, were they? Because his dick really was shoved into her mouth. The more his misgivings compounded, the more she tightened her lips around him. He responded with deeper thrusts until he suddenly cursed and released himself down her throat.

Still panting, he placed his fingertips underneath

her chin and tilted her face up until she met his gaze. "Are you okay?"

She nodded, out of breath herself.

He stood and reached down to help her up, then pulled her onto the bed and under the covers with him. Half asleep already, he rolled on top of her and kissed her long on the mouth. The way their bodies craved each other, he knew it wouldn't be long before he rose into her again.

She woke once more, blinking at the afternoon sunlight glinting off the other casinos through the window. Sore from his manhandling and too much lying down, slowly she rolled under his caging arm to face him. He watched her through sleepy eyes.

She raised her eyebrows in question.

He gave her a devilish smile, grabbed a condom from the nightstand, and crawled on top of her. As the night had crept into morning and bloomed into afternoon, they'd talked less, and she'd lost her jokes. All that was left was his body joining with hers.

After she reached climax and he spilled himself inside her, he stayed in her, covering her body with his, nuzzling her neck. "Wendy."

"I know," she said to the ceiling. "We have to go soon."

"I need to fly to L.A. and see what's wrong with Victor," he said. "But I'm inclined to blow a client off for the first time ever. Could you?"

"Nothing has ever sounded better," she said truthfully, "but I can't. Everything's probably fixed with Stargazer, but I can't afford to assume. I need to be in the office bright and early on Monday morning, talk with my bosses, and seal the deal."

"I shouldn't have asked." He smoothed his hand down her belly and cupped his hand between her thighs.

"We have a few hours, though," she said. "You said you regret never experiencing the cities you visit for work. If we hurried, we could check one cheesy Vegas tourist experience off your list."

"Besides getting married?" he whispered in her ear.

"Yes, besides that." She glanced out the window. Her eyes landed on the Eiffel Tower, and she remembered that Sarah had warned her they wouldn't be able to describe falling in love to their kids if they didn't get more romantic. "It's been two whole months since I was in Paris. What do you think?"

17

Wendy realized too late that they should have stayed in the room. They hadn't even made it out of the casino when their afternoon went south. No sooner had they stepped out of the hotel elevator and started across the crazy casino carpet, hand in hand, than Daniel stopped and swore. Wendy looked in the direction of his gaze. Colton sat at a blackjack table.

"He was supposed to ride back to L.A. with Lorelei last night. What is he doing here?" Wendy exclaimed needlessly, because Daniel was obviously wondering the same thing. Angrily.

He dropped her hand. With Wendy trailing behind him, he stalked to the blackjack table and stood there with his arms folded. She had the briefest thought that the man at the table wasn't Colton after all but the rumored lookalike, the phantom of Rick.

But she didn't have time to put her hand out and back Daniel away before Colton—and it *was* Colton—looked up at them, then did a double take. Turning away from them, he peeked at the new cards the dealer slid him, gave up on his hand, and stood up smiling. He came toward Daniel with his arm outstretched for a handshake.

Daniel kept his arms folded, his face expressionless.

Colton glanced at Wendy in question. She didn't have any answers, so he slowly withdrew his hand and explained in a rush, "Lorelei and I had a fight. The limo dropped me off at the outskirts of town and I took a taxi back here. Look, nobody notices me when I don't have my posse with me. Of course, you're about to ruin that." He chuckled nervously.

"I quit," Daniel said.

Colton gaped at him. "You can't quit. You said I can't fire you. I have a contract with your company, not with you."

"Then talk to them," Daniel said, "but I'm not working for you anymore. I told you what to do, and you didn't do it." Without another word, he headed across the casino for the front doors onto the Strip, seeming to forget Wendy completely.

She was left standing awkwardly with Colton, who asked her, "*Now* will you work for me?"

"No," Wendy said impatiently, "but I'll talk to Daniel for you when he calms down. In the meantime, for God's sake, don't pee on anything. Or post anything online. And no call girls."

"I haven't!" Colton protested, but she was already following Daniel across the floor. She was pissed that he'd gotten so angry. She was more pissed that he was taking it out on her, leaving her to trail after him like a puppy.

He must have realized this because, though he didn't look any happier, he was waiting for her by the exit. "Sorry," he grumbled, opening the door for her. "I hate this job. I hate it more now that it's going to prevent us from being together."

As she moved into the hot, too-bright sunlight, she tossed over her shoulder, "There's always Senator Rowling," half hoping he would consider this an option now that he'd clearly gone off the deep end.

He drew even with her on the sidewalk. They passed the paparazzi camped on the edge of the casino property, six or seven photographers hoping to snatch a shot of one of the lesser stars who'd appeared on the awards show last night.

When they could talk privately again, stepping into the crosswalk together, he said automatically, "I have to work for my dad."

"You don't *have* to work for your dad," she said. "I'd be willing to bet that before today, you said, 'I *have* to do everything my dad tells me,' but you just recused yourself from a case. That's not going to go over well in New York." She laughed humorlessly. "You could work for Senator Rowling, and the next time I get in trouble at Stargazer for speaking my mind, *I* could work for your dad."

"I don't think so," Daniel said. "He wants everyone in the company to be reserved."

Wendy humphed. "You have to use your inside voice? Yeah, that probably wouldn't work for me."

He opened the door of the Paris casino for her. She knew she should be looking around at the vast interior, designed as a vague approximation of outdoors in the real Paris, near the base of the Eiffel tower. But as they rode an escalator in silence to the second floor and she charged tickets for them to take an elevator to the top of the tower, it was all she could do to hold in her tears. His words stung. She knew she wasn't reserved. She seemed to be the only person who wasn't bothered by this. She'd *thought* he liked her style of speaking, but apparently he only covered up his distaste for her when he was trying to get her into bed.

The elevator was crowded. The observation deck was crowded, too, with tourists peering through the iron bars at a more distant, higher-up view of the fountain at the Bellagio. Daniel waited until some of them had bored of the mediocre view and escaped back down the elevator before he leaned one shoulder against the bars next to her and delivered his next blow. "Why don't *you* quit? We can't stay together when you're working for Stargazer and I'm with the Blackstone Firm, so you're trying to convince *me* to quit. I'm not going to work for Senator Rowling. That's a moot point. But if there's another job out there for me, I'm sure there's one for you, too."

She tried to keep the clipped anger out of her voice and sound reasonable as she said, "For Senator Rowling, you're talking about going into a completely different branch of PR, a jump from movie stars to politics, and from a large firm that handles lots of clients to the political campaign itself. Apples and oranges. If I wanted to get another job doing PR for movie stars, in New York there's Stargazer, there's the Blackstone Firm, and then it starts to go downhill."

"True," he said grudgingly.

"I could move to Hollywood. Lots of great firms there."

He stood straighter, towering over her. "Are you threatening me?"

She was starting to feel ill. "Don't look so angry."

"This is not my angry expression," he snapped. "This is my expression of rapt attention."

"And I'm not threatening you," she snapped right back. "I'm trying to solve a problem. Obviously I'm the only one."

He put his elbow on a guardrail, his chin in his hand, and looked toward Fremont. His face didn't give away how frustrated he felt, but his body language did. At least he was listening to her.

"What about your sister?" Wendy ventured. "You said she's interested in the family business. Can't she take it over instead of you?"

"Eventually, but she needs to finish her degree first. And my dad has been looking forward to retirement forever. He and my mom have a trip around the world planned. They haven't left New York except on business since . . ."

"2001?" Wendy asked.

"2001," he confirmed.

"But the Blackstone Firm is a large company," she said. "Surely there's someone else there who can take over until your sister graduates, and steer her in the right direction for a few years afterward."

"There is," Daniel agreed, "but that's not what my dad wants. He wants the Blackstone Firm to be run by a Blackstone, always."

"Why is that your problem?"

"Why are you bringing that up again? He's my dad. It's my family."

"Right, but why does that mean you have to do what they want? Why can't you do what *you* want?"

"I just can't."

"Since when? When your brother died?"

He took his arms off the guardrail and turned to her. Though his face remained impassive, the speed of his movements told her how angry he was. "You're psychoanalyzing me like I'm one of your clients. You should do a lot less of that."

"You should do a lot more of it," she countered. "All you're doing is putting a bandage on your clients' problems, stopping the hemorrhaging, and disguising them from the public. If you don't try to get to the root of the problem and fix that, the problem will just recur. Did it occur to you that Colton might have a gambling addiction? I'll bet that never crossed your mind."

"Somehow we've gotten back around to this same argument," Daniel said, "you telling me that you're doing this job better than me. At least, that's what you're pretending. But what you're really trying to do is get me to quit my job."

"I'm not trying to get you to quit your job, per se," she said. "I want you to be happy, and you don't seem happy."

"You know what would be easier? Let's get divorced, which is what we agreed to in the first place."

Face burning, she glanced around to see if they'd been overheard. They were the only ones left on the observation deck. Possibly they'd scared everyone else off with the accusations and threats they were hurling at each other.

Of course, that was ridiculous. Daniel would never have mentioned divorce if he'd thought someone else was listening. He'd made sure they were alone before he dealt her that blow. Decorum and appearance before everything.

With tears stinging her eyes now, unable to hold them back, she asked, "You would divorce me over your job?"

"You would divorce me over yours."

He held her gaze until she couldn't meet his anymore. She turned and looked out over the view from the romantic Eiffel Tower. All she could see were the roofs of the nearby casinos and traffic crawling by on the Strip on a dusty, unhappy afternoon.

"You *will* divorce me," he insisted, "if I don't do what you say. And I can assure you, that is never going to happen."

She could picture him staring her down angrily as he said this. She thought she could feel his stare. Determined not to look weak in front of him, like she couldn't face him, she turned to him angrily.

He was looking down at the walkway. His expression was a blank, but the hunch of his shoulders and the downcast direction of his eyes made him look hurt.

If he was hurt, there was a chance for them still. They could talk this out. He would have to look up at her, though, and want the same thing. She waited for him to do it.

His head moved, and her heart leaped. But his eyes slid over her and off again. He turned to look out over Vegas. He was waiting for this to be over.

"I'll go get my things from the room, then," she said, "and on Monday I'll have my lawyer work out the divorce and send you something. We don't have to see each other again."

She turned and walked around the observation deck toward the elevator, not expecting him to call her back, not feeling his eyes on her anymore, shifting her mind away from him completely. Her thoughts moved effortlessly back to New York. Her time with Lorelei had been a success. Lorelei still liked her. She would return to the office triumphant—unless there was a nasty contract or some other surprise waiting for Wendy when she got back to New York, but she didn't expect such a thing. Archie would make good on his promise of a promotion and a raise. She would move on to save the next spoiled star. She would be fine, so long as nobody ever mentioned Daniel Blackstone's name.

Waiting for the elevator, she looked down and realized she was still wearing her diamond ring. Correction: Daniel's ring. She should have given it back to him. That's what jilted brides did, right? She certainly didn't want this reminder on her finger, the band feeling cold now, like a medical instrument that would squeeze her finger off.

Sliding the ring off and slipping it into the pocket of her jeans, she turned around on the deck and looked back the way she'd come, half hoping Daniel had followed her and tiptoed a few steps behind her even now, waiting to apologize.

But that was a ridiculous idea. Daniel didn't tiptoe. She thought about him saying coldly, *Let's get divorced, which is what we agreed to in the first place,* and that pushed the memory of him looking down and seeming hurt out of her head. The elevator arrived. On the ride down, she held her breath, feeling that she was descending into the depths of a mineshaft. Back in the casino, she rode down the escalator and headed for the door to the Strip.

She paused beside a bank of giddy slot machines, unable to go on. She took a few shuddering breaths, trying to collect herself before she broke down in tears in public. PR professionals did not make scenes. Not over their own unimportant lives, especially.

Her skin turned to fire as a sharp point jabbed through her blouse and into her side. "It's Rick," a voice growled in her ear. "Remember me?" He wrapped his arm around her waist. "Don't scream. I've got a knife and I will gut your pretty belly. We're going to take some pictures."

18

Daniel moved from the side of the Eiffel Tower overlooking the Strip to the side with the dull view of concrete suburbia stretching toward brown mountains, because it matched his mood. His heart had been racing ever since Wendy mentioned moving to L.A., which had shocked him into blind anger. She couldn't leave New York. She just couldn't. Couples had fun together all the time and then let each other go because a relationship would be inconvenient. People in love did not let each other go.

Daniel knew this. He'd known it when he asked Wendy to marry him. He'd known it when he asked for a honeymoon. He'd known it when he picked this fight with her, but in the back of his mind he'd been hoping she would be the one to cave so he wouldn't have to deal with the inevitable.

But of course she'd been right. She'd been grasping for a solution to the problem and he'd refused to budge, but the solution was obvious. He hated his job. He'd always hated it. He'd taken it because he felt guilty that his brother was dead and he was not. He'd accepted that fate for years, right up until Wendy made him laugh. Now he remembered how happy his life could be. From now on, he wouldn't settle.

Rapping his knuckles on the iron rail to bring himself back to reality, he hurried to the elevator, half expecting to find Wendy along the way. He looked for her again in the casino and on the walk back to his hotel room. Outside the door, he rehearsed in his mind what he would say to her, more nervous than he'd ever been meeting a megastar, because this really mattered. He slid his card through the lock and cracked the door. "Wendy?"

Nothing.

Damn, he'd missed her. She must have packed the same way she unpacked, by flinging things. But as he walked in, he saw that she hadn't touched her clothes. She hadn't been back to the room.

He called her, texted her, and e-mailed her, increasingly alarmed when she didn't answer. She *always* answered *something*. She must be more pissed at him than he'd ever been at her.

He didn't have much time before he needed to leave for the airport to catch his flight to L.A., but he packed his suitcase as neatly as he could. He really needed to leave and she hadn't shown up. Pacing, he wondered whether he should pack her suitcase for her, on the off chance she suddenly appeared and they needed to rush out. If he didn't pack it, they were strangers. Enemies. If he did pack it, they were a married couple who'd had an awful quarrel.

He packed it.

She didn't show.

He sat on the bed, beating his brow with his fist. He would have to miss his flight and stay. He couldn't leave without her.

His phone rang and he dove for it. Thank God!

But it wasn't her, he realized as the ringtone played a few more notes. It was his father, barking at him in his clipped British accent that Olivia Query's baby daddy couldn't take the pressure anymore of his family living with another man. Though the world would find out with just a little digging the terrible secret that he'd served time in juvie, he'd agreed to be interviewed on a gossip show tomorrow, outing Victor Moore. *That* was the reason Daniel had to fly to L.A. tonight. He couldn't stay until Wendy returned.

Cursing his job, his father, Victor, and all baby daddies who had never heard of condoms, Daniel scribbled a note for Wendy on a hotel notepad: *Call me! I love you & I'm sorry.* This time he had no regrets leaving it on her suitcase, because he meant it.

At the airport, already making calls to pinpoint what had gone wrong in Olivia and Victor's marriage, besides everything, he sat down to wait at the gate for Wendy's flight. The call for first class was announced.

The rest of the plane boarded. The door was closed. The plane took off without Wendy.

Daniel called Sarah.

"She's angry with me," he admitted. "Would she decide to stay another day in Vegas on a whim? That sounds like her."

"Yeah, she might," Sarah said. "But not when she's been in so much trouble here lately. She loves this job more than life itself."

"So she said," Daniel murmured. "And if she did decide to stay an extra day, she would call you and tell you that, wouldn't she?"

"See, you know her pretty well."

"I do," Daniel said. "And no matter how mad she was, I don't think she'd disappear without checking in, especially because we got married, and—"

"You did *what*?" Sarah shrieked through the phone.

"Two nights ago we got married, with Lorelei and Colton at the ceremony," Daniel explained, "so the media would assume it was Lorelei and Colton tying the knot. Things were going okay, but this afternoon we had an argument and decided to get divorced. I didn't mean it, and I hope she didn't, either."

Sarah was silent so long that Daniel was about to ask if she was still there. He couldn't afford a dropped call right now—

"You got *married*?" she yelled. "Is that why she made Tom and me leave town, because we would have stopped her?"

"Yes, but—"

"You manipulative ass! I knew she was up to something. I let her get away with it because she hates my husband, *hates him*, and she's never said a word about it. We don't have to agree about everything just because we're friends. But I thought you were going to screw her, Daniel. I never would have left her alone if I'd thought you were going to *marry her*!"

Daniel rubbed his brow. "So you don't have any idea where she would have gone or who she would have contacted—"

"What if Rick really is after her, like you guys were thinking at first?" Sarah insisted. "Do you know how terrified she is of that guy? Do you know how hard she is to terrify?"

"Yes," he said, jogging through the airport with his suitcase rolling behind him. "I'll find her."

Back in the taxi, he phoned Detective Butkus, who dutifully took down the latest details of the saga but said he couldn't file a missing persons report until Wendy had been gone twenty-four hours. It sounded to the detective like Wendy was furious with Daniel and would come back when she was ready. If Daniel had been Detective Butkus, he would have thought the same thing. But as Sarah had said, Daniel knew Wendy pretty well. And he was scared for her.

Then he phoned his father and said he couldn't go to L.A. Someone else could go, or his father could go. When his father predictably started yelling, Daniel shouted back, "I am having a family emergency!" then hung up and blocked his father's calls.

The taxi dropped him off in front of the Paris casino. He wheeled his suitcase just inside the door, slipped the security guard he recognized from that afternoon a hundred-dollar bill, and showed him Wendy's picture on his phone. "Long blond hair," Daniel added. "Beautiful woman."

"Yeah," the guard said. "She left with some movie star, the one who's in town because he was on that TV show last night? He had his arm around her."

Daniel swallowed. "Colton Farr?"

The guard snapped his fingers. "Exactly!"

Daniel ran across the street to the casino where he'd been staying, dragging his suitcase, cursing the whole way. Just inside the door, he handed his suitcase off to a bellhop, along with another hundred and his business card, and asked him to call if Wendy was in the room or her suitcase was gone.

He hurried across the casino floor to the blackjack tables. Maybe Rick had been following Wendy around town. More likely, Colton himself, boor, emotional abuser, asshole, who'd wanted her from the very beginning, had taken her.

Daniel assumed what was becoming his usual position on the periphery of Colton's blackjack table and waited for Colton to notice him. Colton did his usual double take. He cursed with a vehement shake of his head, scooped up three ten-thousand-dollar chips and some change, and slammed away from the table. All his former deference to Daniel was gone.

He approached him with his own arms crossed and demanded, "*Now* what?"

Daniel nodded toward a door at the back of the huge room. "We need to talk in private." He led the way into the service corridor. He'd worked in this casino enough times to know that the hallway where they were headed had no traffic and no security cameras. After he'd closed the door behind them, it was the perfect place to ball his fist and sock Colton in the eye.

"Hey!" Colton hollered, holding his cheekbone. "What the fuck, man?"

Daniel hadn't hit anyone since high school. The searing pain in his hand just made him madder. "I'll tell you what the fuck." He lunged at Colton, knocking him into the wall, and pressed his arm across Colton's throat. "Where's Wendy?"

"With you!" Colton choked out.

He sounded sincere. He was also an actor. Daniel eased some of the pressure off Colton's neck, making him think he was being released. Then, while he was still off balance, Daniel slammed him into the wall again. "Tell me where she is and I'll walk away. If I find out later that you know where she is and you lied, I will fuck you over so hard that you'll wish you were still doing community theater in Des Moines. You know I can do it."

"I have no fucking idea! Get *off* me!"

With a final curse, Daniel threw Colton to the floor and paced a few steps away, running his hands through his hair. He was out of ideas. If Colton wasn't lying, Rick must have Wendy after all. And Daniel had no clue how to find them.

"Have you lost your mind?" Colton exclaimed from the floor. "You sound British all of a sudden, like you've always secretly wanted to play Hamlet."

Daniel's pesky British accent had come back, which made sense. He'd never been so stressed in his life. He asked Colton, "Have you ever heard of a guy who looks like you getting into parties or hanging with the paparazzi?"

"No," Colton said, sitting up against the wall and touching one finger to the bruise under his eye. "But if you have a question about those prying assholes, you should ask Lorelei. She makes friends with them for some damn reason."

"Call her," Daniel said. "Right now."

Colton coughed, spat blood on the floor, and pulled his phone out of his back pocket. He glared at Daniel as he waited for Lorelei to answer, but as soon as she did, his voice was friendly. "Hey! Listen, strange question. Ever heard of a photographer who looks like me?" His fair countenance grew darker, and the fluorescent lights of the hall seemed to dim as Daniel watched.

"Hold on," Colton said. "I'm going to give you to Daniel. Tell him everything you just told me." As he handed the phone up to Daniel, Colton said, "I don't know what's going on, but it doesn't sound good."

Taking the phone, Daniel noticed in passing that his hand was shaking. "Tell me," he demanded.

"He's been hanging with the crowd outside my house for a few years," Lorelei said. "I thought that was creepy at first, because he showed up right about the time I started dating Colton, like he was trying to take advantage of looking like Colton, planned it or something. He seemed really nice, though. We joked about his looks. I got comfortable with him, I guess because he reminded me of Colton so much, and then—come to think of it—he's the one who told me last weekend that I should call Wendy."

Daniel took one pained breath. "What do you mean?"

"I was just talking to him outside when I was on my way to a club, because sometimes I tell the guys where I'm going to help them out a little, you know? And he said if I was having image trouble, he'd heard of this kick-butt girl at Stargazer who seemed to be saving ass for everybody he's been taking pictures of lately."

"What's this guy's name?"

"Rick."

Daniel put one hand to his forehead. "Have you seen him in Vegas this week?"

"No, but that doesn't mean he's not there. I haven't been looking. You know what, though? I've seen a friend of his, Billy. He's probably still out in front of the casino. He has a handlebar moustache and he always wears a hat. The paparazzi dress a little weird—"

"Thanks. Bye."

"Hey!" she exclaimed. "Why do you sound British?"

Daniel hung up on her and tossed the phone down

to Colton. "Sorry." He barged through the door, back onto the glittering casino floor.

"Hey!" Colton called. He was out of breath when he caught up with Daniel. "If Wendy's in trouble with this guy, let me help you."

Daniel didn't want Colton's help, but he might need it. As they wound their way through the banks of slot machines, he told Colton about the attacks on himself and Wendy.

"You're kidding!" Colton exclaimed as they pushed open the exit to the Strip, neon glowing everywhere in the night. "We thought you guys kept leaving the party early to screw."

"I wish." Daniel led the way down the sidewalk to where the paparazzi sat on folding chairs. They all jumped up as Colton approached. Cameras blazed as they took his picture. Daniel's instinct was to guide Colton calmly away, because every bit of what they did next would be at the top of the gossip blogs tomorrow. It didn't matter anymore.

Blinking into the flashes, he called, "Is Billy here?"

"I'm Billy." Sure enough, the old man stepping forward wore a Wild West moustache and a floppy fishing hat.

Daniel drew him out of hearing of the other photographers, though they had no time to get out of shooting range. As the cameras flashed on, he handed Billy his last hundred, then asked, "You have a colleague who looks like my friend here?" He put a hand on Colton's shoulder.

"Sure," Billy said, folding the bill into his pocket. "Rick."

"Do you know where he is?" Daniel asked, trying hard not to sound like he was afraid for his wife's life.

Billy gave the worst possible answer to a man whose wallet was empty. "I might, if I didn't have to work for a living."

Daniel had no idea what to do now. He thought Detective Butkus might finally help him, but by the time the detective took Billy to the police station and pressed the truth out of him, it might be too late for Wendy. Daniel glanced toward the paparazzi, then back toward the security guards at the entrance to the casino, and calculated how quickly the two groups might come to Billy's aid, and therefore how long Daniel could kick the shit out of him.

Colton reached into his pocket and drew out the three ten-thousand-dollar chips. "Would this pay your salary for a few days?"

Billy looked over his shoulder at the other photographers, grabbed the chips, and threw them under his hat. "I been drinking beer with Rick at his hotel room all week. Him and his friend Paul."

"Paul's balding?" Daniel guessed. "Likes Hawaiian shirts?"

"That's the one." Billy gave them the address and room number of the hotel.

While Billy was still talking, Daniel walked into traffic on the Strip and hailed a taxi. Colton called over his shoulder to Billy, "If you're bullshitting us,

I'm coming back to find you, because that was some expensive bullshit." He climbed into the taxi behind Daniel.

Daniel gave the driver the address. "Step on it." Then he realized he had no bribe to get the driver to go faster. He had a credit card to pay for the fare, but plastic didn't talk like cash.

Colton produced a hundred and tossed it into the front seat. The engine revved higher.

"Thank you," Daniel told Colton sincerely.

"When we get there," Colton said, "I'm coming in with you."

"All right." One more time, Daniel pressed the button on his phone to call Detective Butkus. The detective would maintain that Daniel had no proof of what was happening and nothing to go on.

Daniel Blackstone was about to lose his cool.

"Take your clothes off, Wendy," Rick said smoothly. "Nice and slow, so we can enjoy it."

Wendy had heard those words from him before. She'd been eighteen and excited that he considered her an alluring grown woman. When they'd had sex, they'd been in her bedroom or his tiny apartment. Both places were shabby and poor. Either would have been an improvement over this seedy dump of a hotel room five blocks from the Strip.

Paul, a stranger to her with a receding hairline, hadn't been in the room back then to take pictures of them with a state-of-the-art camera and a special lens. Rick hadn't relaxed in a chair, watching her, with a gun and a hunting knife beside him on the table—the same knife he'd shoved against her side in the Paris casino, and which he must have used to hack her hair off three times that week. And Rick's own camera bag hadn't waited on the floor, the padded canvas handle replaced with a sturdy braid of three thick hanks of Wendy's hair.

When she'd known Rick before, he'd been a possessive bully. Now he was out of his mind.

"How much money did you make from the picture of Lorelei on Colton's phone?" she asked as she pulled her blouse off over her head. She wished she knew some kind of stealth move to catch two men by surprise and overpower them while she was taking her shirt off, but her mind was a blank.

"We made a *lot* of money," Rick said. Paul echoed Rick's satisfaction by laughing.

"This gig has cost me, though. I had to dip into the funds when Colton changed his style," Rick said, fingering his suit, a cheap version of the outfit Colton had been sporting since he traded in his usual trucker hat. "You gotta do what you gotta do."

"We knew you were here in Vegas," she told Rick. "People kept sighting Colton when he wasn't there. We figured out it was you. We told the police about you. If you've made so much money already, why are you taking the chance of hanging around and kidnapping me to take *another* picture?"

"It's what we do," Paul said without emotion, adjusting a dial on his camera.

"And the opportunity was too perfect," Rick said. "I think I might have a *little* leeway, don't you, since we've been here all week and a cop hasn't so much as questioned me?"

Wendy agreed. Detective Butkus had pretended to listen to her and take notes, but he might as well have laughed at her for all the following up he'd done.

"Besides," Rick said casually, "the risk is worth the reward. Ten years ago your little bitch friend called the cops on me in New York, Wendy, when all I wanted was to *talk* to you. I *told* you that." His voice cracked, but he maintained his charming, wisecracking demeanor like nothing had gone wrong. "Because of the warrant, I haven't been able to work for the movie studios like I planned. Like *both* of us planned, remember?"

She nodded solemnly, heart racing, skin cold, stomach turning flips. She wanted desperately to tell him that if he'd dreamed of a Hollywood career, domestic violence and evading arrest weren't his best course of action. But his fingers drummed impatiently on the arm of the chair, dangerously close to the gun and knife beside him on the table. She didn't dare speak.

"You ruined my job for me," he said, "so I'm going to ruin yours for you. I've been to your fancy parties. I've seen Colton Farr coming on to you. I know he's still in town. So Paul will take a couple photos of you blowing me, from just the right angle so I look like Colton and you look like . . . you." He smiled at her.

"Lorelei will break up with Colton again. Your company will kick you out on your ass for ruining your star's publicity just to satisfy your own lust. That bastard you've been fucking will see you for the whore you really are, if he didn't figure it out already when you were dry humping that pole at the strip club." He picked up the gun from the table and waved it at the waistband of her jeans. "Keep going. You obviously remember how to strip."

She swallowed and shook her head no.

He burst up from the chair. Before she knew what was happening, she was sliding down the wall, head exploding with pain, fingers pressed to her cheek. He'd only slapped her, she realized as she moved her jaw, noting that it still worked. But the ache in the back of her head, which had faded over the last few days, had worked its way loose again.

The guilt was worse. The embarrassment that Paul had seen Rick hit her. The feeling that she must have done something to deserve all this. Those emotions from ten years before rushed back at her and settled like a weight in her lap.

"Sorry, baby," Rick whispered, holding a hand down to her. "I didn't mean to hit you that hard." Unlike ten years before, he was grinning as he said it.

She reached for his hand. Her hand trembled.

He pulled her up to standing, then backed across the room to sit in his chair again. "Now." He sounded exasperated, as if their fun game kept getting interrupted. "Take your pants off."

With shaking fingers, she unfastened her jeans and pushed them down her legs and off—carefully, so that her ring stayed in her pocket, just in case she made it out of this alive. For once, she wished she was wearing crappy granny panty underwear like Sarah favored. When Rick saw that, if he hadn't canceled the photo shoot and sexual assault, at least he would have delayed them until he could make a side trip to buy her better lingerie. But her bra and panties were red and matching for Daniel, damn it.

Kicking her jeans aside with one stylish high-heeled sandal—again, she looked like she'd dressed up especially for this nightmare—she thought of another argument she could make to stall Rick. "What tabloid would believe these pictures are real?" Her cheek felt stiff where he'd slapped her, but she had to keep talking. Anything to put off the inevitable. "Nobody will buy photos that are obviously fake. Colton might get drunk and let someone take pictures of him with a girl in a hot tub, but he wouldn't let someone take pictures of him getting a blow job. Even he is not that stupid."

"It's not about stupidity," Rick explained. "It's about jealousy. I can tell by what he's been saying about Lorelei online. He loves her. She's beautiful and she left him. He would do anything, *anything*, to fuck with her and ruin her, even if it ruined his own life, even if it took him ten years. Come here and kneel down in front of me, Wendy." He laughed. "I like the sound of that." He sat up on the edge of his chair and unzipped his pants.

With a gasp, she looked to Paul for help. He simply leaned forward in his own chair, camera poised. There was no horror in his eyes at what she was being forced to do, and no lust, either. Just the jaded resignation of a professional who made money from other people's misery.

She turned back to Rick. Heart pounding so hard that she could feel the throb of blood in her ears, she said, "I'm not going to do that."

His eyes narrowed. He was still as handsome as he'd been at twenty-one—more so, in fact, with a man's thick muscles and sharp features. But that shift in the set of his eyes hadn't changed at all. It still signaled that she'd crossed a line with him. He was about to call her a bitch, get rough with her, put his forearm across her throat.

He said smoothly and clearly, "You *are* going to do that."

"I'm not," she said, panting now. "You can't make me. Kill me if you want." Without another glance at Rick, on legs like rubber she walked toward the door.

A few steps and nothing happened. Nothing was going to happen. The ordeal had been horrible, but now it was over. She had called his bluff. She would reach the door and open it, and she would be free.

Paul barked, "Rick!" Though his yell filled the small room and thudded against the ceiling, underneath it she heard another, smaller sound with excruciating clarity: the meaty *click* of Rick's gun.

She stopped short. Tingles rushed across her bare arms as she realized that she was very lucky the gun had jammed. And that she likely would run out of luck in the next second when Rick tried again and the gun fired.

BANG. She braced for the pain of the bullet to tear through her.

Instead, in slow motion, the door burst open in front of her. Daniel dove through it, locked eyes with her, shifted his gaze past her, and kept coming. Colton was right behind him.

In the next second, time snapped back to normal. Colton tackled Paul, knocking the chair over. The camera smashed into the wall.

"No!" was all Wendy had time to scream before Daniel yanked Rick out of his chair by the throat. As he took him to the floor, their movements were a blur. Daniel had no idea about the gun—

BANG. This noise sounded totally different from the door slamming open. It really had been the gun this time. Heart sinking into her gut, Wendy rushed over. If Rick had shot Daniel, he could still shoot Wendy, too, but this was only a fleeting thought as she slipped her whole arm between the two of them and pulled Daniel away.

His shirt was soaked with a fist-size circle of bright blood.

"It's him," he said, nodding to Rick.

Rick's shirt showed a circle of blood in the same place, the barrel of the gun still pointed toward his stomach. His fingers trembled on the grip, and he stared into space, breathing heavily.

Wendy used both hands to lift his fingers away until she could take the heavy gun. He didn't resist. She leaped away from him and grabbed the knife from the table with her other hand. Passing Colton, who sat on Paul's chest with both muscular thighs squeezing his neck, she stuck the toe of her sandal through the crack in the doorway and nudged the door all the way open to toss the gun and knife outside before Paul or Rick could make a grab for them.

She was blinded by camera flashes that heated her bare skin. Beyond them she could hear sirens chirping and see blue lights spinning. "Clear out!" a man called over a bullhorn. "Police! Photographers, clear out! Lady, we've got guns on you. It's over. Very slowly put down your weapons."

Five minutes later, Daniel had joined her against the wall outside the hotel room. The cameras still flashed, though they'd been reduced to taking telephoto shots from across the parking lot. Uniformed police scurried in and out of the room. Daniel's and Wendy's hands, cleaned of Rick's blood, were cuffed behind their backs, but they hugged as best they could, her head against his solid bare chest. His heart raced. Gently he pressed his lips to her bruised cheek where Rick had hit her.

"I tried to catch up with you right after you left," he said. "I meant to tell you that I don't want to get divorced. Wendy, I love you."

She looked up into his worried face, his dark eyes. "I love you, too."

Their lips met. As they kissed, she marveled that he could make her feel this good while she was half-naked and detained by the police in the parking lot of a seedy hotel. It boded well for the rest of the marriage, she decided.

"Thank you so much for coming for me," she said. "How did you find me?"

"It's a long story, but Colton and I are the ones who led the paparazzi here. That was an accident." He nodded to the distant flashes. "I'm afraid I've gotten you fired."

"Why?" she asked. "Just because Lorelei Vogel's PR rep is going to be on the front page of the tabloid blogs tomorrow, at a shitty hotel, in her underwear, with a gun in one hand and a knife in the other?" She let out one halfhearted chuckle of resignation. "Maybe that won't happen."

Daniel looked over at Colton, also handcuffed, who was talking animatedly to a cop. He moved his elbows awkwardly, trying to talk with his hands. "This is going to be great for Colton," Daniel said. "When the reporters hear what really happened, the public will love that he actually lived these action-adventure movies he's trying to land. The publicity could be great for Lorelei, too."

"And if that doesn't work," Wendy said, "I could tell my bosses the truth."

"The truth?" Daniel repeated. "Innovative."

"Stargazer prides itself on being cutting-edge."

"And if *that* doesn't work," Daniel said, "I know of another difficult case you can tackle to save your reputation. Again. I'm pretty sure Olivia Query and Victor Moore's marriage is about to crumble, and they'll be looking for different PR representation."

Wendy gaped at him. "Why aren't you in L.A., taking care of that?"

"Because I'm here, taking care of you. Finally." He set his forehead against hers and closed his eyes. "Besides, after I give my father two weeks' notice, it won't be my problem anymore. I'm going to work for Senator Rowling."

Wendy stepped back to grin at him. "You *are*?"

He smiled. "I am."

"I think you'll be happier."

"I think I will, too." He leaned down to kiss her again.

While they were still kissing, she felt someone manipulating her handcuffs and removing them. She was able to reach both arms up and put her hands in Daniel's uncharacteristically rumpled hair, and she felt his strong arms encircle her bare waist. They only broke the kiss when a man cleared his throat beside them.

"So you *weren't* making the whole thing up," Detective Butkus said. He dropped Wendy's ring into her hand.

She was about to thank him for retrieving the ring from the crime scene, as she'd asked, when Daniel broke in. Keeping one hand on her hip, he directed at Detective Butkus a string of filth the likes of which she had never heard from his lips. She stared at him, taking it in, memorizing a few choice turns of phrase to use in case she really did get assigned to Victor Moore and Olivia Query.

Detective Butkus held up both hands. "Give me a break! Would *you* have believed this story if you were me?"

"No," Daniel and Wendy said at the same time.

"I mean, what a freak this guy is." Detective Butkus jerked his thumb over his shoulder, where paramedics were wheeling Rick on a stretcher out of the hotel room. He asked Wendy, "Did you see he braided your hair and made it into a camera bag strap? Sicko."

Daniel pushed past the detective and lunged for the stretcher. The detective caught him by the arm and yelled, "Get him!" He and two cops wrestled Daniel back from attacking Rick.

Wendy watched the whole surreal scene, the muscles of Daniel's back and shoulders glowing in the shifting light of the hotel's cheap neon, and wiggled her ring back onto her finger where it belonged.

"You know what?" the detective called to Wendy. "Just get in that car, both of you. We'll let you put some clothes on at your hotel before you come down to the station. Get him in there with you."

The cops gave Daniel a final shove. He glared at them resentfully. Wendy took him by the hand and led him into the backseat of a police car and shut the door behind them. He still looked over her shoulders at the ambulance. Finally, to snap him out of that violent mood, she said, "They're taking us to the room to change. Do you think we'll have time for a quickie? Because we never got around to doing it against the wall."

He blinked at her. She thought he hadn't heard her. Finally he smiled, slowly at first, his grin becoming broader as she slid her hand onto his thigh. "We will always make time for a quickie," he said. "And *that* is a wedding vow."

After midnight, the four of them—Daniel, Wendy, Colton, and Lorelei, who had jumped on a private jet when she heard Wendy was in trouble—lingered over dinner in an exclusive room in the restaurant on top of the Stratosphere tower. The lights of Vegas inched underneath them at one rotation every eighty minutes.

Daniel tightened his arm around Wendy's shoulders as she nuzzled against him in the booth. After hours at the police station, he knew she was beat. He was, too. But they'd also been starving. They could have gone to a cheap diner, but he'd insisted on treating everyone at this tourist trap. The past week had convinced him to look for fun where he could find it.

His phone beeped with a text.

"Again?" Wendy teased him.

"Yeah, again?" Colton asked from across the table, and Lorelei giggled. The last call Daniel had received had been from Colton's agent. The tale of Colton's heroics had spread like lightning through the Internet. Both producers Daniel had talked up in the past few days wanted Colton to star in their action flicks, audition or no audition.

"Pesky multimillion-dollar deals interrupting dinner," Daniel muttered. But he really was reluctant to look at his phone, because the beep was the one he'd set for texts from Victor Moore. He wound a tendril of Wendy's hair around his finger. Now that he finally had her—again—he never wanted to leave her. And if she did end up handling the Victor mess after he quit the Blackstone Firm, he never wanted *her* to leave *him*.

He grimaced as he glanced at the screen. "Oh!" he said in surprise.

"What?" Wendy asked, looking up at him.

"Victor Moore has seen on the news that I might be having a little trouble. He says he's explained the situation to his family, and their problems can wait until I'm available."

"That is ridiculous," Lorelei said, laughing, at the same time Colton said, "This Victor Moore, whoever he is, has no idea how to be a star. I could teach him a thing or two." He glanced at his watch. "I think we're about to close this place down. But Lorelei and I agreed that we have a couple of confessions to make to you first."

Wendy's eyes flew wide open.

"Soooo . . ." Lorelei started slowly.

Daniel glared at her. If it was bad news, frankly, he didn't want to know. He definitely didn't want Wendy to know. Not tonight.

"When you guys made Colton and me sit on your couch and talk to each other?" Lorelei continued. "And then you said we should take things slow from there? We didn't. We slept together."

One of Daniel's hands was still wound up in Wendy's hair. Under the table, he balled his other hand into a fist. He was going to kill Colton yet.

"But the next night," Lorelei rushed on, "at my birthday party, we had a huge argument." She was talking only to Wendy now. "Colton said you and Daniel were only getting married so people would get confused about the ceremony and think *we* were getting married. Daniel was so cold, sorry"—Lorelei waved toward Daniel by way of apology—"that I wanted to stop you from marrying him if that was true.

"Colton said to let you go ahead, because it would save our careers. He said it was all for work. I said *nothing* is all for work. The PR folks, the photographers, they're people and they matter, too. That whole fight was why, when I headed home to L.A. last night, Colton got out of the limo and backtracked to Vegas. Though, considering what happened next, I'm glad he did."

"So are we," Daniel said, pulling Wendy closer.

"Anyway," Lorelei said, "I'm happy you've stayed together. You've given Colton and me hope. Sometimes even when a relationship is hard, it's real."

Unimpressed, Wendy tapped her fingernail on the table. "What's the other confession?"

Lorelei bit her lip. "I didn't follow some of your other instructions, either."

"Really," Wendy said flatly.

"Yes! I used my phone and took a picture at your wedding when you weren't looking." She peered down at her phone and thumbed through the images. "I guess it's the only wedding photo there is. Colton thought it was safe to tell you about it now that the awards show is over and everything has worked out. We're going to get it blown up for you as big as this room. Here it is." She handed the phone to Daniel.

He and Wendy put their heads together and peered down at the picture. They both gasped when they saw it.

"That is the coolest thing ever." Daniel elbowed Wendy. "You look completely freaked out."

She laughed. "You look stoic."

"That's my expression of ecstasy. You know that by now." He looked up at Lorelei. "Thank you."

"You're so welcome, you guys! Hugs!"

Everyone stood. Daniel gave Lorelei the hug she deserved for her part in saving Wendy, and his handshake with Colton turned into a bear hug, too, surprising nobody more than himself. With repeated promises to head straight for their hotel rooms and leave for L.A. again tomorrow, Colton sauntered and Lorelei bounced out of the room.

Daniel and Wendy sank back down onto their seat again. He told her, "Lorelei's ditzy, but she knew we belonged together way before we did."

"She's an idiot savant of love." Wendy interlaced her fingers with his. "Gosh, this whole marriage thing has blindsided me, because we've done it all backward. We have so much to talk about. Whose apartment are we going to live in?"

"We can use mine," Daniel said, "but it's too dark for you."

"Mine's too messy for you," Wendy said. "I want desperately to be neat, but I get in a hurry and start flinging things."

"I'll help you," Daniel said. "Life will be a lot less stressful for both of us now that we have each other's backs."

She beamed at him and brought their clasped hands up to kiss his bruised knuckle.

He had a sudden, terrible thought. "Are you allergic to cats?"

"No, I like cats. Are you allergic to turtles?"

He laughed. "You have a turtle?"

"He came with the apartment." Her face fell. "Uh-oh. I wonder if turtles and cats get along."

"I predict that they'll try very hard and will be utterly unable to hurt each other." He unwound his finger from one lock of her hair and wound it around another. "What do you say we put that off for a few more days and have a honeymoon? Are you sick of Vegas?"

"No, even after the week we've had, I'm not sick of Vegas, so obviously that's not possible. We could re-experience it, sort of write over the bad memories. Can you take off from work?"

"Yeah, now that Victor's let me off the hook for a while. Can you?"

"Absolutely. Earlier today, I thought I'd better get back to New York ASAP. But the publicity for Lorelei—and for me—is working out better than I'd dreamed. All of Hollywood will be asking for the well-armed PR expert in her skivvies."

"I certainly would," Daniel said. Her photo was already appearing on the tabloid blogs, looking like a pulp fiction cover. And her tense call to her boss had turned out fine. After all, Stargazer prided itself on innovative PR.

"Before I left," Wendy said, "Stargazer gave all my clients to other people. I can wait a few more days to ask for them back." She examined Daniel's hand in hers. "The first thing I want to do on our honeymoon is buy you a new wedding band."

"Nope," he said. "This one is perfect."

She eyed him skeptically. "It doesn't go with your Rolex."

"I don't care."

"Senator Rowling's constituents are going to think you married a carny."

"Senator Rowling values difference."

"You're good at PR." Edging closer until her lips

brushed his, she whispered seductively, "What do *you* want to do on our honeymoon?"

He wanted to ride the roller coaster around the New York casino. See cheesy concerts. Fly over Hoover Dam in a helicopter. Hike Red Rock Canyon. Avoid the Eiffel Tower like the plague. And one thing he'd thought was so far beyond his reach that he hadn't even longed for it until Wendy appeared like magic in the Big O bar with a shining zipper down the back of her skirt: he would spend every long Vegas night making love with his wife.

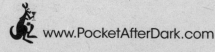

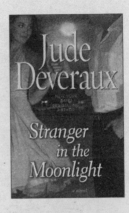

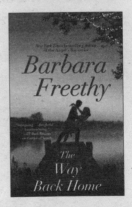